CONCORDIUM

CONCORDIUM

A Historical Conspiracy Thriller

A Novel

A.T. HELM

First Edition, June 2025

Copyright © 2025 by A.T. Helm
All rights reserved.

This is a work of fiction. Names, characters, places, and incidents either are the product of the author's imagination or are used fictitiously. Any resemblance to actual persons, living or dead, events, or locales is entirely coincidental.

ISBN: 9798289083814

For my beloved wife
For my dear son
For my precious mother and father

Concordium

Prologue

1935
Europe

By the fall of 1935, the European political landscape had undergone a violent and irreversible transformation.

Mussolini had been in power in Italy for more than ten years at the time. He marched on Rome with several thousand followers in 1922, an event that would become mythologised as the start of the Fascist era. Previously, he worked as a socialist journalist. To prevent a civil war, King Victor Emmanuel III appointed him as prime minister. Over the next few years, Mussolini declared himself *"Il Duce"*, or *"the Leader"*, of a totalitarian state, dismantled parliamentary democracy, outlawed opposition parties, and censored the media. By 1935, Italy had become a one-party dictatorship, and Mussolini's focus had shifted to imperial territory conquest. Italy's invasion of Ethiopia in October of that year was a defiance of the League of Nations and a sign of the country's renewed desire to consolidate colonial power.

Germany, to the north, experienced a more rapid and devastating political uprising. Adolf Hitler, a failed agitator born in Austria, rose to national prominence through fiery rhetoric and nationalist propaganda, transforming himself from a relatively unknown figure. He was able to dictate *Mein Kampf* during his nine-month prison sentence following the unsuccessful Beer Hall Putsch of 1923. Following his early release, he reformed the Nazi Party through discipline and strategy. He was named chancellor by President Paul von Hindenburg in January 1933. A month later, the Reichstag fire provided justification for civil liberties to be suspended. The Enabling Act, which granted Hitler dictatorial powers, passed in March.

After Hindenburg died in August 1934, Hitler took on the title of Führer und Reichskanzler, which meant he was both president and chancellor at the same time. He now took the oath of allegiance to the Constitution. Germany became a one-party state governed by decree and enforced through terror.

Throughout 1935, both regimes tightened their grip on power.

Italy's invasion of Ethiopia demonstrated the fascist regime's profound disregard for international norms. Meanwhile, Germany violated the Treaty of Versailles by reinstating mandatory military service in March. In September, Germany passed the Nuremberg Laws, which stripped German Jews of their citizenship and established racial ideology as a legal doctrine.

The continent waited patiently for the results. Some hoped that diplomacy would succeed. Some people held the belief that they could reverse the rise of nationalism and militarism.

However, Berlin and Rome had already decided on a course of action. By November 1935, peace had left Europe.

It was simply a matter of waiting.

Part 1

Return into the Shadows

1

November 1, 1935
Berlin

As November dawned, it arrived cloaked in a hushed anticipation, a whisper of secrets waiting to be revealed. A weighty embrace of fog swirled through the streets of Berlin, like a spectral presence. The trees loomed, stripped of their foliage, their gnarled branches curling into forms that murmured hidden tales, casting an eerie spell over the stillness of the streets. The frigid air had woven a delicate shroud of mist across the glass, shrouding the world outside in an enigmatic silence.

As the train neared Berlin, it violently lurched around a bend. The rhythmic metallic clatter of the rails momentarily faltered, a fleeting disruption in the symphony of motion. A soft murmur floated through the carriage, causing passengers to briefly lift their gazes, only to once again sink into the depths of their thoughts. Only a single passenger stirred—a young man, his gaze fixed out the window, nestled in the last car of the train. The furrow between his brows deepened, and his eyelids danced with a restless urgency.

Ernst Adler sat, the collar of his coat turned up against the biting chill, his arms crossed tightly over his chest, a fortress of resolve against the world around him. He stood as a figure cloaked in shadows, a silhouette woven from mystery and unvoiced secrets. He gazed into the desolate expanse that rushed past, enveloped in a thick fog that clung to the glass like a secret longing to be uncovered. The silence weighed heavily on him, and the world around him dissolved into encroaching shadows as he stood there.

From the very beginning of his journey, he sealed his lips, deliberately steering clear of the gazes that surrounded him.

The seat beside him lay vacant, its emptiness shrouded in mystery, a question of fate or deliberate decision lingering in the air.

Beyond the pane, he stared at the outside world, where colours and shadows swirled and blended in a captivating mist. Before him stretched a landscape cloaked in ambiguity, yet it ignited a flicker of recognition: the haunting vestiges of industry as the train sliced through the shadows toward the eastern fringes of Berlin—gravel yards, brick factories with chimneys still breathing out wisps of smoke, and the silhouettes of weathered warehouses fading into the mist like phantoms from a forgotten time. Everything lay beneath a haunting veil of pale grey, a hue that appeared ready to consume the very essence of existence itself.

Berlin draped itself in a sombre cloak of grey, an ever-present companion weaving through its streets. Yet, the grey of this morning bore a weight unlike any other—heavier, more suffocating, and more exhausting.

Familiar, and yet somehow foreign... He pondered this in silence.

He was making his way back to the city he had once abandoned, a place that now felt like a distant memory, as he himself had transformed into someone entirely different. His former self had vanished, taking with it the last remnants of the hope he had clung to so desperately. This morning, the train surged forward, carrying him not just toward Berlin but also into the murky, elusive shadows of his past.

He gradually lifted himself, pressing his forehead against the cool glass of the window. From the depths of the swirling fog, a shadowy figure emerged, gradually taking shape—a hauntingly familiar silhouette: the ancient St Thomas Church in Kreuzberg. Once, it stood as a clandestine haven for fervent protests and hushed gatherings of resistance, where whispers of rebellion echoed through the shadows. It had succumbed to the relentless howl of the wind and the chilling embrace of desolation.

It bore a striking resemblance to the city.

The train's interior held a dense, stale, and suffocating aroma reminiscent of a forgotten cellar. It appeared to protect mysteries that stayed hidden. The air was thick with the acrid scent of sweat, clinging stubbornly to the worn fabric of the ancient seats. In the dim light, the spectre of cigarette smoke hung in the air, weaving its way into the very fabric of the walls. The air was saturated with the metallic tang of iron, a sharp and bitter echo of secrets buried far beneath the surface. It whispered of tales yet to be unveiled, of shadows that danced in the recesses of recollection. The atmosphere hung thick, laden with unspoken truths hidden beneath the surface. It appeared to have languished for eternity within a chamber, haunted by the whispers of unvoiced terror.

Ernst cast his gaze toward the window, each movement deliberate and unhurried. He leaned in, his face mere inches from the frigid glass, watching as his breath transformed the surface into a swirling mist. He swept the back of his hand across the surface, revealing a delicate glimpse of the world that lay beyond. Through the slender crack, a glimmer of intrigue beckoned to him. A poster clung desperately to the crumbling brick wall, its edges fluttering in the wind, a silent plea for recognition.

It was written in bold black letters: *Ein Volk, ein Reich, ein Führer!* [1]

A figure stood boldly, a well-known face that drew the eye: *the portrait of Adolf Hitler*. He stared into the distance, captivated by the vision of the horizon, oblivious

---

[1] One people, one empire, one leader!

to the world around him. His lips formed a tight, resolute line, and his face reflected the burden of stress.

The paper rested slightly moist, its frayed edges dancing in the breeze, fragile like a secret shared softly. However, no one had addressed it or rectified the situation. Perhaps it was apprehension that restrained them. Or perhaps from weariness so deep that it numbed the soul and rendered everyone indifferent.

As the train glided into Berlin's Friedrichstrasse Station, the harmonious blend of metal and rail reached a serene finale. It quivered briefly, a last flicker of vitality, and then it rested in silence. Ernst rose, serene as the early light, gliding alongside the others in the soft glow of dawn.

He had no luggage with him. He possessed a wallet, a neatly folded map of the city, a sleek metal cigarette case, and a compact notebook tucked away in the inner pocket of his coat.

The station buzzed with the energy of countless individuals, each in motion, each in anticipation, a vast array of expressions immersed in contemplation. The swift rhythm of footsteps echoed around, accompanied by the sharp clink of suitcase wheels against the stone floor. Announcements resonated sharply from the loudspeakers, merging into a symphony of urgency. Ernst glided through the crowd, silent as a whisper, his head lowered and his eyes focused and resolute.

He averted his eyes from the faces surrounding him, and in response, they shifted their gazes away from him too. In Germany, it has transformed into something much more significant. It had grown into an essential drive, a crucial element of existence.

He forced his way through the imposing iron doors of the station, and the biting Berlin wind hit his face with the force of an undeniable revelation. An icy blaze seared his skin. He took a deep breath, embracing the quiet calm of the city, and then moved down the street with determination, each step deliberate and quick.

The stone buildings loomed in quietude, their façades heavy and imposing, casting a shadow over the tired streets below. He glided through the shadows, aiming to transform into a mere whisper, an essence of emptiness. At every corner of the street, shadows hung in the air, creating an atmosphere that captivated the imagination. Lost in thought, a young man in a brown shirt rested against the wall. Under the warm glow of a streetlamp, a man lit a cigarette, its flame briefly dancing in the night air. Eyes sweeping the darkness, a uniformed officer stood vigilant and unwavering.

Ernst tilted his head further. In Germany, the art of blending in had emerged as the essential rule for staying alive.

He lingered before a bakery sign, its letters aged and faded, whispering tales of the past. The paint had faded; once a vibrant red, now it rested in cracks and flakes, a reflection of time's unyielding march. Yet within, life thrived, a subtle heartbeat in the silence. He edged closer to the window, squinting as he peered inside.

The charming little cafe had only two occupied tables. An old man savoured his coffee at a relaxed pace, while a young woman, her back turned to the window, quietly perused the pages of a book.

He remained motionless, his eyes locked in focus, as the surrounding world slipped into a serene hush for an instant. His eyes absorbed the world, seizing every detail, every movement with a subtle intensity. He strode confidently, veering into the slender alleyway. He approached the metal door at the back of the bakery. It remained ajar, with no protection. He nudged it softly, and the old hinges creaked, a noise reminiscent of a hushed lament in the quiet.

Inside the walls, a profound stillness enveloped everything. The soft, consistent sound of the coffee grinder resonated throughout the space, creating a soothing backdrop to the calm of the morning. Beyond the door stretched a corridor, slender and shadowy, its light faintly grazing the walls. The old tiled floor felt chilly and moist beneath my feet, a poignant echo of time gone by. The wallpaper clung to the walls, its yellowed and peeling surface telling a story of time's relentless march. At the end of the corridor, beneath a gently arched ceiling, a slender flight of concrete steps descended into the shadowy depths below.

A storage room... or perhaps just an illusion crafted to look like one.

He strode confidently, every step deliberate and unwavering. With every step, the cold, damp stone beneath him seemed to murmur softly. He paused before the door to the storage room, enveloped in the surroundings. He took a deep breath, tilted his head just so, and focused intently to hear even the faintest murmur from inside. Silence enveloped the space, dense and profound, akin to the burden of thoughts left unexpressed. He extended his hand, calm and purposeful, and pushed against the door. The door swung open with a deliberate creak, its heavy frame pressing down on the stone below.

A woman stood by herself. Lina Berger.

She perched on the edge of a weathered trunk, her eyes locked onto a tattered piece of paper lying on her lap, the stillness enveloping her. The bare bulb swayed softly, casting a flickering glow upon the muted walls. In the flickering light, shadows swirled, and Lina's expression hardened, revealing a deep, thoughtful intensity.

A weathered, forgotten shelf stood quietly in the back of the room. The shelf held aged magazines, half-empty cigarette packs, and a collection of old wine bottles with worn labels. The rich scent of the stone walls intertwined effortlessly with the notes of aged paper and the faint trace of tobacco.

Lina lifted her gaze delicately and whispered tenderly. "You've made it here sooner than expected." Her tone was calm, yet every syllable carried an air of alertness.

Ernst stepped into the room, offering a subtle nod as he entered. "The train exceeded my expectations in speed. I had no desire to linger at the station."

Lina folded the paper with meticulous attention, her fingers expertly crafting the creases, then slipped it into the inner pocket of her coat, as if concealing a precious secret from the outside world. She stood and shot Ernst a look, quick but intentional.

"There were individuals around the station," Ernst remarked softly. "Still as a statue, yet fully conscious. They deliberately avert their eyes, a decision steeped in purpose. Berlin is a city where the art of observation has developed into a skilful practice, a subtle choreography of looks and silhouettes."

Lina nodded with a weary, empathetic sigh. "In today's world, everyone behaves in the 'appropriate' way."

Ernst replied with a hint of a wry smile dancing at the corners of his mouth. Still, his eyes held no trace of a smile. "That is exactly why everything is wrong now."

Lina carefully reached into the inner pocket of her coat and gently pulled out a small, folded piece of paper. With deliberate and confident strides, she made her way to Ernst and quietly presented it to him.

"We should make our way to the address on that paper," she whispered. "Yet, Matteo has not arrived."

Ernst held the paper, feeling the rich, timeworn texture under his fingertips. He quickly scrutinised the concise phrases written in worn ink. His eyes fixed on a solitary line, and a furrow formed on his brow.

"What is this place?"

Lina gave a slight nod, conveying her understanding effortlessly. "A historic pathway. Currently out of service. The entrance seems locked tight, but there's a subtle stir inside... or maybe it's just a passerby."

Without diverting his attention from the page, Ernst asked, "Who?"

Lina offered a gentle shrug. "I currently lack certainty. A person consistently arrives and departs from the same spot at regular intervals. Regularly throughout the night. Throughout the day, there was a complete absence of any evidence."

Ernst paused for a moment, lost in thought. With precision, he folded the paper and discreetly placed it in the inner pocket of his coat. "Either an observer... or someone hidden."

"Maybe a bit of both," Lina responded, lost in contemplation. "Yet, whatever it is, it waits patiently. Whether it's for the ideal occasion... or for us."

Ernst offered a quiet acknowledgement, lost in thought. "We'll move when Matteo arrives," he declared with unwavering resolve.

A subtle hint of a smile danced at the corners of her mouth. "That's exactly what he would suggest, too."

The room remained profoundly silent for several minutes. The air, heavy with dust, clung to the shelves and the spines of the books. Then, the deliberate yet cautious sound of footsteps echoed on the metal stairs. Moments later, a voice that felt familiar, laced with irony yet gentle, resonated through the stairwell.

"Looks like you two got a head start."

As Matteo Vellini stepped inside, the moisture had soaked into the shoulders of his coat. His cheeks held a delicate flush from the cold, while his eyes stayed sharp and observant as ever. Upon entering, he surveyed the space, taking in every nook, each shadow, and all the subtle nuances.

He then remarked, "At the train stop, there were three men. They kept their distance, but their actions conveyed so much more. One stood still, watching intently; another scanned the surroundings, while the third hung back in the corner, puffing on a cigarette." He glanced at Ernst, a subtle, wry smile dancing at the corners of his mouth. "The individual who frequently smokes presents the smallest risk. He possesses a remarkable talent for crafting diversions, a skill that frequently outshines others."

Lina broke the silence, her voice a soft murmur, deliberate and precise. "So, were we being followed at that moment?"

Matteo softly declined with a shake of his head. "No, we were being watched. Frequently, watching can be more perilous than taking action."

Ernst discreetly pulled out the neatly folded piece of paper from the inner pocket of his coat and passed it to Matteo. "Lina thinks we ought to go there," he declared. "Before the onset of evening. She asserts that there's an entity nearby… something hidden away."

Matteo picked up the paper, scanned the lines with ease, then lifted his gaze to connect with Lina's eyes. "Who is there?"

Lina responded gently, "Not someone I'm familiar with. Yet just as silent—and just as careful—as those watching us."

Matteo narrowed his eyes, lost in a moment of deep thought. "None of ours."

Lina gave a slight nod after a moment of thoughtful reflection. "Not at this moment," she responded. She then pivoted gracefully toward the door. She paused briefly, offered a subtle shrug, and spoke without looking back.

"It's time to explore," she declared with a steady, confident voice. "In this city, we are being watched by more than just Nazis. I can sense its breath."

2

The trio stepped out of the quiet of the bakery's back door, charting their path toward the eastern edge of the city. Berlin rested in its muted tones, as though the sun were a far-off indulgence, hidden behind the thick blanket of clouds above.

The streets glistened, with puddles pooling in the dips of the cobblestone pavement. They made their way onto the sidewalk. Lina stumbled as her foot snagged on a stubborn cobblestone, its uneven surface challenging her balance. She faltered for just an instant, yet that was all it took. She hesitated but continued, resolute.

"Walk normally," Ernst instructed, his voice barely above a whisper, his lips barely moving. "To pause is to draw the attention of those around you."

"I thought this was the way one walked," Lina remarked, her tone calm and unwavering.

Matteo trailed slightly behind, his gaze flickering from side to side, always alert. In the stillness of Berlin, the unsettling sensation of being watched intensified with every step taken.

As they passed the newsstand on the corner, he paused for a moment, uncertainty flickering in his mind. He grasped the newspaper, its fresh pages unfurling like the dawn, uncovering the stories of the world inside. Although he pretended to read the headlines, he watched the bus stop across the street. He noted the figure beside it. He donned a dark overcoat and a fedora hat; his head inclined just a touch. He might have been just another Berliner, blending seamlessly into the throng. Yet Matteo sensed a growing discomfort within him.

"That's the second time I've seen him today," he murmured, a fleeting darkness crossing his expression. "He was at the station this morning."

Ernst leaned in, his voice a whisper. "Is he monitoring us?"

Matteo folded the newspaper with a smooth motion and set it down, his voice steady and composed. "No. His eyes are empty, lacking any clarity. An individual without a specific focus notices all that surrounds them."

They pressed forward on their journey. Now, their steps had become more subdued, and their breathing was steadier. It felt like Berlin, hidden in its depths, was watching them closely. The absence of people was palpable, yet the ambiance was undeniably present. In Berlin, the greatest danger stemmed from the very reality: the lack of clarity.

They glided past the bus stop and turned onto a slender dead-end street to the right. At the far end, partially hidden by the wall, stood a door that had clearly seen better days, its rust unmistakable. The door appeared frozen in time, its paint flaking delicately, its lower corner encrusted with years of hardened bird droppings. The dark bricks encasing it amplified the eerie essence of the stillness.

Matteo moved forward with quiet confidence, placing his hand gently on the door. The harsh metal gripped him tightly, leaving him breathless. "Not locked," he whispered gently, examining the hinge with care.

Lina expertly scanned her surroundings. The empty windows of abandoned buildings stood still, clinging to the walls like haunting echoes. "No one is around. Let's get going," she said, examining every corner.

The door swung open, releasing a haunting creak that echoed through the silence. A thick cloud of dust hit their faces all at once—damp concrete, rotting fabric, and rusted metal... an all-consuming blend.

As they stepped inside, the sound of crunching stone and broken glass echoed beneath their feet. The floor seemed shadowy, but a keen eye would soon reveal fresh footprints etched upon the thick layer of dust. Each one is a subtle reflection of the thoughtfulness behind its placement. Only one path lay ahead. Guiding from the core—no one comes back.

"It seems someone has recently travelled this path," Ernst remarked, crouching down to examine the footprints closely. "Or they stay inside."

"Stay alert," Lina instructed, her tone unwavering as the sun sank beneath the horizon. Her voice was soft, yet it carried a depth that hinted at hidden perils.

The expansive room unfolded before them, surprising and grand. Every footfall echoed, a sound that hung in the bare expanse of the walls, bouncing back with an unsettling hollowness that stirred the spirit. The ceiling soared overhead, but in certain spots, the plaster had crumbled, exposing a framework of corroded iron underneath. The dust hung thick in the air, swirling gently through the soft beams of light that filtered in from broken windows.

Beyond the decaying walls, the entrance to a tunnel emerged. The enduring concrete arch stood resolute against time, while the tunnel's conclusion slipped away into shadow. At the centre, a massive barrier of fallen stones obstructed the way forward. It felt like a deliberate choice to lock away the hidden truths that lay beneath the surface.

Ernst advanced deliberately toward the ruins, each step laden with the significance of what once existed. Upon first inspection, the wall displayed signs of deterioration, a clear sign of the unyielding march of time. Upon closer inspection, subtle lines emerged within the stone's rugged surface—almost faded inscriptions, the lingering essence of letters etched in the past.

He glided his fingers softly across the surface, sensing the delicate impressions hidden beneath his touch. "There's a message inscribed here," he murmured gently. "Etched in...only to be erased."

Lina approached him in graceful silence. Her gaze rested on the wall, and then, compelled by an inner urge, she sank down to the ground. With careful precision, she unearthed a piece of wood, partially hidden beneath the debris. A small metal box lay beneath, its surface tarnished by rust and the relentless march of time. A lock dangled from the door, its edges worn by time. "Look", she said; her breath was sharp.

Matteo appeared in an instant, poised to support them. Ernst gently opened the box, revealing its contents with a sense of anticipation. The ancient timber creaked, yielding to the passage of time. Inside rested an ancient pocket Bible, its pages tattered and worn, documents faded with time, and bits of paper adorned with letters drawn in charcoal.

Ernst grasped the Bible, sensing the significance of its pages and the narratives woven throughout. He unveiled the cover. A tiny folded note slipped from the pages. He bent down and grasped it in his hand. The paper showed signs of wear, its edges delicate and vulnerable, but the message within was unmistakably vivid.

Non solum credere. Cognoscere.[1]

Ernst uttered it gently, his gaze revealing a mix of wonder and purpose. "Who might have written this? This is not the familiar language of the Church."

Lina delicately lifted a frayed fragment of the book's pages. Her fingertips brushed against the delicate surface—

---

[1] Do not just believe. Know.

so fragile it appeared it could break with the slightest touch. The words remained aged, yet undeniably vivid:

Ordo, Veritas, Vox [1]

Her fingers glided over something. A circle, subtle yet unmistakable. You could sense it, the faint trace of an impression, imprinted and almost faded, yet still vibrant beneath the touch. A seal.

In the fading glow, a word lingered, solitary and almost lost to memory. Lina tracked the word with her eyes. Then, her voice lifted gently, a whisper breaking the silence.

"Concordium."

"What does it mean?" Matteo asked, his voice softening to a hushed tone, tinged with a deliberate sharpness.

"I'm not familiar with that," Ernst remarked, his brow furrowing as he glanced at Lina. "You?"

The weight of the universe seemed to anchor in Lina's mind as she shook her head intentionally and heavily. "No. I haven't encountered it previously."

Matteo stayed crouched, his gaze following the shapes and shadows inside the box, seeking significance in its diminutive nature. He gazed into the box, its inner surface captivating him like a subtle vow. The wooden interior showcased a deep stain, flowing unevenly across the grain like a whisper of darkness in the dimming glow. He remained there, quiet, his eyes steady.

His voice emerged, deep and resonant: "It seems to be dried blood…"

---

[1] Order, truth, voice.

They locked eyes for an extra heartbeat, the stillness enveloping them. The stillness thickened around us.

"Someone brought this box here," Matteo declared gently, yet with unwavering certainty. "This person had sustained injuries."

Lina scanned the room with a discerning gaze. She leaned in closer and whispered, "Whoever it was… It seems they aimed to convey a message."

The door creaked unexpectedly, breaking the thick stillness of the tunnel. They all recoiled in unison, straightening as if guided by an invisible hand.

"Hide," Lina urged, her voice barely a whisper in the quiet.

Ernst glided silently, manoeuvring behind the shelves that bore the marks of time, their wood aged and tired. Matteo, almost crawling, stealthily made his way into a shadowy corner. Lina deftly returned the box to its place, swift and silent, before slipping into the shadow created by the nearby column.

The room was still. An oppressive hush enveloped the space, creating a palpable tension in the atmosphere. The gentle resonance of heartbeats remained suspended in the atmosphere, a subtle rhythm weaving through the confines.

Footsteps resonated in the quiet. They moved with a measured grace, each step imbued with a thoughtful care that reflected the burdens they carried. Every footstep echoed against the stone floor, resonating through the quiet that enveloped the space. Suddenly, two silhouettes appeared out of the twilight.

In the soft glow filtering through the broken window, one figure loomed large, while the other appeared smaller—two shadows frozen in the night's quiet. They remained quiet; the atmosphere enveloped them in tense stillness. As the sun dipped below the horizon, the two silhouettes drew nearer, their whispers soft and deliberate.

Their words flowed gently, enveloped in a whisper of sound that blurred the syllables into a dreamlike mist.

Then, a single word sliced through the silence, distinct and precise as a blade cutting through mist: "…Concordium…"

Ernst, with an unwavering focus, allowed his eyes to wander toward Lina. In that instant, Lina redirected her attention towards him. The silence enveloped the space, heavy and foreboding, a palpable tension that loomed with an unvoiced threat.

The enigmatic silhouettes hung in the atmosphere; their weight was palpable and lingered just a heartbeat longer. Then, they moved deliberately and steadily until they vanished, like shadows dissolving into the twilight. Their footsteps vanished, a gentle sound consumed by the stillness of the night. And then it vanished, as if the universe had consumed it entirely. Silence enveloped the room again. Yet this silence was unlike any other—it bore the gravity of a caution.

From the depths of obscurity, three figures ascended, verging as though burdened by the enormity of existence itself. Their eyes locked, intensely and briefly; a quiet agreement formed in the air surrounding them. Words were superfluous. They all held a silent understanding, unmistakable and profound: staying here at this moment would invite calamity.

Someone had unveiled their presence. And now… they stood on the edge, the space between them just a whisper.

3

Emerging from the shadows of the passage, they beheld Berlin, a city cloaked in shades of gloom. The streetlamps glowed brightly, but their light provided no comfort. Instead, they cast elongated, shapeless shadows across the cobblestones and the walls, as if the very essence of night had materialised in the darkness.

They glided through the stillness, the burden of existence resting heavily upon them. With hands buried deep in their pockets, they advanced with a disciplined cadence, gazes fixed unwaveringly on the distant horizon. The street was quiet, with only the rhythmic sound of their shoes tapping against the pavement.

One word resonated in their minds, a persistent refrain: Concordium.

But what was it, truly?

A manuscript that reveals the essence of the world, its narratives unveiled across the printed pages. A community shaped by time. Is it a fellowship rooted in the Catholic tradition or one that aligns with Protestant beliefs? Is it simply the name of a phantom carved in shadows, tied to no spirit?

The Latin meaning exuded a captivating charm—tranquillity, balance, and structure. The unsettling thought persisted: someone could warp such a virtuous and elevated concept into a tool for the darkest intentions.

Lina was the first to break the silence. "We have to head to Humboldt," she declared. Her voice was soft, yet it carried an undeniable conviction.

Matteo slowed his pace, raising an eyebrow in subtle curiosity. "University?"

"Yes. The archive department houses the historical printing records, the church manuscripts, the reports from secret societies, and the journals dating back to the 19th century. If that name appears in these records, we will reveal it."

Ernst took a deep breath, a slight nod accompanying it, as though the burdens of existence were heavy upon him. "But how do we gain access? They currently restrict access. They scrutinised the documents of identity."

Lina gracefully opened her bag. She pulled out a worn identity paper with ragged edges, its surface dulled like ancient parchment—but the embossed seal stood out, sharp and unmistakable. "Typesetter reserve personnel. Emulation, but impactful. It will grant me access."

Matteo grabbed the document and examined it intently for a moment. He directed his attention to Lina. "That grants you access. What about us?"

Lina presented a delicate smile—just enough to lift the corners of her lips. "Then I will go in alone."

Ernst paused momentarily. "Alright. We'll go to the Humboldt archives. But first... I need to speak with an old contact of mine in the centre."

"Who?" Lina asked.

"Pharmacist Johann."

"Is he trustworthy?" She asked, her tone laced with a mix of wariness and doubt.

Ernst narrowed his gaze. "In this city, trust has transformed into a precious rarity."

4

The area around the pharmacy exuded a serene quiet, a tranquillity that hung in the atmosphere. Matteo lingered in the dimly lit alley, a figure cloaked in mystery, watchful and poised. Ernst advanced with determination, his hand reaching out to connect with the cold metal handle of the door.

The bell chimed gently, its tone rich with the essence of history.

Inside those walls, the atmosphere was heavy with the echoes of time past. Bottles, glass jars, and small boxes laden the shelves; their aged and faded labels whispered tales of a time long past. The walls, heavy with age and fatigue, drooped beneath the burden of the low ceiling. The atmosphere was thick with the scent of old paper, potions, and traces of desiccated herbs.

In the shadowy nook of the shop, a man with grey hair and a face marked by passing years raised his eyes from a pile of prescriptions. As he gazed at Ernst, his eyes narrowed, and a delicate change in the atmosphere enveloped them. Then, a subtle smile, tired yet genuine, touched his lips.

"Ernst Adler..." he whispered, the name lingering in the atmosphere like a faint memory. "Is it really you after all this time?"

Ernst lingered in the doorway, the significance of the moment enveloping him. With a measured breath, he moved in, each step purposeful. "It is I, Johann. You have changed a little."

Johann let out a low chuckle, his voice carrying a rugged charm. "You remain the same, just a year or two older."

Ernst's eyes wandered over the old shelves. He reached out, his fingers brushing against the dusty bottle with a delicate touch. "The pharmacy—still the same. Even the smell: as if time stopped here."

Johann nodded, his hands coming together in a serene gesture, embodying a tranquil acceptance of the moment's calm. "The city beyond has withered, Ernst. The streets were quiet, and whispers filled the air. Yet this place... this place stayed the same. In order to maintain a sense of self, one holds on to the constants in life."

A veil of sadness enveloped Ernst's expression, profound and resolute. "In Berlin, circumstances lead to people being forgotten or lost... or people discover a way to thrive in the shadows." Johann's gaze remained fixed on Ernst's face, his voice barely above a whisper. "You continue to walk among those shadows, don't you?"

Ernst's eyes wandered around the room, glancing over at the medicine bottles and the tarnished glass jars, before settling back on Johann's expression. "And yet here you are—still at that same desk, still shuffling the papers, still processing the orders."

Johann remained quiet, the tension of his silence palpable in the atmosphere. He adjusted his glasses, a subtle smile playing on his lips, hinting at a profound understanding and a wealth of contemplation beneath the surface. He exhaled deeply, his head nodding slowly and purposefully. The smile faded, revealing the deep lines of time etched into his face.

Ernst spoke gently, his words a quiet yet resolute murmur. "Has anyone been here recently? Someone... extraordinary. Did someone say something?"

Johann shrugged, a subtle movement that conveyed a wealth of meaning. He gazed into the gap between the shelves, ensnared in the realm of what was and what could easily fade away. "Every day, a few wander in and out. Countless individuals swallow their pills and move on, burdened by the weight of the world. Even their everyday existence holds the burden of an unspoken reality."

Ernst edged closer, his voice a soft murmur in the quiet atmosphere. "Yet some... seek more than just medicine, do they not, Johann?"

The clock on the corner ticked steadily, its heavy sound slicing through the silence that enveloped them. Johann gazed deeply into Ernst's eyes, the silence hanging between them like a finely tuned instrument, poised for the faintest hint of revelation. His face reflected a moment of uncertainty, yet underneath it flowed a profound sense of acceptance. He remembered a profound truth, concealed and unspoken, one that had remained locked away within him. Finally, he lowered his head, burdened by the immense weight of the world. He removed his glasses and set them down on the edge of the counter.

"Certain individuals... They do not depart from here in the same manner they arrived, Ernst. Some allow their pain to fade into the background, while others carry the weight of their silence. Each one undoubtedly leaves a lasting impression. It was present, concealed in the darkness, yet unmistakably clear."

"How do you mean?" Lina asked, a hint of concern crossing her face.

Johann's eyes moved from one person to the next. His voice dropped to a hushed tone, carefully, as if the walls themselves were listening.

"Some never speak. But the air changes when they're here. You can feel it... They carry an invisible weight, a profound influence that moulds each stride they take. Their presence hangs in the atmosphere, dense and unwavering, yet invisible."

Ernst's hand glided into the deep pocket of his coat, exploring, the fabric brushing against his fingers. He pulled out a small, wrinkled slip of paper, its edges frayed and stained by the years, the ink blurred and indistinct. He opened it with great attentiveness.

"Have you ever seen this before?" he asked, his tone calm and unwavering, as he offered the paper to Johann.

The elder gentleman adjusted his spectacles on the bridge of his nose, his hands trembling slightly as he completed the task. He gazed at the paper, the words dancing in his mind, time flowing away like sand through fingers. His expression grew tense, a slight change, lips separating, but the stillness hung heavily around them. The stillness deepened, marked solely by the unyielding tick-tock of the wall clock.

Finally, his voice broke through—gentle and trembling. "Absolutely... I am familiar with it. It remained hidden. I have only ever come across it. Just in select locations. The words appeared to be meant for specific listeners only."

Ernst narrowed his eyes, his expression sharpening as he advanced. "What is preventing it from being heard by a wider audience?"

Johann responded. His gaze remained fixed on the page before him. "For it is not for the ear to grasp... but for the silence to embrace. It was a reality that only the keenest observers could fully comprehend. That is what they believe to be true."

"Who possesses such a conviction?" Lina asked, her voice carrying a sharp determination.

Johann pivoted his head, with a measured and intentional grace, in her direction. His eyes carried a profound depth, and his voice flowed gently, like a whisper in the twilight. "It seems you still do not know their names."

"No," Ernst replied, his tone resolute. "Only one name stands out: Concordium."

Johann took a deep breath. His shoulders sagged, and a tired doubt lingered in the lines of his expression. He removed his glasses and set them down on the table, the light glinting off the lenses briefly before they came to rest in quietude. He grasped the coffee cup, yet it remained suspended, never touching his lips. He placed it down once more, softly, as if the gesture carried a significant meaning.

"I can't keep you here any longer," he said, his voice calm and unwavering. "Yet, if you still have the bravery to pursue the right companions... explore the university's archive level."

Ernst's eyes narrowed, revealing a glimmer of something profound within them. "Is someone there?"

Johann nodded; his head swayed gently as he pondered deeply. "Yes. His name is Elias, an old typesetter. He now dedicates himself entirely to translation and documents. He keeps to himself—lives as if invisible. But if he speaks, one must listen to him carefully. As far as I know, he's still there…"

Lina locked eyes with him, her expression firm, a mix of determination and caution. "How about sharing a bit more with us? Why do you only guide us on our journey?"

Johann's gaze wandered, enveloped in contemplation. An unwelcome echo from the past resurfaced in that instant, piercing and undeniable.

"Because…" he murmured, his voice a soft echo against the gentle breeze, his head lowered as if guarding a hidden truth, "those who bear certain revelations… rarely enjoy a long life."

Part 2

The Trace within Silence

5

Lina paused for a moment at the entrance to the archive wing of Humboldt University. She slipped her hand into the inner pocket of her coat, her fingers gliding over the fabric, and retrieved the well-worn, faded identity paper of the auxiliary staff. She handed it over discreetly to the guard standing by the door. The man shot a quick, vacant glance and then tilted his head slightly to show she could go by. He stayed quiet. He requested nothing at all.

She confidently pushed the door open and stepped inside. The noise of the outside world faded, enveloping everything in a profound stillness. Tranquillity wove through this location, a heavy veil of memories enveloping it. Dust motes danced in the air, gently settling among the shelves, blending with the inviting aroma of leather-bound books. In the soft glow, aged wax stains on the stone walls shimmered gently, reminiscent of timeless guardians keeping their vigil through the ages.

This transcended mere memories. It was a stone passageway where the whispers of centuries intertwined gently.

She moved forward, determined and unwavering. The gentle click of her heels was the only sound that pierced the stillness of the stone floor. She glided past the archive desk, her head lowered in contemplation. Her fingers brushed against the spines of the books, a momentary caress, as she continued on her way.

Her eyes darted across the titles with remarkable speed, but then she paused, ensnared in a fleeting moment.

A figure glided silently through the aisles. A lone silhouette occupied a desk, shrouded in the soft glow of the distant corner. He stood with a subtle slouch, his head lowered in contemplation. He grasped a document in one hand, a pen poised in the other. The hold was firm, as though the nib could pierce right through the page. The dim light cast shadows across his face, but it was his subtle intensity that captivated Lina.

She approached quietly, her movements gentle, like a phantom rising from the shadowy depths of the bookshelves. She lingered at the edge of his desk, her voice a soft murmur, deliberate and controlled.

"Excuse me... is your name Elias?"

The man lifted his head with measured grace. He appeared to be around the age of forty-five. His complexion was fair, with the darkness under his eyes intensified by fatigue. Sharp features marked his face, etched by anxiety and countless sleepless nights. His hair tousled, a vivid reminder of the previous night's adventures. His eyes, tinged with uncertainty, sparkled with a keen awareness, poised for the challenges that waited. He observed Lina intently, absorbing every nuance from her head to her feet.

"Who's asking?" He asked, his voice calm, eyes narrowing. His voice carried a subtle uncertainty, not menacing—rather, a cultivated caution, the kind forged by a life intertwined with danger.

Lina moved ahead, her hands relaxed at her sides, signalling her readiness to welcome whatever was to come. "A friend... sent from Johann's pharmacy," she stated, her voice calm and unwavering. She aimed to ensnare his attention with her eyes. "You are Elias, aren't you?"

He glanced to the left and then to the right, his fingers tapping gently on the edge of the desk. He gave a slight nod and gestured toward the chair across from him. Lina grasped the situation and confidently settled into her role.

She pulled the old wooden chair nearer, the soft creak resonating in the quiet, and eased herself into it with a deliberate elegance. The atmosphere was thick around the shelves, a stillness that felt poised, anticipating a moment that would shatter the quiet. Elias fixed his gaze on her, the silence expanding between them like a tightly drawn string.

"What brings you to this place?" he asked. His voice bore the burden of exhaustion, yet it resonated with sharp insight.

Lina paused momentarily, then tilted her head gently downward. "We uncovered a word."

Elias's expression, previously devoid of emotion, transformed in an instant. His gaze locked onto hers—as if he were not exploring the features of a stranger but unravelling the echoes of a long-buried enchantment. "Was that word...Concordium?"

Lina stayed quiet. She held her gaze steady. The stillness surrounding them expressed a profound connection that words could never fully capture.

Elias tilted his head forward just a touch, but his eyelids stayed resolutely open. When he spoke again, his voice resonated with depth and gravitas. "Then it's settled; remain."

She leaned in slightly, her words flowing softly like a captivating story. "Can you clarify what you're trying to say?"

Elias ran his fingers thoughtfully along the edge of the desk. His gaze drifted far away—but every word that came next struck with remarkable clarity.

"Concordium transcends a simple definition." His voice resonated with a depth that transcended mere words, carrying an intensity that captivated the listener. "Concordium stands as a remarkable structure—one that defines the home of knowledge and who holds the power to unlock different truths. Some view it as a hidden extension of the Vatican. Some think it is merely a secretive scholarly group formed by experienced archivists. Yet, it is… none of those. And far more dangerous than any of them."

Lina inhaled deeply. Her voice emerged softly, as if stifled by the heavy stone walls surrounding her. "What exactly is it?"

Elias's gaze drifted past her, into the dim recesses that lingered beyond the shelves. His voice dropped to a whisper, but every word landed with undeniable impact.

"Concordium represents a group of individuals who shape the course of history, yet their contributions often go unnoticed in the records of time."

A brief pause of tranquillity followed. In the room's stillness, the only sound was the deliberate, rhythmic ticking of the ancient wall clock—unwavering and constant. Elias tilted his head, lingering in the shadows that concealed his features.

"Have you ever considered who wrote the foundational texts that set the stage for Hitler?" he asked gently. He settled into his chair, his eyes fixed on an unseen target—not the shelves, but the imposing walls steeped in history. He appeared to peer beyond the veil of time, observing a narrative that was both present and yet to be penned.

"The papers that enabled Hitler's rise..." he whispered finally. "These records are absent from all official German archives. They lack documentation in any state. Someone crafted them, as if they had never existed. Crafted, contemplated... and then thoughtfully eliminated."

Lina leaned forward in her chair, her knees drawing nearer to the desk. Her gaze sought Elias's in the dimness, as if searching for a hidden key in the shadows—a key to the truth.

"What were these documents?" Lina asked, her voice calm and determined.

Elias held his gaze steady and unyielding. The tone of his voice had transformed—now it was not just informative but also filled with caution and intention.

"In 1919, Germany was in ruins. The empire had crumbled into disarray. They disbanded the military and left the economy in ruins. People were grappling with hunger, overwhelmed by a sense of despair and frustration. Amid the chaos, Concordium emerged with a striking presence. It extends beyond Berlin... " He paused, locking eyes with Lina. "...simultaneously—in Rome, Munich, Zurich, Paris... and particularly earlier, in the Vatican."

"Mussolini was still just a journalist then," Lina remarked, her voice laced with a confident doubt.

Elias nodded thoughtfully, his eyes drifting back to the hidden stories that awaited discovery on the shelves. "Certainly... he was already being monitored. Or maybe..." He turned to her once more, his voice taking on a gentler quality. "...he was already being advised."

Lina's breath caught in her throat. She intently watched his face, determined to catch every word. "And what about Hitler?"

Elias locked his eyes with determination. His facial muscles tightened, as if the truth he was on the verge of sharing carried a weight too great to bear. "In 1923, Concordium held simultaneous meetings in Berlin, Munich, and Rome." The stillness of the room grew heavier with the impact of his words. "In every case, the aim was clear: identify the right person, elevate them, and shape them into a leader who can inspire the masses."

He gently lowered his eyelids as if trying to shield himself from the haunting memories he was about to summon. "Mussolini and Hitler... They did not ascend by their own volition, as many assume. Concordium expertly developed the projects; the results of a thoughtful, systematic, and relentless design strategy. Their voices, their slogans, their speeches... Concordium continued to function seamlessly behind the scenes. They are always hiding in the shadows and always concealed."

Silence shrouded the room; nobody spoke a word. The silence in Lina's throat was thick—heavy, clinging, and impossible to swallow. Her hands trembled softly as she rested them on her knees. As the truth unravelled, it seemed to shroud clarity even further. As they journeyed deeper, the boundary between past and present became increasingly elusive.

"What's the reason for that?" Lina asked. Her voice emerged with a raspy quality, barely more than a whisper. "What are the goals of Concordium?"

Elias took a deep breath. A sharp, insightful expression settled on his face. "It is not to stop the chaos," he said, his voice lowering to a hush, "but to design it."

Lina's brows knitted together, a hint of tension in her expression.

Elias spoke again. "From the outside, it may seem they are creating a sense of order. Yet that command is merely an act of surrender—crafted in stillness. No one asks. No one guarantees answers. Those who have the courage to express their opinions... find themselves muted."

His voice turned heavy, rich with unexpressed realities. "They dispatched the diagrams to Mussolini, cloaked in the pretence of *celestial direction...* phrases wove seamlessly into the essence of sermons... Hitler's words, the foundational elements of his theories of *racial superiority*, remained clear and resolute. Instruments of a sinister design, they moulded thoughts and destinies in a logic-forsaken realm. They did not create these for people. Despite embodying the people's beliefs, they only reinforced the existing structure. Not the intelligence reports. Not the burden of political ideologies. They were directives cloaked in the appearance of conviction."

Lina reclined in her chair, her breath a subtle challenge in her throat. The genuine horror lived not in the actions of Concordium. *The manner in which they executed their plan was remarkable—especially considering that no one seemed to see it happen.*

She found it challenging to articulate her thoughts. "Is there any proof?" She enquired, her voice a husky murmur, softly piercing the stillness.

Elias lifted his eyes. His gaze locked onto Lina—devoid of life, yet unwavering. "You are not adrift in your quest," he said, his voice calm and assured. "However, I cannot yet determine if you are here at the right moment…"

He dipped his head for a moment, then slowly rose from his chair and turned to face the shelves behind him. His hand glided over the old leather spines of dusty folders—purposeful, yet confident. At last, he revealed a blank, unadorned folder. It lacked a title, a code, or a label—its very being seemed to contradict itself. The thick layer of dust on its cover spoke volumes: it had remained undisturbed for quite some time. He placed it gently on the desk and delicately raised the cover with the lightest touch of his fingertips.

The stillness deepened, wrapping all in a weighty aura.

The delicate tremor of the pages seemed to echo the depth of the mysteries they contained. Elias looked down at them, a brief recognition passing over his features, as if he were facing a well-known wound. "These documents… date back to 1923," he remarked. "A blend of Latin, German, and Italian. Most people wouldn't even think about looking at them."

Lina keenly observed Elias's focus and picked up the foremost document. As her fingers glided along its edges, a blend of aged ink and dust caressed her face. As she turned the page, a familiar typeface emerged — the striking Gothic script often found in church records and ancient manuscripts. The text did not begin like a revered prayer or a ceremonial excerpt. The nuances hidden within the words were remarkably intricate. It was rich in precise terminology, yet concealed within the prose was an unwavering mathematical precision. Commands, instructions, lists... it resembled a detailed blueprint of a mechanism rather than an expression of conviction.

She immersed herself deeply in the text. The text contained words that seemed like deliberately crafted symbols. On their own, they seemed insignificant, but together they exuded a haunting, metallic significance.

Elias acknowledged with a quiet nod. "This is the language of Concordium," he declared. "Not wholly divine or completely worldly... A language that functions in the background of both."

Lina gently turned the delicate page with her fingertips. In the gentle light, the words seemed to sway in the shadows — almost alive. Her lips parted slightly, her voice barely a whisper. "*Volksgeist... obedientia absoluta... custodire silentium...*" Her eyes sharpened, searching for deeper insights concealed within the text. "Spirit of the people... absolute obedience... preserve the silence..." she translated softly.

She paused for a moment, then turned to Elias with a concerned expression. "To what do these texts belong?"

Elias kept his head down, his fingertips tracing the edges of the lines as his gaze stayed locked on the documents. As he spoke, his voice carried a weighty clarity: "These are... documents not issued by the Church, yet presented as though they had its endorsement. This embodies the genuine operational strategy of Concordium." He stood confidently and met Lina's gaze with unwavering intensity. "These weren't for governments... but for leaders. Not to forge a public legal framework, but to cultivate a deeply personal sense of sacred legitimacy.

Lina fell silent, the weight of Elias's words pressing down on her.

He continued, "The initial documents sent to Mussolini showed the nation-state as a divine order. The documents presented holiness not as something born from the people's desires but because of their adherence."

He whispered, almost as if sharing a secret. "The papers that reached Hitler were nearly identical... just adapted for Germany. Various versions of the same structure, the same ceremonial language."

Lina subtly shook her head, remaining silent. Her mind wrestled with the words she had just heard, caught in a tension between acceptance and denial.

"Concordium goes beyond mere manipulation," she stated, her voice soft. "It forges an entirely new existence—through unwavering belief, through vibrant expression, through the core of fundamental principles."

Elias narrowed his eyes and whispered, "And the most terrifying part... is that its actual power lies in not making a sound. A system built in silence survives because there's no one left to oppose it."

Lina raised her gaze, her eyes sharpening with clarity. Her voice now carried not curiosity but an undeniable sense of urgency. "Then why aren't they in Rome? What leads documents like these to a forgotten university archive in Berlin rather than the Vatican?

Elias nodded thoughtfully. He carefully opened the folder and pulled out another aged, yellowed page. The ageing process had deepened the edges, much like charred paper, and the ink kept a subtle sheen, as if it had never fully dried, even after decades.

"The originals are in Rome," he said in a gentle tone. "*Codex Altus*. Hidden away in the deepest recesses of the Vatican Library. Shown to no one. These... are only copies. Yet, even these—they do not desire for them to last."

Lina scrutinised the page in her hand with keen focus. Someone had crumpled the corner, as if gripping it in a fleeting moment—just before it vanished into the ether.

Elias continued, his voice steady and composed: "Look... someone blacked out some lines, and someone deliberately soaked some pages. As if someone had tried to save them before their destruction. In haste. In panic."

Lina traced her fingers over the wrinkled edge of the page. She spoke in a hushed tone. "Who came to their rescue?"

Elias responded while maintaining steady eye contact. "I am unaware of his actual name. Nobody does. However, one title consistently emerges throughout the documents: *Frater Cinis*."

Lina contemplated the words in her mind. They escaped her lips in a soft whisper. "Brother of Ashes..." In that instant, the stillness in the room thickened once again. The dust particles swirled softly in the candlelight, and for the first time, Lina felt the profound depth of Concordium's shadow—its timeless essence, its deep-rooted presence... and its dangerous allure.

Elias nodded thoughtfully, his gaze drifting over the dimly lit shelves as if he were hunting for a hidden spectre. "Someone from within Concordium," he whispered, his voice barely audible. "Not necessarily of high status, but having the ability to reach the deepest levels. Once he had successfully smuggled out the documents, he vanished without a trace. Vanished without a sound, leaving nothing behind. He disappeared."

His words filled the room, crafting an unmistakable ambiance. The soft glow flickered among the shelves, intertwining with the floating dust on the worn pages, as the stillness grew, becoming increasingly palpable.

Lina gently caressed the worn edges of the old papers. Their delicate, intricate surface trembled softly—echoing a faint heartbeat from the past. She released her trapped breath, then gradually raised her head. The contours of her face became more defined in the dim light. She locked her eyes on Elias, her voice dropping to a soft murmur.

"These documents..." she remarked. "What led to their being in your hands?"

Elias took a moment before he replied. He settled back in his chair, his eyes slowly drifting to the dusty window. Outside, Berlin's hazy, heavy morning swirled like an elusive spectre in the fog. The sky felt limited, as if the entire universe held its breath in eager expectation. In that moment, silence transformed into something profound—it carried the weight of memories, heavy with the echoes of what once was.

At last, Elias found his voice. His voice carried a gentle clarity, shaped by the depth of the memory. "Last year", he remarked. "Late November. A gentleman entered from Rome. He stayed quiet. Resembling a silhouette. He stayed out of sight. He failed to mention a name. I chose not to ask." He turned his attention to Lina. "Sometimes, in the quest for answers... one only uncovers even more daunting questions."

Elias continued after a moment of silence. "He carried a rugged, dark metal box. There was no seal on it. He stared at me and said, *'Look at this city. As the quiet settles... hand over the documents.'* He then left. I never saw him again. I discovered his name is Frater Cinis. And that he stays hidden."

Lina gave a slight nod of acknowledgement. Her voice felt hollow, devoid of any warmth. "This is... It extends far beyond Berlin. It suggests that Europe is deteriorating from the inside."

Elias shifted his focus towards her. His tired yet sharp eyes seemed to distil a lifetime of knowledge into one profound remark.

"Concordium has consistently made its mark. Still lurking in the background. They were never at the war itself. They were the ones who laid the groundwork for war.

And now... the darkness has lost its purpose. His voice became richer. This structure is presently in operation. At this moment, more than ever before."

Silence once again cloaked the archive room. Yet it was no longer the serenity of comprehension—it was the stillness before an approaching storm. The books on the shelves stood quietly, while the ancient stones embedded in the walls seemed ready to unveil their tales.

6

As Lina stepped out of the university's stone-paved corridor, an intense weight pressed down on her chest. Each step seemed to draw forth an invisible, endlessly growing burden from the depths of her soul. Elias's words resonated in her mind; each phrase revealed a fresh opportunity, but none offered solid ground to stand on. Beyond each threshold was an endless abyss—a silence so profound, it resonated with power.

Outside, the sky seemed to have drawn closer to the ground. The moment hung in perfect harmony between light and shadow; a gentle fog danced in a quiet contest with the looming night that sought to shroud the city. The silhouettes of the structures elongated, weaving through the crevices of the cobblestones, gliding around corners with an air of quiet menace.

The air was freezing, yet an even more ominous force lingered than the cold: something unseen, yet undeniably felt. Like a presence that was watching.

She quickened her pace. As she exited the courtyard, a figure captured her gaze in her peripheral vision—just to the right, at the foot of the stone wall. A silhouette draped in an elongated black coat. He was merely there. Immovable, as if chiselled from the solid stone that surrounded him. He kept his head straight, never glancing away, but Lina felt certain he was watching her.

It was more than just a passing glance from a stranger. The atmosphere was chilly, calculated, and intentional. A gaze that unmistakably targeted its prey.

A chill ran down her spine. With a swift motion, she clutched her bag more firmly. The documents Elias had provided her—nestled within the inner compartments—now felt heavier, infused with a profound significance and an air of danger.

The man stood motionless. Yet Lina was nearly certain that his gaze lingered on her back. An unsettling quiet enveloped the street, her footsteps echoing against the stone pavement in the calmness. She pressed on seamlessly. As she crossed the threshold and entered the main road, the street lamps cast their soft, flickering glow.

She delved into her pocket and pulled out a small, round metal mirror—nestling it in her palm and tilting it perfectly to glimpse what lay behind her.

He was gone. But the feeling remained.

With every step, an elusive presence seemed to close in—hovering just out of reach, teasingly close to brushing against her shoulder. Lina took a deep breath. But the knot in her throat wouldn't loosen.

7

Ernst and Matteo waited calmly under the shimmering light of the streetlamps. As Lina's quick yet deliberate footsteps broke the silence, the three of them exchanged a brief glance—strategic, unvoiced. Quietude surrounded them.

In silent agreement, they turned and headed towards the abandoned tram depot. It remained a testament to Kreuzberg's industrial zone—a place so neglected that it had disappeared from every official map. The walls showcased a tapestry of paint, each layer gracefully peeling away to reveal the stories beneath. The weathered tracks sank into the cracked ground beneath, as the cold radiating from the concrete edifice seeped into their very bones.

The broken windows welcomed the breeze, gently swaying the hanging chains and producing soft, echoing sounds—evoking the faint toll of a bell long left behind.

As they stepped inside, the sharp scent of corroded metal and rotting wood overwhelmed their senses. Moonlight poured through the shattered glass in fragmented rays, twisting shadows into strange and silent shapes.

They stood still for a moment. The stillness appeared to have sealed their mouths shut. Finally, Ernst's voice broke through—gentle in tone, yet brimming with resolute conviction. "What did you find out?"

Lina gently placed her bag on the ground. She took a deep breath. Her hands remained unwavering, while her expression took on a determined clarity. With a sense of relief, she carefully retrieved the bundle of papers she had been safeguarding, as if releasing a weight that had pressed down on her shoulders. There was no need for words. The answer was on the paper. And that should break the stillness.

She handed the file to Ernst. He accepted it without hesitation. Under the dim light filtering through the rusted metal beams overhead, he unfolded the pages with care. The ink had faded, but the words continued to echo with strength.

As his gaze lingered over the words, his expression shifted—starting with confusion, it quickly intensified into a simmering, palpable anger. Finally, his expression grew stern, his lips forming a tight, resolute line. He delivered his words while keeping his gaze fixed downward. His voice was barely audible, yet underneath it surged a current of restrained rebellion.

"Are these real?"

Lina carefully arranged the stack with her fingertips before turning to face him. Her gaze was steadfast. Her voice rang out with sharpness and elegance. "According to Elias, they're real," she said. "And this text… it's not an ideological manifesto. Not a call to action. Not propaganda."

She paused for a moment. Then, without a moment's pause: "It's a blueprint. Cold-blooded, systematic and long-term. A schematic for building a structure—in silence."

Ernst redirected his attention from the text. Feeling an unexpected weight pressing down on him, he took a few steps back. The soft whisper of his shoes gliding across the uneven concrete floor broke the stillness. He lowered his head. The lines on his face had deepened, revealing a sense of unravelling within him, as if a more daunting landscape lay just beneath the surface.

His voice came forth as barely more than a whisper. "Does this have any ties to the Vatican?"

Lina softly shook her head. Her reply was prompt, straightforward, and resolute. "No. At least… not officially." The brilliance in her gaze was unwavering. Her voice lowered further, yet somehow gained more gravitas. "Elias stated Concordium developed under the influence of the Vatican. It undeniably exists, though official records may not reflect that. It has always existed. Quiet. Unseen. For it to exist—it needed to stay hidden. A framework that forges its own path… only to obliterate it. It helps you overlook its presence."

A moment of quiet enveloped them. When she finally spoke, her voice was gentle yet resolute. "I successfully encouraged Elias to share his thoughts. His understanding is exceptionally deep. He will provide us with the details tomorrow morning. He is going to be here."

Matteo was at the edge of the room, quietly sifting through the scattered papers atop an old crate. His fingertips paused at the faint trace of a seal on the corner of a yellowed sheet. The weight of the years embedded in the parchment seemed to hum against his skin—like silence captured in the paper's very fibres.

"If these documents aren't forgeries..." he said, his voice low, nearly a whisper. The sentence hung in the air, unfinished. But the thought—its *weight*—spread through the room like smoke.

Lina turned her gaze to Matteo, her eyes steeled under the flickering light. This time, her voice was clear—unshaken, resolute. "We know one thing for certain," she said. "We're not alone in Berlin."

Ernst slowly lifted his head. He fixed his eyes on a distant, vacant point—yet behind them, he felt the storm building in the depths of his mind. He leaned back against the wall. The cold crept up his spine like a shadow, but it no longer mattered.

When he finally spoke, the words came slowly—but the conviction in them was as unyielding as the cracked stone behind him.

"We're not alone… *anywhere* now."

8

The following morning, they gathered once more at the abandoned tram depot of Kreuzberg.

Lina knelt next to an aged train seat. She meticulously retrieved the documents hidden beneath it and laid them out on the wooden crate they had converted into a temporary table. She opened each page with meticulous care, her fingers softly smoothing the curled edges. The breeze seeping in through the broken windows made the pages tremble as if filled with the essence of memories.

Ernst kept a vigilant watch in the faint glow of the rear doorway. His eyes swept across the end of the street, taking in the quiet corners, vigilant for the slightest hint of movement.

Matteo strolled along the rusted tracks, pacing thoughtfully, his gaze sweeping the surroundings—deciphering the city's pulse like a heartbeat, sensitive to a sound that seemed oddly misplaced.

A figure lingered in the doorway, hesitant and quiet. A moment lingered, then crossed the threshold. It was Elias.

He wore a black overcoat, worn, its collar turned up against the chill, guarding his face from the wind. His hands lay deep in his pockets, seeking warmth from the biting cold, yet his stride remained taut and purposeful. His eyes held the weight of a night spent awake, shadows of uncertainty lingering in their depths. He pressed his lips into a hard line, his face bearing the weight of a long-ago choice—one he knew was irreversible.

Ernst and Lina sat still, their eyes fixed upon him, the air thick with unspoken words. Elias paused, a slight nod of acknowledgement passing between them—quiet, measured.

"Did anyone follow you?" Ernst's voice was unyielding, deep yet tinged with the wariness of one who understood the deceptive calm of a morning.

Elias took a step closer. He gave a subtle shrug, then slowly shook his head. "I changed stops twice. Choose the hidden pathways. I have completely lost all trace…" His voice trembled, turning gritty and raspy. "One cannot find out with complete assurance."

"Please take a seat," Lina said, gesturing toward the worn chair next to her.

"Before we start... is there anything we ought to know?"

He paused; a moment stretched between them. Then he nodded, slow and deliberately, turned away, and settled into his seat. "Before we start..." His voice was distinct now. It was no longer the possession of a man who held wisdom. It bore the burden of a voice, one that had known the hard edge of survival, etched deep into his very bones. "Understand this: those who bear this knowledge become prey. Concordium erased its past, for it stilled every hand that sought to mark it. Silence stands as their only command, from the beginning to the end. Only the structure remains, steadfast against the passing time."

Elias drew his bag onto his lap with a deliberate motion. He unfastened the clasp, steady and sure, without a tremor in his hands. He paused. A moment stretched thin, weighing the burden of what was to come, just once more. He took a deep breath and pulled from the shadows a thick file, its pages yellowed with age.

This one stood apart from the rest. It was weighty, encased in an aged paper that had a texture reminiscent of fabric. The worn yellow stains and the tattered edges—these were not signs of disregard, but rather of time, mystery, and purpose. The cover bore no title. No seal present. Just quiet—and heaviness.

He set the file in front of them. For a moment, his hands lay gently upon it. He then raised his head slightly.

"If you are ready... I will speak about Concordium."

9

Elias lifted the cover of the file, his fingertips moving slowly, as if the weight of the world rested upon them. Within, there lay but a solitary page.

Ernst's and Lina's eyes fell to the lower corner, where a seal, bold and striking, caught the dim light. It was round, shaped by a careful hand. Delicate embossing adorned its surface, and intricate geometric patterns wove through it like a story told in silence. At its heart, hidden like a secret in the fabric, there lay a phrase in Latin. Plain and clear. Yet laden with significance:

Custodia Pacis [1]

The paper was brittle and fragile, like the remnants of a forgotten story waiting to be told. The ink, dark and rich, had seeped into the fibres, yet the handwriting remained deliberate and precise, a testament to care.

Anno Domini MCMXXIII
Roma, Berlin, München
Sub umbra, pactum factum est.

They all stood close together, staring at the note, and the air was dense with ideas that weren't voiced. Matteo carefully reached for it, raising the fragile paper and tilting it just enough that the faded lettering might catch the light from the candle. They moved gently, as if the ink had breathed across time. His words rolled from his lips like a spell he had forgotten, reverberating in the still room.

---

[1] Guardian of the Peace.

"In the year of 1923. Rome, Berlin, Munich. The pact was forged under the shadow."

A shadow of confusion passed over his face. He furrowed his brow and tilted his head, a slight movement that spoke of thought and weight. He spoke in a low voice, almost lost to the wind: "An agreement made in the dark..."

Elias lifted his gaze. His eyes wandered to the shadowy corners of the room, and when he spoke once more, his voice had taken on a deeper tone. Every word landed with the weight of a verdict, measured and intentional:

"Yes. Three cities; three silhouettes. Roma, Berlin, and Munich. A contract that one can understand without speaking. Diplomats are absent. There have been no official agreements created. No official documentation exists. However, Concordium was present. With a profound understanding of the Reichswehr... when Mussolini was not yet at the height of his power, he had already pledged his support. They carried out actions quietly."

Matteo and Ernst exchanged a glance, each sensing the gravity of the words, the subtle aggression hidden within their shared past. Lina's voice cut through the air, shattering the tension that hung between them:

"What about the Vatican? Did they provide support for this as well?"

Elias inclined his head slightly. He stayed quiet for a considerable time before he finally spoke—his voice now slower, laden with meaning:

"Officially, not at all. However, within the Vatican, there was a long-standing—but formidable—faction. People dismissed the collective's presence outside the Vatican, but they murmured about it within." He paused for a time, choosing his words carefully. "A framework introduced with the assurance of *'maintaining peace'*... yet, in reality, crafted to impose authority, control, and unwavering compliance."

Lina shifted her gaze from the document to Elias, then returned her attention to the seal. She asked in quiet tones, "This order... who does it serve?"

"Certainly not the people," he replied with a chilling clarity that was devoid of any pretence.

Ernst deliberately traced the charred marks with his finger, as if he were deciphering the fingerprints of history. His voice was distinct and firm when it first emerged: "Why did they attempt to set this on fire?"

At that moment, Elias exhaled. He met Ernst's gaze, which was laden with the fatigue of an individual who had endured an inordinate amount of difficulty for an extended period. "This is Concordium's birth certificate, or more precisely, its rebirth. Their centuries-old strategy of denial will collapse if this document ever reaches the outside world," he continued. "If that were to occur, it would be imperative that they acknowledge their presence in a public setting. This motivated our transition from mere shadow tracking." His voice faded into a gentle murmur. "They have identified us as targets."

Elias continued to speak, his voice resolute and steady as it penetrated the inert atmosphere with precision.

"Just weeks before Hitler's failed coup in Munich..." he remarked, "... three senior Concordium representatives gathered in secrecy with select individuals from Italy and Germany in a historic Benedictine monastery just outside of Munich."

"When I first heard about it", Elias confided, "I was sceptical as well." He opened his bag once more, his hands shaking now—not out of fear, but from the awareness of what he was about to reveal. He picked up another old sheet; its edges curled and darkened, and placed it carefully on the wooden crate. "This leaves no room for doubt. This document stands as proof of that meeting."

Ernst leaned in gradually. He glided his fingers across the page, sensing the texture of history—as if the paper had absorbed the whispers of every secret shared that night. In a soft yet consistent tone, he read:

"Geistige Führung durch göttliche Disziplin." The words resonated with a deliberate and substantial cadence as they drifted across the room. "Intellectual leadership through divine discipline."

He shifted to the second line, his tone growing deeper: *"Ubi silentium regnat, ordo nascitur."* His eyes became still, as though gazing into the emptiness that lies between words. "Where silence reigns, order is born." The words echoed against the cold stone walls, not as mere facts, but as hidden truths—an encoded declaration of a reality constructed not on honesty, but on quietude.

"Veritas non semper prodest." With the precision of a blade descending point-first, the words exited his lips. "Truth is not always useful."

A dense and unyielding silence followed. Each of them remained seated, their gazes fixed on the document. However, their minds wandered far from it, as they pondered the words like stones in the dark, evaluating their importance and the responsibilities they imposed. Concordium was not merely a historical force that influenced events; it was an entity that redefined the concept of *"truth"* to suit its own objectives.

Lina's voice had undergone a transformation, with no trace of dread or apprehension. It had become more distinct, methodical, and sharpened by determination. "These are not mere slogans," she declared. "This serves as a schematic. A system design that is comprehensive. A structure of authoritarian dominance that is meticulously detailed and encased in belief. The concealment of reality when necessary is of paramount importance, as are compliance, faith, and quietness. This is a practical guide, not a statement of beliefs."

Elias nodded, a resigned comprehension dawning on his face.

He said, "Every word serves a useful purpose in the real world." His finger slid across the paper, emphasising each sentence. "*Silence* — complete control over the media and public opinion. *Spiritual discipline* entails the covert infiltration and silent enslavement of establishments like scholarly circles, universities, and the Church. *The propagation of lies as official policy*—the pointlessness of truth, manipulating perception and the art of changing people by distorting reality."

Matteo remained silent as he gazed at the document. When he finally spoke, his voice was barely above a whisper: "So Hitler's failed coup... Was it merely a distraction?"

Elias gradually shifted his gaze toward him. "No. The coup's failure was not part of Concordium's plans." He let out a deep breath and said, "But the chaos it caused turned into an opportunity. As attention focused on Hitler, the streets, and the rallies, a significant structure was quietly taking shape behind the scenes. Without noise. Without a doubt."

Ernst carefully set the document back on the crate, his fingers shaking slightly. He raised his gaze, his eyes sharp and unwavering. "What I encountered during my academic journey... being compelled to depart from the city... They handled it." His voice held the gravity of a conclusion—an undeniable finality. "Revealing this structure... goes beyond merely halting them."

When Elias spoke again, his tone was more deliberate—each word coming from a deep place within, as if he had weighed it before speaking. "They provided Mussolini with a pre-prepared strategy—to redefine the Church's position in Italy," he stated. "Concordium's advisors had previously prepared the framework for negotiations with the Vatican long before the Lateran Treaty. The public role of clergy, their influence in education, and the language used in sermons..." He raised his gaze, his voice steady yet resolute. "Everything was meticulously documented. Contrary to policy. As a script."

Lina nodded softly. Her face was expressionless, but her eyes burnt with anger. The news she heard was both expected and troubling. Instead of being surprising, it validated. This revealed an even more unsettling truth.

Elias's voice rang in the quiet. "Using the same framework, they reinterpreted Hitler's antisemitism as *'divine purification'*. They devised a celestial plan. They elevated hatred in politics to a sacred duty. Antisemitism went beyond racism. It posed as spiritual purification."

With his fists clenched at his sides, Matteo stood motionless, staring at the file. His expression twisted in a mixture of incredulity and anger. His eyes never left the document's faded lines. He said, his voice full of resentment, "These people weren't just playing politics. They were waging a war of belief, turning God into an instrument of conflict."

Elias gradually dropped his head. He appeared tired behind closed eyelids. "That is the essence of Concordium," he declared. "Combining the distinction between belief and compliance, establishing obedience as a moral obligation—a deep loyalty—and transforming religion into the ultimate instrument of unquestioning obedience." He raised his gaze, his voice soft but determined. "Once they achieve that, they will no longer need soldiers. Or law enforcement. Individuals hold the keys to their own confinement in their pockets."

A profound stillness enveloped the room. Shadows remained frozen around them—immobile, as though the essence of Concordium itself was hovering in the periphery. Ernst was the first to shatter the quiet. His voice sliced through the air with a chilling clarity: "This is not just about Germany… or Italy."

Elias faced him. "No," he replied. His voice was deliberate, yet unwavering. "This was a strategy to dominate all of Europe—through silence. Not with bullets… but with words, with prayers, with tranquillity. A plan crafted to eliminate opposition before it emerges. And the most frightening aspect is this: *it was effective.*"

"Mussolini and Hitler…" he continued, "They represented merely the visible tip of the iceberg. The true strength lived in the principles that supported them—in those that remained unnamed, the ones that were never visible."

Matteo raised his gaze to Elias. "And what about now?" he enquired softly. "Even if we share these documents with the world… Who will take us seriously? Who would accept such a betrayal? How does truth express itself—after it has lingered too long in the shadows?"

Ernst offered a subtle, tired smile. It bore a mix of determination and sadness. "Revealing treachery is not sufficient," he stated. "You must also possess the bravery to dismantle the system that brought it into existence. That is the reason for our presence."

Matteo raised his fingers to his chin. His thoughts surged behind eyes now steeled, as if he were piecing together the last elements of a strategic battle plan in his mind. "This agreement…" he said, his voice piercing yet tinged with apprehension, "…the original copies—records—where are they stored?"

Elias paused before responding. He gradually raised his eyes from the papers and observed the expressions of Ernst and Matteo. In a voice that was low yet undeniably resolute, he responded, "Rome."

Ernst furrowed his brow. "The Vatican Archives?"

"No," Elias replied. "Not found in the official archives. The documents live in a location beyond any catalogue's reach—maintained without titles or documentation. They call it the *Codex Altus*."

Ernst leaned in, his voice lowering. "What is that?"

Elias took a deep breath. As he spoke, he seemed to conjure up images of Rome's hidden maze. "Codex Altus lives deep within the Vatican's underground complex. This is not an official archive. It does not appear in any indexes. Only a few people are aware of it. Only specific orders—or selected cardinals—can access it. Assassination orders, agreements that have stood the test of time for over a century, and declarations of excommunication. Instead of destroying them, they bury heretical, cursed, or forbidden texts. Even the Church did not eliminate them."

"Who put these papers there?" Ernst asked.

Elias put his hand in his coat's inner pocket. He pulled out a small, worn note. He placed it on the table. A shaky old hand had scrawled a single letter in the centre of the page:

M

Matteo leaned forward, a shadow crossing his brow. "What does it stand for?"

"I can't say for sure," Elias whispered. "However, Concordium documents often include it. Sometimes sealed, sometimes handwritten in margins. Although it is not a name or title, it seems to embody them. A person hiding their identity but not their existence." Elias stared at the worn note. "The name *Magnus* is often associated with this letter." Elias lowered his voice after a moment. "Based on my review of the documents... Magnus is a Concordium title, not a person. Shadows loom at the top. The ultimate authority."

Matteo slowly raised his head, allowing his gaze to wander over the bare structure of the abandoned tram depot. He turned back to Elias. "In Berlin... Do you think anyone is already near this structure?"

Elias' expression immediately became tense. "I am convinced that they have already arrived. Even they may be watching us right now."

10

A sudden crack from outside interrupted their conversation, shattering it like fragile glass.

Ernst reached for his bag quickly and instinctively. His fingers quickly moved to the opening of the linen pouch. Lina leapt from the crate with the force of a tightly wound spring, her gaze immediately fixed on the window. Matteo moved quietly and purposefully, positioning himself against the wall and gazing out through the glass.

A faint silhouette appeared just outside the window. Slender. Flexible. A shadow moves gracefully across the wall. Shortly afterwards, the sound of quick, rhythmic footsteps echoed across the concrete floor outside.

"We need to go," Lina said, her voice whispering but cutting like a command. She knelt down and gathered the documents quickly, with deliberate precision.

Elias took a step back, a look of panic in his eyes as his hands frantically rummaged through his coat pockets. "They didn't follow me," he whispered, his voice trembling and tinged with regret. "I am sure…"

"Now is not the time for certainty," Ernst snapped, taking a quick glance at Elias before turning his attention to the door. Under pressure, his voice remained steady. "They are actively observing right now. They're putting us to the test."

Footsteps echoed again. Nearer. Make more deliberate decisions. Better organised. In the quiet moment that followed, everyone present paused, gasping. Their eyes met. Only action remained—no more questions.

"Where is the exit?" Ernst asked, his gaze fixed solidly on Elias.

Lina pointed to the shadows. "There is a door behind the tram tracks," she said. "It leads to an ancient maintenance tunnel."

They followed her without a moment's hesitation. Time no longer flowed but became a heavy burden pressing down on them. Their breathing became shallower, and their movements became both silent and deliberate. Every corner and shadow seemed to contain an unseen watchfulness waiting to be awakened.

They tiptoed through the soft glow of light. The scent of dust and rust that had previously defined the depot now carried an acute sense of danger. When Ernst arrived at the old fire door, he pushed down on the handle with force. The door slowly opened, as if to comply; its creaking hinge extended into the darkness, like a last cry against the silence.

They moved through the dark. Lina cast a final glance back, and moonlight poured through the broken glass. The fissure in the glass remained unchanged, but the shapes in the shadows had changed.

A presence hung in the silence now. Invisible, ambiguous, but unmistakably present.

"That was a warning," Ernst said. "It signifies, *'We acknowledge your presence.'*"

Lina's expression changed as she muttered, "We're not alone anymore."

Matteo gave a subtle nod from behind her. "We were never."

11

As they walked through the narrow, chilly underpass beneath the tram tracks, the sound of their footsteps echoed against the steel and concrete walls, only to bounce back to them. Silence enveloped them completely; it had infiltrated the ground beneath their feet, turning every step into a soft murmur.

They found themselves in the heart of Berlin. Except for the distant hum of a passing vehicle, everything was quiet—a fleeting reminder of movement in a city that appeared to be holding its breath.

Elias came to a halt at the end of the tunnel. He rested his back against the cold, damp stone wall, breathing in quick, irregular bursts. Despite his best efforts to hide his fatigue, the perspiration on his brow and the quivering of his jaw revealed the truth. His gaze fell on Lina.

"I cannot say where Frater Cinis is," he said, his voice low but firm. "But as I was told months ago, there is a workshop. Between Kreuzberg and Neukölln. It looked abandoned. However, there was a presence in that place, possibly Cinis."

Lina slowed her pace, her gaze fixed on the shadows that clung to the world's edges. She paused by his side, the air heavy with unspoken words. She looked at Elias, her eyes filled with quiet doubt. "Who gave you this information?" She asked, her tone steady and piercing.

Elias opened his bag softly and quietly in the silence. He pulled out a small, worn piece of paper that fit comfortably in the palm of his hand. There was a single sentence scrawled in the centre of the page:

"Cinis. He does not speak. But he shows."

He kept his eyes fixed on Lina, his voice barely above a whisper. "This is the phrase used by those who found him. Cinis says nothing, but he leaves an impression. Codes and notes, documents dispersed like whispers in the wind. Always indirect and elusive. He doesn't respond directly. Only the right question reveals the truth."

Matteo took a few steps back into the shadows, his voice a whisper, cautious and measured. "Whoever saw us speaking may still follow us. This meeting carries a weight—a danger not only for us but for Elias as well."

Lina's eyes shone with determination. "Then we must separate our ways," she stated firmly. "Elias will leave us. Matteo and I will monitor the perimeter." She faced Ernst. "It must be you who enters. If Cinis is truly present, he will only listen to those he believes deserve it."

Ernst looked at her for a moment. His posture, as always, conveyed a sense of calm and composure. This time, there was absolutely no hesitation. He gave a subtle nod, as if acknowledging an unspoken understanding. "How can I persuade someone to talk who previously attempted to mute me?" He spoke gently. "It will be challenging."

Part 3

Born of Ashes

12

The exterior of the old workshop appeared to have been abandoned for a long time, fading from the city's memory. The windows were cracked or completely shattered, and rust had eaten away the iron shutters. A dull grey appearance, coated in soot, characterised the building's façade. Amid all the decay, Ernst noticed one detail. Door handle. It stood out from everything else because it was so clean. Free of rust. Free of dust. Only the faint, ethereal outline of fingerprints remained, as if it had been meticulously cleaned just hours before. That was sufficient. This was not abandonment. It was a stage: a meticulously planned deception.

He reached for the doorknob with deliberate, unhurried movements. The cold brass bit into his palm, causing him to shiver violently and unwaveringly. The door opened with a soft creak, leaving a lingering sound in the quiet room. It was open and unguarded.

As he crossed the threshold, his eyes adapted to the shadows, and the scene became clear: someone had neatly organised the tables. The shelves were in quiet order, with each stack of paper carefully placed to show mental discipline. This place was still breathing, albeit in its own way.

He tiptoed. After a few cautious steps, he spotted a figure behind the old printing machine. The figure stood tall and stiff. There was no withdrawal or sign of an exit. It's just existence.

With a steady, icy determination, Ernst inquired, "Is your name Cinis?"

No response. A heavy silence settled between them. Even time appeared to pause in anticipation. A worn sheet of paper on the desk fluttered gently. Quietly and deliberately, the figure pulled an old pencil from under the paper. Upon the yellowed surface of the paper, he inscribed a solitary, minor question: *"Who are you?"*

Ernst advanced another step. He lowered his voice yet maintained its clarity.

"My name is Ernst. Those who were pursuing you are now also pursuing us. Concordium's influence looms over all of us. That is why we must have a conversation."

The silence lingered for a moment. The pale winter light streaming through a window gradually illuminated the man's face. He appeared to be in his late fifties. Dark hair that faded to white at the sides stressed sharp, weathered features. His face showed the signs of years spent fighting, with an unwavering alertness. But his eyes remained unyielding. They reflected a tired but sharp intelligence, a memory that assessed every movement but chose not to forget.

"Speaking is dangerous," the man finally said. His voice was hoarse, like a bell left to rust for years—thick and corroded. However, the words arrived with surprising clarity.

Ernst acted without pause. He kept his gaze fixed on the man and responded with equal tenacity: "No—being silenced is what's dangerous."

Again, silence enveloped the surroundings. However, this time it was different. Not aggressive. In that moment, two strangers fell into a profound silence, realising they were both in danger. A quietness that now served as the foundation for trust.

The silent history was about to speak up.

13

Cinis gave a subtle nod, his eyes unwavering and unblinking. He slowly and deliberately pointed to the small, square box in the centre of the table. The dark wooden surface bore the marks of time, with fine cracks etched into it that appeared to support the weight of something long buried.

Ernst extended his hand. His fingers dabbed at the lid. He cautiously opened it. Within the box was a carefully folded document from 1923. The texture was brittle, the once-white surface had faded to pale ivory, and the edges had frayed because of time's impatience. At its core, the writing was firm.

A Latin title glowed with refined sophistication, echoing through history with a mix of beauty and foreboding. Below, three signatures:

The initial, quaking but undeniable: *Adolf Hitler*

The second is inscribed with the same enigma. *Benito Mussolini*

And the third—*a seal* is present: two interlocking circles with a broken cross in the centre.

Ernst held the document with great care in his hands. He raised his gaze to Cinis, who remained motionless on the opposite side. "Is this...?" he asked.

Cinis nodded slowly. "A pact", he explained. "Hitler, Mussolini, and three high-ranking Concordium officials made the initial agreement." He paused before continuing in a measured, thoughtful tone: "But this is not a standard agreement. It is neither a definitive law nor an officially issued manifesto. There is no date set for its enactment. A common belief prevails: the decision to change the framework of European thought. To elevate thought to the divine level. Changing thought from a means of inquiry to a mechanism of compliance."

Ernst let his fingers glide over the faded ink marks on the document, feeling the gentle whisper of time beneath his touch.

Cinis opened his mouth as if to say something, but no words emerged. He turned quietly and extended his hand toward the dust-covered shelves behind him, which contained artefacts lost in time. His fingers glided with deliberate confidence until they came across an aged metal artefact. He cradled the item in his palm and presented it to Ernst.

Ernst accepted it with caution. The object in his hand was more than just metal; it bore the weight of history. *A signet ring*; time had muted its sheen, but the engraved symbol remained boldly preserved.

M

Ernst muttered, "Could this be Magnus?"

Cinis slowly shook his head. He focused his attention on the ring Ernst was holding. "Yes," he answered, his voice hoarse and weary. "But it's not a name. Magnus is not a person. Magnus represents anonymity. A function that substitutes for the identity. From that point forward, the person no longer exists. Only the framework communicates. Those who believe they understand him actually inhabit his space. His voice and decisions become theirs. And that person... disappears."

Ernst gently returned the ring to its box. His gaze swept over the documents. He whispered, "These texts... whoever gets them..."

Cinis nodded quietly. His eyes were now filled with undeniable certainty. "They become a target," he stated. "Concordium's primary concern is the spread of knowledge. We can still communicate. At the moment, only a few people possess this ability. Excellently used."

He then shut the lid of the box. Ernst kept quiet for a moment. In the room's dimness, the flickering light of the old lamp on the desk cast shadows across his face. Finally, he spoke softly but clearly: "How do we enter Codex Altus?"

Cinis sat in the chair opposite him. He smiled subtly, neither derisive nor comforting.

"You cannot," he declared. "You cannot access a nonexistent location. Codex Altus was a deception. It never existed."

Ernst's gaze was steady and unwavering. "We were told that's where all the secret documents are hidden. They conceal the true manuscripts there."

Cinis made a slight nod. "That is exactly what the upper echelons of the Concordium intended for you to believe. The intention was obvious: to deceive those seeking the truth. To give them a map with no destination. It was successful."

A moment of silence followed. Cinis extended her hands toward an old piece of paper resting on the table's edge. He lifted it with great care. The creases had nearly split it apart. He extended it to Ernst.

Kraków—Collegium Maius [1]—Archive 3

Ernst squinted against the light. He whispered the words to himself, a soft echo in the silence of his mind. "Is that the place we are to go?"

Cinis nodded. "Yes. The Codex was a deception, but the past lives on within its pages. There, the first signs of the Concordium's fading remain. What you discover there will help you get to the next mark." He paused for a moment before speaking softly. "Now, go. You must be the last to speak before the silence returns."

14

Ernst rose to his feet. He folded the note carefully and tucked it into the inner pocket of his coat, as if it were the weight of the world. He faced the door. He continued walking, the road stretching ahead of him, without looking back. Footsteps rang out in the corridor and then faded into silence.

He stepped out of the building. The night had fallen over the street. The street lamps stood like tired sentinels, their dim yellow lights spilling onto the cobblestones below.

Lina and Matteo stood at the end of the street, waiting. Their gazes conveyed one question: *Did he speak? What did you discover?*

Ernst stayed silent. Words had lost their importance—perhaps even their safety. Instead, he reached

---

[1] The oldest building of the Jagiellonian University, dating back to the 14th century.

into his bag and gently lifted the linen-covered file of documents. A paper appeared from the shadows.

Lina leaned forward gradually. Her gaze swept over the file. "The document that cast a shadow over Europe," she whispered.

Matteo slipped his hands into the pockets of his coat. He inhaled quickly, and his voice was calm but firm: "What is the plan?"

Ernst reached into his coat pocket again. He carefully extracted the small piece of paper Cinis had given him. Then he raised his gaze, responding calmly and decisively, "We cannot stay in Berlin any longer." His voice steady, but weariness hung over him like a shadow. "We will go to Kraków."

Lina and Matteo exchanged a quick, unexpected glance. Their faces betrayed them, revealing unmistakable shock.

"Kraków?" Lina enquired.

"Codex Altus was never real. It was all a deception," Ernst continued. "People believed for years that Concordium kept its archives there. Even Elias believed this. They dispersed the actual documents. They hide in multiple locations. Kraków is only the beginning."

Lina gradually lifted her gaze away from the document Ernst held. She spoke softly but with unwavering determination: "And if an archive is truly there... we will be the ones to open it."

They grew quiet. Beyond language, only certainty remained—advancing inch by inch.

15

The train left Berlin at 5:30 a.m. According to the records, the shipment of coal to Wrocław was standard freight. If anyone had looked closely at the cars, they would have discovered a different cargo hidden beneath the layers of black dust: three human silhouettes shrouded in silence: Lina, Ernst, and Matteo. Three shadows; motionless, observant, and ready to act at any moment. They would take the train to Wrocław and walk to Kraków from there.

The freight car's windows were covered with soot, which prevented any light from entering. It was almost completely dark. The very sound of breathing was silenced. The quiet had become both a protective barrier and an oppressive burden.

Lina huddled in the corner of the wooden floor, her knees tucked close to her chest and wrapped in her coat. Her eyes were closed, but she remained awake. Each jolt and screech of the brakes rang out in her mind like a warning bell. Departing from Berlin was not an act of fleeing; it was simply the beginning of a new conflict.

Ernst leaned against the sidewall of the freight car. He kept reaching into his inner pocket to ensure the linen pouch containing Cinis' documents was still there. The feel of aged paper under his fingertips provided a brief sense of comfort. These were no longer just written pages; they were the first stones to break Concordium's cover. Perhaps there were hints that would eventually lead to their demise.

Matteo climbed to the corroded ventilation grate of the car. Although he saw nothing in the darkness, he heard the sounds beyond perfectly. He became accustomed to the rhythm of the train wheels striking the rails, discerning speed, direction, and station proximity through subtle changes in tone. In those moments, he moved with the instincts of a scout through a foggy battlefield. The sky remained dark, but the faint light of dawn appeared along the eastern horizon.

The fragile barrier of silence, built throughout the night, accompanied them into the morning, carrying shadows and secrets toward Wrocław.

16

Lina spoke in hushed tones over the metallic groans of the rails. Her voice was extremely low and delicate, as if the constant clatter of the train wheels could consume it. "Berlin is behind us," she said, her voice steady as the sun lowered in the sky. "Yet we remain in the dark about what lies before us."

Matteo, who had been quietly listening at his post by the corner, turned his head for a moment, breaking out of the role of silent observer. A subtle, almost imperceptible smile appeared at the edge of his lips.

"It's more like... we still do not know what—or who—we've gotten ourselves tangled up with," he replied.

At that moment, the train lurched violently. The wagon floor creaked, and tremors along the rails rose and fell like the earth's breath. Then there was a sharp and prolonged screech of brakes, piercing the silence like a knife. In an instant, sharp awareness seized everyone.

Lina drew her legs beneath her and took hold of the hem of her coat, rising silently. Ernst closed his satchel with a sharp motion, pulling his belt tight to the last hole. Matteo slipped through the dusk, a silent figure approaching the wagon doors. He stood there, as still as the night, his ears tuned into the surrounding silence.

The silence outside weighed heavily, leaving a lingering presence in the air. It carried a heavy burden. The voice then arrived, sharp, clipped, and with a German accent. A call with a clear and pressing demand:

"Inspect every carriage. One by one!"

The footsteps approached, each measured and sure. Steel boots struck the ground in a steady rhythm, each step ringing out like iron thorns against the closed wagon's walls.

Ernst knelt in silence, the weight of the world pressing against him. He reached into his satchel and retrieved a small black jar. Inside, a mixture of coal dust and thick, rancid oil sloshed quietly. He opened it slowly, keeping his hands steady and deliberate. The scent hit them right away—heavy, oppressive, with notes of burnt iron and rot.

Lina and Matteo instinctively pulled back. The burning sensation in their throats occurred immediately. Their stomachs churned with the urge to vomit.

Ernst silently pushed the jar toward the wagon door. He fastened his coat, lowered his cap over his brow, and hid himself deep in the darkest corner, where the coal sacks stood like sleeping giants. He leaned against the dark mass, steadying his breath.

"Camouflage", he muttered. "The odour itself will suffice."

Lina counted, the numbers flowing like a quiet stream. Three steps. Four. Five. The wagon door groaned, a sound of rust and cold steel echoing through the silence. A narrow beam of pale morning light pierced the darkness, sharp and unforgiving. Shadows pulled back as if afraid of the light.

The figure in the doorway, strong and broad, leaned forward, casting a long shadow throughout the room. His tired eyes scanned the heaps of coal, heavy with the weight of the day. The sharp lines on his face showed exhaustion, a man stretched too thin by the weight of the same day, over and over. He crinkled his nose in a quick expression of disgust. He stopped. The world around him was holding its breath. Then, a deep sound of revulsion rose in his throat. He raised a hand and pressed his fingers against his nose.

"Scheiße..." he muttered, a bitter truth escaping his lips. "This place smells of decay. Just leave it. Look to the next."

The door closed with a familiar, unsettling creak from the worn hinges. Footsteps faded—steel boots clanging against metal, echoing through the corridor before falling silent. Then, a recognisable vibration appeared beneath the floor. The locomotive shuddered, let out a low groan, and continued its slow advance. The sharp, piercing sound of metal grinding against metal resurfaced, forming a cadence with the floorboards beneath them. Once again, darkness engulfed the surroundings.

Initially, the silence appeared to be a rescue. However, it twisted into a tight, oppressive tension. Everyone stayed still. Only the steady rhythm of their breathing and the repetitive melody of the rails filled the air.

Lina brushed a small bead of sweat from her forehead with the back of her hand. Her fingers were steady and composed; however, when she spoke, her voice was so faint that it almost vanished in the darkness. "It was incredibly close..."

Ernst gently closed the small container. He set it next to the document pouch, the jar's weight still evoking fear.

Matteo stood by the narrow, soot-smudged window, his eyes fixed on the fog-covered horizon. "We were fortunate," he mumbled. A subtle smile played across the corners of his mouth. "What an awful odour... Even hell wouldn't have such an unpleasant odour."

In that fleeting moment, despite their exhaustion and all odds, all three of them shared the faintest, most genuine smile. The tension broke, if only for a moment.

The train sped up with an abrupt jolt, picking up speed once more. The only sound was the monotonous, metallic cadence of wheels hitting rail joints. Dense mist shrouded the outside world, reluctantly accepting the first light of dawn. Fog crept across the horizon like a thick curtain, enveloping the train's wheels in silence. The sky above seemed uncertain, as if the sun were only a whisper, an invisible but palpable possibility.

The border crossing occurred around midnight. They remained perfectly still, sensitive to every vibration in the car. Every shift of the rails, every brake, every moment of silence—any of these could signal a checkpoint. Nobody did. The oppressive atmosphere inside the wagon was no longer part of Germany. It was air from Poland. The shadows had shifted, but the danger persisted.

17

The train moved onto a long-neglected freight line near Wrocław. Despite the absence of snow, a hard frost had frozen the ground beneath a fragile, silent layer. The locomotive gave one last hiss, and then there was silence. It had come to a stop.

Lina raised her collar to her cheekbones, her breath creating a fine mist in the cold air. Matteo knelt in silence, tying the laces of his boots with a double knot. In an instant, every detail must be steadfast and loyal.

Ernst moved forward, step by step, through the quiet landscape. His boots struck the ground with purpose, but his face revealed no signs of relief. Safety didn't come with a breath.

Matteo arrived near the end, trailing behind the others. He hefted the bag onto his back and took one last look into the wagon's dark interior. He closed the door quietly, saying nothing. The sharp scrape of metal rang out briefly, like a cry swallowed by the wind.

They stood there, watching the train disappear from view, its whistle fading into the distance. A low groan of iron against iron faded into the fog and then vanished. They sat silently, the weight of time pressing on them. When the last whisper of the shadow faded, Ernst led them down the tracks with measured steps.

A small shack loomed ahead, obscured by the thick morning mist, its outline faint and uncertain. The walls bore the signs of age, cracked and worn. Moss covered the roof, suggesting years of abandonment.

When they were about to leave the shack, silent as shadows, the door groaned open. A warm, smoky breath escaped from the old iron stove, which was still alive with fire inside. A man stood in the doorway, dressed in railway coveralls, his age etched on his face, possibly in his sixties. His face bore the weight of deep lines and weary years, but his eyes were sharp—calculated and watchful.

"Who are you?" he asked. His voice bore the marks of time, but it exuded the authority of an experienced leader.

Ernst responded, his voice firm. "Passengers disembarked from the train."

He narrowed his eyes. His gaze travels between three of them. Their simple clothes offered no respite from the tautness in the air, a quiet murmur that hinted at hidden truths beneath the surface.

"You will not find another train from this location," the man said, his voice devoid of warmth.

Ernst nodded lightly, a brief but meaningful gesture. "We understand. We'll walk."

The man's expression remained unchanged. Uninterested. Not aggressive. Evaluating. "Where?" he asked.

"Kraków", Ernst replied.

A slow nod, deliberate and measured, as if time itself was holding its breath. His tone was steady, but his words carried the weight of truth. "A dirt road stretches to the east. On dry days, you will find a way. No one at that location seeks answers."

"Thank you," Ernst replied, his voice low and steady.

The man moved to close the door but paused. His last words hung in the silence, a soft breath intended for ears that could hear. "You didn't see me. I didn't see you."

Part 4

Fragments of the Unseen

18

November 7, 1935
Kraków

By morning, the cold enveloped all three, freezing them to the bone. They had walked the narrow, muddy forest path through the dark hours of the night, each step numbing their toes until pain set in, every bend of the knee and ankle filled with countless unseen ice shards.

They approached Kraków from the southeast, following the mist-covered shores of the Vistula. The river flowed alongside them as a silent observer, offering no greeting. The city's silhouette gradually emerged through the misty dawn, with towers, chimneys, and dilapidated buildings looming like sleeping giants.

Lina noticed the Wawel Castle's remarkable shape, which stood out against the sky. In the morning haze, the fortress rose, its shape merging with the sky. It stood there, not as a guide, but as a silent observer of everything that had happened before.

They possessed only one clue: a scrap of paper as small as a hand. Its faint, trembling script contained no plea or riddle. It was a command—clear, direct, and unambiguous:

"Collegium Maius. Archive floor. Section Three."

They had gained access to the archives by claiming to be scholars researching Kraków's architectural history. However, neither the authorities nor anyone else mentioned such a section. The Collegium Maius records only mention the building's surface levels. A 1902 document explicitly declared that no substructures, hidden chambers, or materials from earlier periods remained. There was no mention in the city plans, no proof in the construction permits, and no sign on any emergency schematics. The structure appeared to have reached a quiet agreement with time, hiding the truth not beneath its floors but deep within its stones.

However, Matteo had not given up. He had been searching for days, relentless in his pursuit. He discovered it in a forgotten corner of the city archives: a brittle, nearly disintegrated Austro-Hungarian architectural drawing. The paper had cracks along its edges and a deep fissure running through the centre, stained by the passing of time, a relic on the verge of oblivion. A single breath could have transformed everything.

That night, beneath the flickering candlelight, Matteo leaned over the delicate parchment; his fingers traced the worn lines and faded script written long ago. He moved calmly through the tangled web of sewage lines and maintenance shafts. Then his gaze fell on something. There's barely a whisper in the vastness.

The western sewer branch of Kraków's historic network ran remarkably close to the northern wall of Collegium Maius. At that point—hardly discernible, written in a nearly unreadable hand—was a subtle note:

"Section Three"

Matteo raised his head, a sparkle of excitement in his eyes. His voice was soft but true. "This is it," he said. "If this plan holds true, the western branch of the sewer line lies just beneath the archive level."

Lina leaned in, her eyes narrowing as she studied the arrangement intently. Her fingertip lingered softly at a branching point. "If we are to enter from here, we ought to seek another way out—just to be prudent."

Ernst looked at the drawings, his expression heavy with contemplation. He traced the line with his finger, guiding it to another point where it intersected the old mill, worn and steadfast in the dim light.

"We will go this way," he said. "We might find a way out through this second line. Mark this location near the old mill. It might still be within reach."

Matteo spoke softly, with his gaze lowered. "The map shows the route. However, we are still unsure of what lies within."

The tunnel, dark and silent, guarded its secrets closely. One couldn't tell if it was safe, because safety is a delicate thing that is frequently lost in the shadows. The air was thick with uncertainty, and the walls seemed to whisper of unknown dangers. Is the entrance blocked? Is there a flood now? There are no guarantees to be had.

Lina fixed her gaze on the plan, the world around her fading into silence. Her voice was heavy, firm, and unwavering. "If we are to know", she insisted, "we must first enter."

19

That night, as they approached the sewer entrance, Kraków lay motionless, enveloped in a heavy silence. When they lifted the iron cover, the stench that rose from below hit their lungs with a powerful force. Rust clung to the damp stone, and moss grew over the dried sewage. It was a heavy, thick breath of rot, a sign of decay.

Ernst struck the match and watched as the small flame came to life. The yellow light flickered against the stone walls, creating trembling shadows that moved like ghostly hands in the corners. Matteo spread the worn map, its creases whispering of previous journeys, and let the light shine on it. With trembling fingers, he traced the delicate lines.

The tunnel descended gently, a quiet slope into the earth. The ceiling hung low, and the floor stretched out beneath it. Dark water pooled in the hollows, gathering quietly, a testament to the passing of time. The walls held the chill of dampness and the stillness of ages, and each step seemed to bring back the ghosts of long-forgotten troubles.

"Three hundred metres," Matteo said, his voice carrying through the still air. "Then we take a right. A path begins, following the line of the northern wall."

Their footsteps echoed on the stone floor, each one a ghost of the last, swelling and fading like the tide, creating the illusion of many where there were few. Lina moved with quiet grace, her knees soft, and one hand brushing against the rough wall for stability. The silence grew thicker with each step as they moved deeper into the dark tunnel.

Ernst walked ahead, holding the light steady in his grip. He paused at each turn, his eyes searching for any sign of life, a shadow that could reveal a presence, or a whisper of movement in the dark. Matteo followed behind, clutching the map with a fierce grip, as if it were more than just paper—as if it were the only thing keeping them alive.

The tunnel bent before him, a dark promise hidden in the shadows. Silence was more than just the absence of sound from the world above. It had taken on a weight, an unseen force pressing in on them, its breath brushing against the back of their necks. Cracks marred the ceiling above them, and the weary, worn stone walls leaned inward. However, a striking detail emerged: some stones appeared freshly scrubbed.

"It seems as if someone cleaned some of these stones," Lina said.

Ernst came to a stop. He knelt low, his fingers brushing against the rough surface, sensing the world below him. The stone was damp, but there was no grime on its surface, which appeared nearly polished in the low light.

"You are right," he whispered, his eyes narrowing against the shadows. "We may not be alone."

The tunnel opened gradually, its walls receding into the shadows. They walked a short distance and arrived at a door. It stood firm, a guardian of memories long forgotten. Iron, heavy and rusted, stood there. Its old paint had peeled and blistered in places. It had no colour, just a worn-out cover in muted shades of grey and brown. Someone deeply etched an ancient symbol onto the door. Surrounded by a rough and uneven frame, a handwritten Latin inscription that had nearly worn away over the years lay just within sight.

Matteo moved the torch closer, and the flickering light cast shadows on the rough walls. The light played on the cracked stone, revealing the letters one by one, like secrets long hidden beneath the earth. He spoke the words gently, as if breathing life into them with each breath.

"Hic intrant qui veritatem quaerunt." [1]

The door stood unguarded, without a lock to keep it closed. Ernst extended his hand, feeling the cold metal beneath his fingers. Time and rust had etched harshness into the surface. He pushed slowly, as if the weight of the world was on his shoulders. The door creaked open, its old hinges protesting, making a sound reminiscent of a wounded beast.

A small chamber lay before them, carved from the cold, unyielding stone. They stood still for a moment, holding their breath before moving on. The room held its breath at that moment, engulfed by the stillness that hung

---

[1] Here enter those who seek the truth.

over it like a heavy cloak. The air that drifted out was heavy, scented with stone and moisture, as well as something older—a whisper from the past pressing down on their shoulders.

A thick layer of moss, green and silent, covered the walls. On the floor, a dark pool of water lay motionless and heavy. Above, dark stains lingered from an old leak that had once bled through the ceiling. But what drew their attention the most was a weathered metal plaque affixed to the distant wall. It resembled a shadowed sun against the cold stone, and the words carved into its surface gleamed softly in the shifting light. Letters are thin and precise, carved with a steady hand and intention.

"Memoria non mentitur. Scriptura manet." [1]

Lina placed her foot on the ground, the weight of the world resting on her shoulders. The tip of her boot broke the surface of the calm water. She fixed her gaze on the plaque and whispered, "It's time to find those writings."

Three corridors stretched from the chamber's shadowed rear walls. Each one leads to another path from a long-forgotten past. Matteo spread the plan under the flickering light of the lantern. His gaze swept over the fine cracks in the paper, tracing the faded lines with quiet intensity. He pointed to the narrow passage on the right, his certainty unspoken but clear.

"This way," he replied.

They tiptoed along the corridor. Remains of old inscriptions—half-letters and faded marks—spoke of hands long gone, leaving their mark in this quiet darkness.

They reached a second door at the end of the tunnel. This one was stronger than the first. In the centre of it all, a

---

[1] Memory does not lie. The writing remains.

heavy cast iron handle loomed, surrounded by a spiral of etched symbols.

L V X

Matteo moved quietly, the lantern's light unwavering as it illuminated the ground in front of him. He traced his fingers across the symbols. "These markings... they bear a similarity to the inscriptions seen on the doors of ancient churches in Rome. They could be the initials of prayers or the symbols of hidden brotherhoods."

He examined the nearly faded inscription engraved on the metal's edge.

"Lux Veritas Xenos."

Lina said softly, "Light, Truth, Stranger." The words hung in the air, engulfed by the chill of the stone and the deep shadows that surrounded them.

Then Ernst grabbed the cold iron handle. He inhaled deeply and exhaled with purpose. The sound that followed was not a click but a groan—deep and ancient, like the breath of something awakening from a long sleep. A harsh sound, produced by metal scraping against stone, shattered the corridor's silence. The door slowly opened; each creak a reminder of time passing.

20

Something in the room set it apart from other rooms; a weight, a presence. The air, once thick with the pungent odour of damp moss and decaying stone, was now clear. A lightness filled the air, free from worldly burdens. Time hadn't simply passed; something had caught and held it fast, as if intentionally.

The walls were bare, with large stone alcoves hewn from the rock itself rather than man-made shelves. Some alcoves were worn and weathered, but they remained firm—silent guardians of lost ages. Each niche held relics that had weathered the years: thick leather-bound scrolls, sealed linen sacks, and yellowed, steadfast handwritten volumes.

The weak light flickered, creating long shadows that danced across the cold stone. They slipped through the alcoves' shadows, silent as the night, like spirits reclaiming their watches.

Matteo moved forward, taking each step carefully and deliberately. He carefully lifted the light, a deliberate action in the evening's quiet. Cracks ran through the ceiling, and symbols were etched into the corners of the shelves. Inscriptions — their meanings faded over time — glowed in the flickering light. His voice fell softly, like a breath in the stillness. "This place..." he mumbled, his gaze drawn to the lines carved into the wall, "has a pulse. It was like a creature of the night—quiet but always vigilant."

Lina moved closer. Her fingers grazed the rough edge of the heavy, sealed linen sack before her as she reached out. She examined the wax seal pressed into the surface, which featured *two circles and a broken cross in the centre*. She whispered, "Nothing held here was silenced to be lost. It lay quietly, waiting to be read again."

Within those walls, the weight of history hung in the air. Finally, the weight of history was ready to reveal its truths.

Ernst carefully lifted the cover of the first scroll. He gently pried the edge apart with his fingers. The cover slowly opened, releasing the aroma of aged parchment and dried ink into the still air. Amid it all, a faint but undeniable emblem caught the light: Concordium's seal, raised and proud. A steady, unyielding hand carved a date beneath it.

1253

The pages remained unblemished and untouched by time. The words danced on the page, fresh and vibrant, as if the ink had recently dried.

Matteo moved the lantern closer, its light flickering against the shadows. The letters stood in their ranks, narrow and sharp, like soldiers waiting for the dawn. The words were straightforward—sharp and authoritative.

Three names appeared on the first page. In the mid-13th century, amidst the chaos and corruption that raged like a storm, these men created a secret order. Power struggles raged within the Papacy, and they moved through the shadows, focused on their goal. Their purpose was clear and unwavering:

"Guide with sermon, protect with fear, endure with silence."

Lina leaned in closer. Her voice was low, but it conveyed unwavering confidence. "This is the heart of Concordium."

Ernst's eyes traced the lines with intensity that grew with each passing moment. His brow furrowed in thought. "Not the rulers," he replied softly. "The men who started it all, the minds that designed it, the ones who commanded the power of fate."

In the dim light of the small chamber, the heavy stone walls appeared to close in. They felt it together. They were not alone in their endeavours. The mark of those who had written these words lingered—quiet, unseen, but undeniably felt. He watched silently, perhaps weighing the value of what lay before him.

Ernst extended his hand toward the second scroll, which lay motionless on the stone shelf, waiting. It was thinner than the first, but it stretched out longer. The leather, worn and cracked over the years, had a strange allure beneath the fingers. He opened the cover with deliberate fingers. At the top of the first page, carved in old Latin numerals, a solitary date looked back:

1347

Pestis Nigra [1]

The plague swept through Europe that year, dark and relentless. They stood still, caught up in the moment, as if the world had stopped around them. Ernst turned the pages with a measured hand, each one offering a quiet moment in the silence. Amid the words were maps—bold lines etched in dark ink, charting cities, harbours, and rugged mountain paths. Some areas held the weight of dark strokes, the marks of a hand that understood its purpose. The margins bore strange marks, single Latin words like small warnings, each a whisper of caution.

Initially, they expressed their fundamental philosophy during this period in a single Latin sentence.

"Mens primum cedit, corpus sequitur." [2]

Matteo leaned in, his voice barely audible: "This is more than the plague."

The silence was overwhelming in the room. Lina drew back, a subtle retreat in her stance. She stared at the page, her voice trembling as she said, "For them, the plague

---

[1] The Black Death

[2] The mind yields first, then the body follows.

was more than just a disease. It was a device used to cast shadows over many and instil fear in the hearts of the countless."

Ernst traced the chill on the book's cover with his fingertips. He nodded slowly and whispered, as if confiding in the silence. "When fear grips a people, thought disappears. Then you can lead them with a firm hand, unwavering in your commands. The body moves on, but the actual struggle has always been with the mind."

Matteo lowered the lantern, and shadows returned to the corners between the shelves and the cold stone walls. The truth hung thick in the air, heavy and undeniable. This was more than just a historical account of cruelty; it was a quietly admitted cunning design.

Another volume rested on the bottom shelf. It was thick and dark, a presence among the rest. They drew it out deliberately. The cover bore the marks of time; its embossments were nearly faded, but the date in the lower corner remained visible.

1478
Inquisitio Ecclesiastica [1]

They opened the book. The words were bare and unyielding: court verdicts, names etched in cold ink, confessions whispered in shadows, and records of suffering that revealed a harsh reality... Lina's fingers lingered in the upper right corner of a page. Her eyes widened. It was present and unmistakable. The seal lay there. The years have weathered Concordium, but it still powerfully projects a presence.

She turned the pages with quiet resolve. The same words echoed across every page, forming a solemn chant.

---

[1] Ecclesiastical Inquisition.

"Puritas ex obedientia, non ex voce." [1]

She spoke softly, each word drawn out like a long-held breath: "Not to confess... but to remain silent." The weight of these words remained in the air. "To them, confession of sin was not important. There was just silence. They sought the quiet that held its breath, rather than the clear voice. True mastery exists in the quiet moments."

They knew at that exact moment. *Concordium's greatest weapon lay in the silence that surrounded them. The most perilous act of defiance was to break the stillness.*

Lina unrolled another scroll. She examined the faded ink with keen eyes. At the top, the date glowed in the light. And the title sat heavy on the page, etched deep like a stone embedded in the earth.

1917
Post Sanguinem [2]

Lina held her breath as she read the first lines. The papers carried the weight of strategy, with notes on how to guide the rising tides of popular movements across Europe in the aftermath of Russia's Bolshevik Revolution. But one phrase kept reappearing, striking the three of them like a sudden wave. *'Divine chaos.'*

Matteo furrowed his brow and traced the lines with a steady finger. The theory spoke clearly, with its propositions laid out for all to see. *'Amid great chaos, when the noise is loud and the confusion thick, a few chosen words can steer the hearts of men. They can find their way again, guided by the light of those messages, like ships returning to harbour after a storm. Chaos comes before the*

---

[1] Purity through obedience, not through voice.

[2] After the Blood.

calm. But whose command it takes rests on the voice that rises amid the chaos.'

At the bottom of the page, one sentence stood out in bold letters:

"Concordium veritatem tenet. Populus numerus est." [1]

Lina spoke in hushed tones. "This is not merely about control... They have no regard for us. To them, a man is simply a weight to be counted."

Ernst placed his hands on the document with measured slowness. "Truth is not what they wish to claim," he stated, his voice resolute. "This is what they wish to hide."

Matteo nodded. "The people", he explained, "are just variables in the equation. No one asks about the absence or excess."

The room was still, heavy with silence. The lantern's light flickered, casting shadows that danced across the stone walls, like lost souls floating among the shelves. Concordium's weight hung heavy—not just in the words, but in the walls, in the quiet cracks of the stone.

21

A soft noise came from the back corridor, breaking the silence. Matteo moved with precision, extinguishing the lantern's glow. Night fell over them, heavy and silent. They stood still, three figures against the backdrop of the world,

---

[1] Concordium holds the truth. The people are numbers.

as if time had stopped to watch them. Even their breaths became silent.

Then, a voice broke the silence. **"Omnes silentii filii."** [1]

Lina spoke quietly, her lips barely moving: "Take all the documents you can carry." Her voice had a quiet power, a whisper that hung in the air.

Ernst moved purposefully, slipping the papers quietly into the linen satchel. Matteo's hand rested firm on the knife at his belt, ready to use. He moved through the tunnel without a lantern. His hand trembled, a silent reminder of the weight of the world bearing down on him.

Then the first shadow appeared, followed by another one. They emerged from the deep shadows. Lina noticed them at the edge of her vision. She didn't speak. Her lips parted, revealing the word "Run".

They approached the door marked on the map, the old escape route, with purpose and determination. Matteo walked ahead, his hand on the cold, rusty lever, ready to push it forward. The metal groaned, and the door slowly opened, as if held back by an unseen force.

A voice emerged from the shadows behind them, breaking the silence. It emerged as a whisper from the stone walls, rising from the depths of history. It resonated with the burden of time, the decree of the Concordium: **"Silence! Obedience! Order!"**

It was something else entirely. It was an unequivocal declaration. A simple note to remember.

---

[1] We are all children of silence.

22

The corridor sloped gently, a peaceful descent that led the way forward. The ground was slippery. With each step, their feet faltered, causing a brief sway before the body straightened itself, instinctively avoiding the ground's embrace.

Ernst took the lead. The lantern in his hand flickered in the darkness. It did show no shadow. Instead, it tracked the movements of unseen objects, leaving quivering shapes on the walls. Lina followed him, her steps steady and confident. The bag hung heavily on her back, pulling on her shoulders. Inside, the documents lay, their secrets pressing down like a chain around her. Each step she took was on a shadowed trail etched into the earth by history, not just a stone path. Matteo lingered in the back, observing the world unfold before him. He closed the last door softly; the sound was drowned out by the stillness. For a moment, his gaze lingered on the shadows they had left behind.

He noticed the sound right away. Steps echoed through the silence. They grew steadily and deliberately, with a cold, relentless cadence. They lingered. It was a solemn procession rather than a military march. The fire of discipline had forged them.

He muttered, the words barely escaping his lips. His voice was tense, heavy, and undeniable. "Our scent has been detected. They no longer remain in the shadows. They are following in our footsteps."

They made a sharp turn to the right. However, the corridor remained immeasurable. Another bend in the road, and another arrived. With each bend, the tunnel closed in, the roof descended, and the air became thick and stifling. The stone walls loomed, heavy and unyielding, as if they planned to consume them completely.

They passed through three more narrow passageways. The walls had become more than damp; they bore decay marks, streaked with sewer remnants, mud, and creeping moss. The scent floated in the air, thick and suffocating. However, the smell had lost its ability to disturb. At last they reached a door. Cracks marred the surface, and time had darkened the hinges, yet the door remained steadfast.

The sound of footsteps splashing in the water behind them became clear. Matteo stood still, immersed in the moment, as if time had stopped around him. He measured the sound. "Two... perhaps three," he said, his voice low and sharp as a blade. "However, they are no longer slow. They are now hunting us."

Ernst stayed silent. He pressed his body firmly against the door, feeling the wood yield under his force. The wood squeaked, and the hinges cried out. With a last effort, the door slowly opened. Beyond the door, a narrow passage lay before him, with stone steps leading down into the unknown. They came down one after another. The steps led down into shallow water. It crept up to their ankles.

Lina stepped closer to the wall, her breathing steady. She traced her fingers across the cold, wet stone. A line seemed etched into the stone, giving it a unique, softly indented texture. "There is something here..." she mumbled. She slowly pushed her hand into the hollow, as if the world outside had vanished. She felt the feel of air on her fingertips—a slender vent, or another way out. As she approached, a faint shimmer appeared in the shadows. "There is light," her voice low and determined. "It opens to the world beyond."

It wasn't a window, but it did offer the possibility of escape. Matteo leaned forward intently and focused. Rusted iron bars stood in the way, creating a small barrier to the passage. The years had worn the metal down, corroding its strength, but it maintained a stubborn resilience. Ernst opened his bag with purpose and drew out a short, strong metal rod. He pressed it between the iron bars, leaning his entire body against them. The metal let out a deep, weary sigh. Then, as if awakened from a long sleep, it shattered with a sudden, piercing crack that echoed in the silence. The bars fell inward, a silent surrender to the weight of time. A narrow tunnel stretched before them, beckoning to the unknown beyond. Ernst spoke softly, but his voice carried a weight that demanded attention. "We go. Now."

They moved slowly, inching their way along. Hard and unrelenting, like a wave crashing on the shore, the cold air hit them. The pale light of dawn crept across the horizon. The decaying back wall of an ancient mill towered over them. A secret exit lay hidden behind the rubble. From the outside, it appeared to be nothing more than debris, a dismantled piece of the world. But they had arrived. They had emerged—breathing—from the dark, narrow passage.

Matteo leaned against the mill's stone wall, which was damp and rigid. He took a sharp breath. His gaze returned to the darkness from which he had previously escaped. The footsteps ceased, but the echo remained in his mind. His tone was low and rough, similar to the gravel underfoot. "Did you see it?" He shifted his gaze to Ernst and Lina. "They might have stopped us. But they didn't."

Lina looked inside her bag. The papers were bound, firm, and unyielding. She slowly rose, lifting her head to meet the world. "We are not their true aim," she said, her voice steady but heavy with unspoken truths. "They observe our movements, connections, and the words we exchange. They want to follow the lines that pass through us - the rest of the chain."

Ernst furrowed his brow, a bitter smirk playing on the corners of his lips. "We are not a threat," he stated softly. "Not yet. We are their path, guiding them through the unknown. They sought a method for building their snares."

Lina's voice barely cut through the thick shadows that surrounded her. "At the moment, we are just carriers. Not targets." She took a deep breath. "They will break the chain if they take our lives. However, if we persist, they may trace it."

Matteo nodded with a quiet acceptance in his eyes. His gaze remained fixed on the mist-covered streets, the formless shadows lurking within. "When we speak and show our papers, we become more than just instruments. Then we become the danger." He paused for a moment. "And that is when they will arrive."

23

They walked into the heart of Kraków, silence hanging heavy between them. Each window stood like a sentinel, a silent warning of danger beyond. Their footsteps echoed throughout the narrow streets, bouncing off the stone walls, creating a chorus of sound that filled the air. Under the ancient city walls, with the weight of centuries pressing down on them, they clutched the darkest stories of history tightly in their hands.

When they arrived in the Vistula district, the streets were bare and empty, as if the world had turned away. A building remained, long forgotten. The roof had collapsed, plaster hung in tatters from the walls, and the windows, which had once been bright, were now dark and blind, leaving a deserted and silent print house covered in soot. It would give them a chance to release their burdens.

Ernst approached the door, his shoulders burdened with the weight of the world. The creak of the rusted hinges broke the morning's silence, sharp and piercing, like a cry in the quiet. The door creaked open slowly and mournfully. Mingling with the dust motes, the light shone through, creating a pale curtain that hung in the emptiness.

The room appeared empty, a void waiting for something to fill it. Lina's keen eye caught the details: the remains of a recently extinguished candle on the table; the faint mark left by a body that had occupied the chair not long ago. In the silence, something unseen took a breath.

Lina's voice was low, a mere breath in the stillness. "This place isn't abandoned," she said. "A presence lingers in this location."

At that moment, a dim light appeared in front of them. Someone deliberately drew back the thick curtain in the back room slowly. A cane struck softly against the cold stone floor. The footsteps moved at a measured pace, deliberate and unwavering. A figure appeared from the shadows.

An old man; his long beard fell to his chest like the weight of years. The lens of his glasses had a crack, a thin line that obscured its clarity. He carefully fastened the buttons on his worn coat. His hands were steady, with a firm grip on his fingers. His gaze shifted from Lina to Ernst and then to Matteo, unwavering and steadfast — a look heavy with passing time but still bright.

24

Ernst posed the first question. "Who… are you?"

The man's stance was quiet and determined, with the tip of his cane against the floor. The sound echoed softly across the worn stone below. Then he sat down in the chair, slow and deliberate, as if the weight of the world was on him. His shoulders drooped with age, but his eyes were clear and unwavering. He observed their faces through the cracked glass of his spectacles.

"I am a child of this land," he said, his voice clear despite the whispering winds. His voice had the weight of years, but it remained strong. Its tone reflected the steady gravity of someone who had seen the world in all of its harshness.

Stillness hung in the air, fleeting but heavy. Then he said, "My name has lost its meaning. But you can call me Sebastian. For many years, that was my name." He inhaled deeply. "But, in that place I once called home, names had no meaning. Only the call to duty reverberates through the silence. Names fade into the silence of memory. And I stood there, with the weight of the world pressing down and the silence stretching like a taut line in the air. My thoughts were a jumbled mess, each fighting for freedom but none finding their voice. Then I realised the truth. And," He lowered his head slightly. "I am no longer in service."

They all drew in their breath and waited in the silence. Sebastian spoke, and his words landed like stones. The air thickened, and the room became a courtroom, reserved solely for his confessions. Lina leaned forward, her hands gripping the top of the cane. She knelt, but not in submission. Her gaze remained firm and unwavering. Her voice carried a weight, gentle yet piercing, as if calling forth a truth long hidden: "You... were in the Concordium?"

Sebastian nodded slowly, as if weighing the world in his mind. It was not a declaration but rather a quiet understanding. The deep lines on his neck bore the marks of a dark past, as if time itself had pressed down on him, leaving indelible scars.

Lina's voice fell to a whisper: "Then tell us." Her gaze remained focused on Sebastian. "We want you to share it all." Her voice breaking the silence of the room, each word with a sharp edge: "How was the Concordium founded? When did it lose its way, and how did the rot begin? Why did they turn away from the Vatican? And why do they harbour such hatred for the people?"

Sebastian lowered his head, the weight of the world pressing down on him. A long, heavy silence pressed down on what remained. His gaze lingered in the distance, as if he were measuring the weight of years rather than words.

Then, quietly but firmly, he said, "1253." The word hung in the air, heavy and palpable, not bouncing off the stone walls, but sinking like a stone into the heart. "Three men gathered as the light faded. One was a theologian, one a historian, and another a doctor. They stood together, three souls united by a single thought: *'If God is silent, who will protect the people?'*"

He looked at Lina through the broken lens in his glasses. "In those days, faith entailed more than just prayer. It was the most powerful tool of fear, uncertainty, and submission. Plague hung in the air, casting a shadow across the land. The prospect of excommunication loomed like a dark cloud. Hellfire sermons rang through the streets. The people stood, exhausted and waiting for a hand to guide them through the darkness. Even as God remained silent, those three men believed they could create order out of knowledge." His voice dropped to a whisper, heavy with the weight of unspoken truths. "They set their own convictions where faith once stood."

Ernst spoke, his voice low and distinct, "And thus the Concordium was born."

Sebastian nodded; his motion was deliberate and measured. "Yes. They were named after the Roman goddess *Concordia*, who represented harmony and balance. With the wisdom of the ancients, they attempted to lead. They did not openly oppose the church. Instead, they aimed to rule covertly, manipulating invisible forces."

"When did it begin to fall apart?" Lina enquired.

Sebastian shut his eyes against the world. He rubbed his fingers against the cold metal head of his cane, feeling its weight and the stories it held.

"With the first death." The word hung in the air, heavy and silent. "One of the founders stood up to the Inquisition's relentless advance across Europe. He warned that fear would taint men's souls and dim the light of understanding. The other two believed that fear was the most effective way to maintain order. Then, they reached a decision. The man who spoke out against the tide was silenced. His name had vanished, fading into history. As if he had never taken a breath. Concordium revealed its true nature at that moment, a deep and raw betrayal. From that point forward, betrayal was the norm rather than the exception."

Matteo's voice was quiet: "They turned fear into a weapon?"

Sebastian shook his head slowly and deliberately, as if the weight of the world was on him. "Yes. It became law. Knowledge was a treasure hidden from the common people, guarded closely by those in power. All that remained was a heavy silence. Silence was their only language."

Dust motes floated in the soft morning light, and the room was silent except for Sebastian's breath. "In 1347, the Black Plague arrived." The words hung in the air, heavy and oppressive. "Concordium stood ready. They understood men's behaviour, their fear, and how to control them. Sermons and prayer texts were ready, and proclamations remained firm. They planned every detail long before the disease took its cruel course."

Sebastian took off his glasses. He wiped it with the sleeve of his coat, slowly and deliberately, as if the action had some significance in the world. His gaze drifted far away, lost in the shadows of what had been. "Yet the true commands lay concealed in the spaces between those prayers." His voice dipped to a near whisper. "A moment of quiet reflection, followed by a brief, stark command: *'Withdraw into solitude.'* Leave your family behind. Don't ask. Pray and obey."

Ernst furrowed his brow and spoke steadily. "So the plague was not a test for them."

He raised his gaze to Ernst. "None of the crises was ever a test for Concordium. Each was a tool for them, sharp and unforgiving."

He inhaled deeply. "Then the Inquisition arrived. 15th century. The scribes of the Concordium, also known as priests, wrote the orders of execution and court records. They wrote each line carefully to silence the audience. Each statement laid the groundwork for what would come next."

Matteo broke the stillness. "Then... how did the Vatican find itself beyond this structure?"

Sebastian tilted his head. "Initially, it didn't. Some Concordium men toiled alongside the Pope, their fates intertwined in the shadows of power. It was a quiet alliance, forged in the shadowy light of secrecy." He deliberately drove the tip of his cane into the stone floor. "However, as the days passed, a few cardinals came to understand the truth. Concordium attempted to take the place of the divine. They sought dominion through dread rather than belief. They scheduled an internal purge. But it arrived after the sun had set. Shadows dismissed the cardinals who started the plan from their positions. The men of Concordium took their places. Thus, silence found a place to grow."

The room became quiet again. Lina's voice broke through the silence. "Then... are they still inside today?"

Sebastian directed his gaze downward. He firmly gripped the head of his cane. "Yes."

Ernst opened his bag with quiet determination. He took out the cloth-bound dossier, treating it with the reverence reserved for things that held weight not in their substance but in the danger they concealed. He carefully placed the sealed page on the table. His gaze met

Sebastian's. "Who is Pater Magnus?" The words slipped from his lips as smoothly as a breeze.

Sebastian's expression changed in an instant. A shadow passed over his face, deepening the lines that spoke of burdens carried and battles fought. "It is not a name," he explained, shaking his head slowly. "This is a title. It's a man of duty." He went on: "For twenty years now, the title has lingered in the same body, unyielding and steadfast. This Pater Magnus differs from those who came before. He creates a silence that is more powerful than any words could ever be." He looked at the light that filtered through the window. "He met personally with Hitler. In the shadow of power, he handed Mussolini the papers—a quiet exchange. More importantly, he slipped into the shadowy depths of the Vatican."

He let go of the cane and reached for the nearby chest. His breath came in quick gasps, but his movements were steady and precise. He lifted the lid. He reached inside and pulled out a tightly rolled document. The document had frayed edges and softened corners. Sturdy, worn leather wrapped it, holding stories within. On its surface, the Concordium seal rested like a worn scar, telling stories of time and silence. The Latin notes, scrawled in a hurry, mingled with the traces of age, each stain a testament to the passing of time.

He held the scroll in his hands and turned it slowly, as if a quick motion might awaken the ghosts of the past. He directed his gaze at them. "The outline of the plan for the cleansing within the holy city." He reached out, hand trembling, to Ernst. "This is not just a plan... It includes the names of those who were silenced, erased, and forgotten. Everything is present."

Ernst took it in hand, firm and determined. Yet, in the tips of his fingers, he felt the weight of ages, a silence long buried beneath that leather. He was holding a life, not a weapon: a record of betrayal. He carefully placed it in the safest pocket of his bag.

Sebastian faced the wall, his gaze fixed on a distant mark in the stone, as if he saw something beyond the reach of others. His voice fell low, a whisper carried by the gravity of the situation. "There is one more place you must go." He paused and drew in a breath. "Vienna. For there, a soul awaits."

He turned to face them one by one. He pulled open the table's drawer. With purpose, he pulled a thin slip of paper from his pocket. He wrote a brief note and delivered it to Lina.

***Johannes Heller**
Linguist*

25

They slipped away from the old mill in Kraków's Podgórze district early in the morning; the stones surrounding them were cold and silent. The mist hung heavy on the narrow pavements, transforming shadows into ghostly companions who tracked their every move. They huddled together, coats drawn tight against the cold. The cold didn't just brush against their skin; it dug deep into their bones. They carried only one backpack. Within lay sealed parchment documents, chronicling the Concordium's shadowy past.

Each step they took was deliberate, with quiet reflection woven into the rhythm of their movement. Their path stretched ahead, unwavering and certain: Kraków's western borders. They avoided the main roads and instead took less-travelled paths. The road ahead was a long stretch of unknowns, winding and silent beneath the weight of the sky.

They returned to the old print shop in the foggy backstreets of Podgórze before leaving the city. They pushed open the wooden door. The hinges gave out a soft groan. They walked in, and only Sebastian's shadow was visible in the dim light. He leaned slightly forward, and despite his age, his resolve was firm and clear. He nodded slowly and deliberately, acknowledging the presence before him. His eyes met theirs, unwavering, but the space between them remained unchanged.

His voice, soft but clear as a bell, reached them: "Listen closely." His hand reached for the crumpled map that was on the table. "Avoid the Tarnów line."

Ernst knitted his brow as the weight of thought pressed down on him.

Sebastian moved forward, determined in his purpose. "They are observing you. They don't know you're here, but they're watching the road to Tarnów."

Lina's voice pierced the air, clear and consistent. "Are they searching for us?"

Sebastian tilted his head slowly. "Yes. They don't know your names, but they've seen you. They have identified you through your shadows and how you move through the world."

He handed the map to Lina. His fingers traced the paper's frayed edges, worn over time and use. "Go west...to Cieszyn. The land rose sharply, craggy and unforgiving, demonstrating nature's raw power. But the border was less guarded in that location. If they're following you, that's the only way to get away from them."

Ernst leaned close to the map, his gaze following the curves of the roads. "How far is it?" he asked.

Sebastian answered quickly. "140 kilometres is a line drawn through the land. However, crossing the rugged mountains would take at least three days on foot."

Matteo took a quick look at the map, his head nodding slightly. "It could be."

"Be mindful of your footprints and food scraps. When you notice the shadow behind you, let all other thoughts fade away. Only the papers must remain with you."

For a moment, there was only silence. In the dimly lit room, the candle's flickering flame danced, casting shadows that moved like whispers. Lina's eyes met Sebastian's—weathered but steadfast. "You've helped us. You've made our chances better. We understand it well, and we are deeply grateful."

Sebastian lowered his head, a subtle gesture at the moment's calm. "I watch over the legacy of those who came before you. You will see it through to the end. Here, my duty ends."

"I hope we shall meet again at the end of this road." Said Matteo.

Ernst spoke with calm confidence, his voice as steady as the dawn: "The documents will be safe. I give you my word."

Sebastian smiled for the first time. "What you have is of greater value than anything I possessed." He turned his attention to the door. "Don't waste another moment. Depart at once. For the shadows will arrive before you."

26

A silent march began westward towards Cieszyn. On the first day, they tiptoed through the forest's ancient paths, taking care not to be seen. They stayed in the shadows, avoiding the roads that carried the weight of men and their labour. The villages remained quiet, and the farms stood still, unaffected by their passage. The mud clung to their boots, heavy and unyielding, making each step a struggle against the ground's grip. Silence walked beside them, steadfast and true, as they travelled the long journey ahead. Each pause was a fleeting snare; thus, they blended into the darkness and vanished without a trace. They subsisted on dried meat and stale bread, the taste of survival lingering in their mouths.

On the second night, they arrived at the mountain pass that overlooked Zakopane. The air was sharp, and the cold cut through the skin like a knife. The wind lifted the snowflakes, spinning them in a quiet dance that softened the rough stones beneath. Swallowed by the stillness of the winter air, the path vanished into the white. The moonlight pierced the darkness, casting a pale glow across the jagged path, fleeting like a whisper in the night.

They took a moment to catch their breath before moving slowly and steadily toward the border. The border stones lay there, moss-covered, fallen, and forgotten. Time has obscured the original purpose of these significant markers. They moved cautiously into Austria, their feet whispering against the ground.

They soon arrived at the first structure: an old border watch cabin, abandoned and silent in the distance. However, the faint scent of a recently extinguished stove drifted from the doorframe, indicating that someone had lingered nearby.

They stood outside, the door looming ahead of them, but they did not enter.

Lina looked into the void, its shadows deep and unyielding. "We should go," she said, her voice firm and devoid of warmth.

Ernst gave a light nod. Matteo took a last look at the warm cabin. "Yes...we keep moving," he said, the weight of the world pressing on his shoulders.

The moonlight hung above, quietly observing their fate. Three figures moved into the stillness of the mountain, propelled by the wind and darkness. Shadow blended with shadow.

On the third day, after a quiet and unyielding trek, they arrived at an old hunting cabin, abandoned and hidden deep within the dense woods. The cabin stood exhausted and worn on the verge of collapsing into itself. Someone had covered and tightly sealed the windows with wooden planks against the outside world. The cold crept in, relentless and biting, but the location remained hidden from the rest of the world. For now, their most valuable asset was their invisibility.

They arrived quietly, shadows among shadows. Lina searched for the driest corner of the cabin and unfastened her bag. She traced her fingers across the rough edge of the parchment. The papers remained untouched, their surfaces crisp and unyielding. They were the reason for the march and the subsequent silence. Matteo knelt by the door, aware of the surrounding silence. All night long, the wind howled relentlessly. The forest remained still, its gaze fixed on the world. The dawn approached, bringing a quiet promise on the horizon. They retreated into the shadows, waiting for the sun to set before moving again.

They set out into the darkness again at ten-forty in the evening. The moon cast its pale light in narrow beams through the dense woods, and the trunks loomed like silent guardians in the night. They arrived at a place where the trees were sparse, and there lay a vast field of crops surrounded by weathered fences and shrouded in thick fog. A narrow dirt path lay beside the road, a reminder of what once existed. They turned without saying anything, and the silence between them was heavy. The parched earth bore the marks of wheels and footsteps from long ago. They proceeded, measuring each footfall to find the imprints left behind.

They arrived in a small village northeast of Vienna just as dawn broke, approximately 25 kilometres from the city. The village lay still, enveloped in the evening's quiet. No smoke rose from the chimneys of the silent houses, their windows dark as night. The wind occasionally hit the wooden shutters before disappearing into the dark, deserted streets. A dog barked in the distance, the sound coming from a farm beyond the village.

Two notices hung, weathered and worn, on the old wooden board in the village square, catching the attention of those passing by. Lina took a soft step, the world around her still and waiting. She examined the worn papers, the words dim and ghostly in the pale moonlight. The first came as a warning from the Austrian government regarding village security. The second was an anonymous declaration, a silent testament to unspoken thoughts.

"Austria's standing rests on reverence for the common German legacy."

Matteo spoke quietly. "Goebbels probably wrote it. However, they lacked the courage to sign it." Ernst fixed his gaze on the words that lay before him. The words were sharp and clear.

Lina spoke softly, "They're laying the groundwork, spreading the word, their truth, the story that needs to be told."

They turned and left. The silence between them was as thick as the evening air. They passed through the village silently. They walked on, determined to avoid the harsh light of day. Vienna lay just ahead, and the air was thick with anticipation. Fatigue draped itself over their steps, pressing down hard. Stopping, however, would invite the danger that lurked behind them. They measured each step, as if the ground beneath supported the weight of unseen observers.

The plan was simple and straightforward. They refused to take the main roads into the city. Instead, they would disappear into the chaos of the north-eastern industrial districts, where the noise and smoke would consume them completely.

Part 5

The Unseen Enemy

27

November 18, 1935
Vienna

They arrived at Floridsdorf, Vienna's outer ring, as the sun rose at eight in the morning. They walked purposefully through the shadows of factory chimneys reaching to the heavens, past weathered metal bridges and heavy coal wagons. The sharp scent of iron, coal, and oil permeated their lungs, heavy and thick like the weight of the world on their shoulders.

The morning shift lingered in the shadows, waiting for the sun to emerge and the day to begin. A handful of workers moved quickly, casting shadows in the fading light. They wore grey or blue overalls. Nobody greeted them, and no one even looked at them for more than a few seconds.

Ernst noticed a café on the corner of the street. Five men sat in the dimly lit room, their eyes fixed on newspaper pages, the silence heavy with unspoken thoughts. Only the smoke from the cigarette rose slowly, curling toward the ceiling.

Matteo said softly, "We cannot continue in this manner. We may attract an excessive number of eyes. We need to find a place to wait until the sun goes below the horizon."

They sought refuge in the shadow of an old warehouse, its walls worn and forgotten, standing by the roadside like a sentinel of bygone days. Among the rusted doors and broken windows, the stone walls remained silent. They disappeared into the shadows, unseen and unheard. The quiet cadence of their breaths was the only way they could tell time.

They stepped outside at 7:00 p.m., into the fading light. As they entered the Josefstadt district, their pace slowed again. This was an old neighbourhood in Vienna, but its streets maintained a sense of order and quiet dignity. The narrow cobblestone streets wound through town, with old houses leaning heavily under the weight of history, their stones worn and weary. Under the evening's weight, the streets lie bare and silent. The distant sound of trams echoed faintly, reminding that life exists beyond the stillness.

Lina pulled out the note Sebastian had placed in her hand. She studied the address and moved forward at a deliberate pace. "Number 23," she replied softly. She paused in front of the stout, dark green wooden door. She pointed to the brass plaque, the number gleaming in the light.

28

Lina gently tapped the solid door, the paint peeling in spots like old memories fading. The stillness enveloped the room like a heavy cloak. Time passed silently. She knocked again, her hand steady and firm against the door. After a brief pause, the slow creak of a metal bolt broke the stillness. The sound of iron broke through the stillness of the street. A deep and weary voice followed. "Who are you?"

Lina moved closer to the door, her head bowed slightly, as if the weight of the world rested on her shoulders. Her voice came softly. "Sebastian sent us."

The door opened, a slow creak echoing through the silence. An aged figure appeared in the doorway. The thick lenses of his glasses distorted the light, but his gaze remained sharp and unwavering. His white hair, slicked back from his forehead, spoke of a long-standing habit, though it was now dishevelled, a testament to time's relentless march. His face was pale, but it exuded a quiet strength; the years had etched lines on his body, but his spirit stood firm, unyielding in the face of time.

"Come in," he said, his tone steady and welcoming. His voice was soft, but it carried a sense of resolve. "This is not the place for words."

They entered one after another. The door quietly shut, leaving only the sound of their departure in the still air. The heavy bolt slid back, a metallic sound reverberating briefly in the silence. For a moment, it provided a sense of safety and comfort in the quiet darkness.

The old man remained silent, his head slightly inclined, beckoning them to follow him down the narrow, stone-paved corridor. They entered a small room with books piled high on the walls. The ceiling loomed above them, vast and empty, but it bore down on them with a force that was difficult to shake. Heavy velvet curtains swallowed the light that could have filtered through the windows. The air was thick with the smell of dust on shelves, the weight of old ink, the crumbling of dried paper, and a solitude that had seen much in its day.

On the central table, thick-bound dictionaries, notebooks, and a magnifying glass sat in silence. An inkwell sat there, uncapped, as if the man had paused mid-sentence to await their arrival.

He bowed low as he approached the head of the table. He kept his gaze fixed ahead, his head rigid, and spoke to the three without looking back.

"I wish to see what you have brought."

Lina quietly set her bag down. The rustle of the linen pouch she pulled out was loud enough to break the silence in the room. Her fingers delicately drew out the first document. She placed the old, worn parchment on the table.

The ink had faded over the years, but it remained legible. In the top corner, a faint seal remained—the mark of hands that once sealed silence itself.

"We discovered these in Kraków," Lina said, her voice steady but heavy with unspoken emotions. "The parchment, the ink, and the language... each originate from a distinct time period."

Heller delicately lifted his glasses from his forehead, carefully placing them on the bridge of his nose, and leaned in. The front of his garment bore the stains of old ink—traces left by years of contemplation, expression, and codes both deciphered and yet to be unravelled, silent witnesses to his labour.

He leaned over the parchment, holding the magnifying glass with ease. The lens accentuated the texture of the ancient ink, capturing the silence of time nestled among the lines. "What is the date of the first parchment?" he asked, his eyes fixed on the text.

"1253", was Lina's reply.

Heller gave a subtle nod. "It's composed using the Latin alphabet," he said, "yet this is not traditional Latin." He pointed his finger toward one of the lines. Amidst the letters, he discovered a sentence that had travelled through centuries to reach them.

"Veritas initium ex lingua." [1]

He paused for a moment. Then, with the careful, deliberate manner of someone who understands the value of words, he said, "This phrase is not pure Latin. The sentence structure shows evidence of Saxon influence. It is woven with threads of early Middle High German grammar. This is more than just a tongue; it is a reflection of one's essence."

---

[1] Truth begins in language.

He flipped through the papers, each revealing a quiet secret in turn. Each parchment whispered of a bygone era, with its own weight and story. Heller's eyes traced the lines, feeling the rhythm of the words. He listened not only to what they said but also to the music they created.

Matteo approached the table, the wood worn and familiar to his fingertips. He examined the faint lines along the edges of the pages. "They say Concordium came from the Vatican," he said. "Sebastian suggested as much."

He paused for a moment. Then, he said with the careful manner of someone who understands the value of words, "This phrase is not pure Latin. The sentence structure shows evidence of Saxon influence. It incorporates threads of the early Middle High German grammar. This is more than just a tongue; it reflects one's essence."

Ernst shifted his body forward. "So, where did it originate?"

Heller indicated a worn line at the border of one parchment. *"Ordo initium cepit Roma, completus est apud Magdeburgum,"* he read aloud. "The Order began in Rome; its completion was in Magdeburg," he translated.

"During the 13th century, there was a rapid emergence of structures in Magdeburg that appeared religious but lacked a theological foundation. Records show unnamed orders, as well as minor councils that appeared to be affiliated with the Church but operated independently... They all followed a consistent framework when conveying their messages. The same language. The same silence."

Matteo bent low over the parchment, his brow furrowed with concentration. His gaze moved across the pages, then settled on a single line. "Why would a system so deeply hidden bother with ciphers?" he was wondering.

Heller responded quickly. He said, "These texts weren't intended for reading. They were designed for clarity. Understanding is not based solely on words. The soul that seeks them out carries more weight than the words themselves. These words serve as a trial. These words reflect a way of thinking rather than the essence of a soul."

Lina whispered, her eyes fixed on the words before her. "A man who understands these papers finds his place in the framework."

Heller put his glasses back on his face. "No," he replied, his voice firm and resolute. "A person who understands them... is either deceived—or destroyed. This language goes beyond mere information delivery. It demands loyalty."

Lina watched as Heller's gaze vanished behind the magnifying lens. With a measured pause, she asked, "Is it really possible to decipher these ciphers?"

Heller nodded slowly. The lens of his glasses reflected a faint shimmer of light. "They are capable," he said. "However, it would be a long and difficult process. The encryption structure is not uniform. Each period developed its own approach. When comparing texts from the 14th and 17th centuries, structural differences emerge."

Ernst gently pushed forward the parchment he had just unsealed. He indicated the quivering manuscript in faded ink. "Here", he said, "it reads *'Lux silentii regit.'* [1] What does it mean?"

Heller lifted his gaze. He felt as if he had heard that phrase hundreds of times, but each time it struck a different chord in his mind.

"One of the fundamental principles of Concordium," he stated. "Power exists not in the spoken word, but in the quiet moments. For them, secrecy is an essential part of their existence, not just a strategy."

Lina sat motionless, her gaze fixed on Heller as he pored through the papers. "These texts..." she said, her voice steady, "were carefully crafted. A careful hand seems

---

[1] The light of silence rules.

to have placed each word, creating a deliberate rhythm in the lines. What do you think their purpose was?"

Heller spoke without raising his gaze. "Those aren't manuals," he clarified. "They don't give orders; they're more like... a book of methods. These were written for future generations, not for the leaders of the time. What they wished to pass on wasn't just knowledge—it was a form, a method. This is Concordium's actual strength: their ideas outlive their people."

Ernst raised his chin, a question lingering in the air. "So, who could have leaked these documents? Do you have any idea?"

"No," he said. "But it's known that in Berlin, Himmler was working on similar structures."

Lina asked without circling around the question. Her voice was clear, like water flowing over stone. "Was Himmler a part of this structure?"

Heller took off his glasses and carefully wiped them on his jacket sleeve. In that gesture, there was a ritual that carried the weight of the question. "As far as I know, he wasn't a direct member," he said. "But he wasn't entirely outside it either. Himmler wanted to ground his Aryan race theory in historical texts. Some of the concepts found in the Concordium documents... may have infiltrated his research."

Matteo stepped closer. He placed his hands on the table, his eyes fixed on the parchments. "Then could Concordium's ideas have served as a source for SS ideology?"

Heller paused for a moment and then gave a slight nod. "I can't say for certain," he said. "But it's highly likely they were an inspiration. Especially the use of language in identity formation, positioning individuals through bloodlines and symbolic systems... these have very old roots in Concordium's structure."

Lina carefully turned one of the parchments. With her fingertip, she pointed to a faded but still vivid phrase. "It says *Initium ex electis*. What does it signify?"

Heller bent low, his gaze fixed on the taut line before him. He sat motionless, the weight of unspoken thoughts heavy in the air, as if deciphering the meaning hidden in the dark lines on the page. Then he stated clearly, "The beginning comes from the chosen." He continued, "They don't transmit knowledge randomly. Each layer is accessible only to specific individuals. It is not for the public; it is a system designed for those within."

Ernst spoke softly, but in the silence of the room, his words carried a powerful truth: "A hierarchy of knowledge... And in this structure, access is sacred rather than meaning."

Heller raised his head. "Yes," he answered. "Because according to Concordium, the greatest danger is not knowledge falling into the wrong hands — it's everyone having access to it."

A quiet stillness settled over the room. In the quiet of the room, surrounded by books and worn parchments, an old wooden clock ticked steadily, marking the passage of time. Heller moved deliberately, slipping his hand into his coat's inner pocket. His fingers, shaped by time and routine, pulled out a small scrap of paper with frayed creases. He slowly opened it, and a grave expression spread across his features. The heaviness of the words hung in the air, thick and palpable, even before he spoke.

"There's another trace in Vienna," he said, his voice low and sharp as a knife. "To understand the upcoming chapters of the Concordium, you must visit Karlskirche. It appears to be undergoing restoration. However, this is only a deception. A secret place; hidden in the back courtyard. They say Pater Magnus left a permanent mark there."

Ernst leaned in, his eyes scanning the parchments, but his mind had already set a course. His voice was heavy, steady, and firm: "We must make copies of these documents. To carry only one version would be a foolish mistake."

Heller slowly nodded. "There's a small workshop in the university's history department that still uses traditional printing techniques. You can create copies there. But take care. The corridors now carry more than just students—they also carry eyes."

Matteo spoke in short, clear sentences, with each word deliberate and meaningful. "Then we must act quickly: first to the university, then to Karlskirche."

Heller's hand found his desk drawer. He pulled out a tattered notebook; its spine showed creases and wear from use. The yellowed and worn pages bore the marks of time, with darkened fingerprints etched into the surface. "Take this too," he said, passing the notebook to Lina. "It contains the templates for the cipher structures, denoted by their periods. It doesn't provide a direct answer... but it will help you figure out which texts belong to which eras. That's not the key; it shows you the shape of the lock."

Lina lowered her head, the weight of the moment pressing on her, and reached for the notebook. She carefully opened the mouth of the linen pouch, inserting the parchments one at a time, each movement deliberate and measured. Each document contained more than just words; it carried weight, a shadow, and a history etched in silence. "We are ready," she stated. Her voice was gentle, but it conveyed resolve.

They faced the door, a silence lingering between them. Heller stood silently, watching them leave. He said goodbye with only his eyes. He stepped to the door, the cool night air brushing against his skin. With a measured hand, he drew back the bolt, the sound echoing softly in the silence. The door slowly opened, and the quiet streets of Vienna lay before them, motionless and waiting.

The air enveloped them like an old, discarded winter shirt. Night still owned the sky. The street lamps had not turned off; they stood watch over the silence. The city remained silent. But the silence was not peaceful; it was a period of preparation. Standing on the threshold of dawn, Vienna appeared to have forgotten how to breathe.

29

It was three in the morning. They arrived at the back of the main building. The door remained shut. A mere whisper among the shadows concealed the entrance. The lock was ancient, its hinges worn and rusted over the years, but its heart remained firm against the time. Matteo paused, the world around him falling silent as he strained to hear. He took out a small, slender screwdriver from the inner pocket of his coat. He turned it inside the lock with a steady hand, the motion familiar and secure. A quiet click broke the silence, and the door gently opened without making a sound.

Silence reigned within the university's walls, echoing like the quiet of a graveyard nestled in the city's core. The corridor was dark. Dim lights cast shadows in the corners. The walls were bare, devoid of posters, laughter, and life from the students. The marble floor held their footsteps, a sound that echoed through the stillness of the night. It was a whisper that stirred something deep inside.

Silence hung between them. They breathed lightly, their steps measured and sure. They walked through the shadowed halls. Finally, they arrived at a desolate floor, devoid of light and air. They stood before the door labelled

Relief Printing Laboratory'. They lingered for a moment, immersed in the air's stillness.

The door was ajar, unguarded. The door creaked as it slowly opened to reveal the world beyond. They entered the room. The room was small, resembling a cell. There was a large printing press against the wall. Its gears had rusted, but it remained solid, a testament to time. A handful of worn-out metal type blocks, as well as stamping ink remnants and spare rollers, waited in silence nearby. The shelves remained silent, laden with dust-covered parchment rolls. They appeared to linger, as if someone had not forgotten them but had chosen to wait for the right time to return.

Matteo lingered in the shadows, his eyes scanning the room with quiet intensity. "It has not felt a hand in many years," he said softly. "Yet it can still fulfil its purpose."

Ernst approached the press, brushing his hand against the cold metal and carefully testing the lever. The soft creak of gears cut through the stillness of the room.

Lina opened her bag with quiet determination. She loosened the tie on the linen pouch inside. Her fingers traced the worn edges of the parchments, which were heavy from years of use. She drew them out with a steady hand, each movement deliberate and calculated. She slid them under the light, her gaze fixed on them.

The first parchment copy came to life in ten minutes, swiftly and steadily, like a fleeting moment. The printing press arm creaked as it turned for the last time. Like a winter night, the air in the room was heavy and still. The ink lay there, wet and alive, a reminder of the moment. It clung to the parchment, each line crisp and clear, but a simple breath could ruin it all.

Ernst set the second document down with care. Then a sharp clang echoed from below, piercing the silence like a knife. The iron door to the university slammed shut, echoing through the silence. Then a voice rang out, high and piercing, full of authority, resonating off the stone walls, sharp and commanding.

"Stockwerk sichern!" [1]

The words echoed throughout the corridors, breaking the silence like glass. Lina drew back instinctively. Her gaze met Ernst's. Her breath came in fits, but her whisper remained firm: "They've found us."

Ernst moved without pause. His jaw set firm, and his face became stern. "Damn it," he muttered, his teeth clenched tight. "The ink stays wet. If we run now, we will lose everything." His eyes darted around, measuring time and shadows and weighing the likelihood of escape. Then he decided quietly and decisively. "One of us must stay here with the paperwork. The other two must create a distraction."

Matteo's eyes remained calm, like the sea before a storm. "I will remain," he said.

Lina looked into his eyes—there was no fear there, only the heavy burden of a decision shaped by the relentless passage of time.

Ernst nodded briefly and to the point. "Very well," he responded. "Let the papers be. Let them be. Time will take care of things. Burn them if necessary. But never let them be lost."

Lina and Ernst moved softly through the lab's narrow door. They closed it softly. The faint creak of the hinges echoed like thunder in the silence of the corridor. They lingered in the hall, pretending to be students and drawing others' attention to themselves. Inside, Matteo sat motionless in the darkened room, barely breathing.

Lina kept her hands deep in the pockets of her coat, lowering her head just enough to conceal her thoughts. Ernst fiddled with the collar of his shirt, his gaze drifting

---

[1] Secure the floor!

over the scene around him, taking in the quiet details of the world.

At the far end of the corridor, two men appeared. They wore no uniform, but their dark overcoats and stiff posture betrayed them. It was clear they were plainclothes officers. They carried folders—probably checklists. Their steps were heavy on the ground, and their eyes scanned the horizon with sharp focus.

One of them paused, turned his head, and met Ernst's gaze.

Ernst fought to maintain his composure. He kept his gaze steady but did not look the man in the eye. He turned to face Lina, his lips parted as if to speak, but silence held him fast. The man got closer.

"Are you a scholar?"

The voice pierced through the air, demanding answers. It was more than just a question; it carried the weight of a warning. A single wrong word, or even a pause, could shatter everything. Ernst maintained a steady gaze. His face was devoid of challenge or fear, only the simplicity of daily life. He spoke with a blank expression: "Yes. I study history."

The man's eyes narrowed, like the line of a distant horizon, sharp and unyielding. He opened the folder, the weight of which rested in his palm. The papers lay in front of him, and he bowed his head, the words drawing him in.

"What is your name?"

Ernst felt the fog lifting from his mind. He couldn't reveal his real name. Wearing a mask was risky, but stretching the truth was far more dangerous. His mind sharpened, clear as morning light. It must be a name like any others: ordinary, steadfast and 'true'.

"Johann Gruber", he replied, his voice firm and unwavering. His voice was firm and steady, as if it were a natural extension of his being.

The man paused, his breath steadying in the silence. He went over each line on the list, looking for something that might not be there. His fingers brushed the page, slowly lifting it, as if to reveal something hidden beneath the surface. Ernst felt his heart in his throat rather than his chest. The silence lasted only seconds, but each heartbeat drew it out, making it feel like an eternity.

Finally, the man raised his gaze. He took a quick, silent look at the officer next to him. That look contained emptiness, and it was this emptiness that caused a deep unease within.

"Very well," he said, closing the folder with finality that echoed throughout the quiet room. "He's on the list. Let us proceed."

The second man gave a fleeting glance and held his tongue. He made no enquiries and showed no expression on his face. They turned and walked slowly down the long corridor, the end distant and unknown. The sound of their boots on the stone floor faded, leaving a steady beat like the ticking of a clock.

Ernst and Lina sat in silence, their bodies still and the air thick around them. They averted their gazes, and in the silence, a deep understanding hung between them. The sounds faded away down the hallway, leaving only silence.

Ernst exhaled quietly, as if at dusk. He clutched his throat, as if to contain the tightness that had settled within him. He counted himself fortunate this time. *At times, fortune alone is sufficient.*

Lina turned back, her movements deliberate and measured, as the silence settled like a thick fog. She approached the door. Her hand moved towards the handle. She looked down the corridor again, nodded, and opened the door slightly. She said softly, "Clear. Step into the light."

Matteo passed through the door without making a sound. His eyes swept the surroundings with precision, capturing every detail and shadow that lingered in the fading light. He clutched the rolled documents tightly, his fingers gripping the edges as if they were the last traces of a fading truth.

Ernst moved forward, his gaze fixed on the papers laid out before him. He unfolded it and checked the ink. The air was dry. "The papers are fine," he said quietly.

Matteo nodded; a simple gesture that carried weight. "We must reach the service tunnel in the basement." His voice was gentle, but it had a sharp edge that warned against the folly of delay.

They moved without pausing. They glided silently through the corridor; their movements were quick and sure. Lina climbed the stairwell, her steps sure and steady. Matteo followed her, close enough to detect her scent, while Ernst drew up the rear, alert as a sentry in the fading light. Their feet tapped the stone steps, making a quiet sound in the stillness. Each echo was a silent reminder to move quickly but gently.

They descended to a lower level, and the air shifted around them. The cold dampness clung to their skin, a constant reminder of the world beyond. The damp stone walls pressed in, heavy and unyielding, as if attempting to swallow them whole. Every shadowed nook kept its secrets close.

Matteo crouched low and quietly pressed the service door, the weight of the moment hanging in the air. The door slowly opened, a creak echoing in the silence, and there was a dark tunnel beyond.

They came to a halt, with a heavy silence between them. Matteo stepped in first, as silent as the dawn. The rest lagged. The tunnel lay before him, narrow and dark. Low ceilings forced them to stoop with every cautious step. Every footfall broke the silence, a reminder of the company they tried to keep hidden. They considered only escaping.

After two hundred metres, the tunnel gently sloped upward. The air has changed. A fresh wind whispered down from above, indicating what lay beyond. They came across an old maintenance hatch. They heaved it upward. A sharp, sudden crack rang out. Then the resistance gave way, and the edge rose, revealing what lay beneath.

The cold morning air seeped into the darkness of the tunnel. One by one, they emerged from the shadows.

They stood on the edge of Währinger Park, the air heavy with the scent of earth and the whisper of leaves. The morning sun shone through the clouds, casting a muted light over the world. Shadows faded as light broke through, and the world began to breathe again.

Lina tightened her grip on the bag, pulling it closer to her back. Ernst looked around, his eyes steady as he took in his surroundings. Matteo nodded quietly, acknowledging the stillness of the moment. They sat silently, each lost in their own thoughts.

30

They arrived at the Karlskirche as the sun rose high. The church stood tall, its grand front façade shrouded in scaffolding, a symbol of time's relentless march. According to the announcement, restoration work was currently underway. However, closer inspection revealed the truth: there were no labourers toiling, and no building clamour echoed in the air. The marble surfaces were thick with dust, and the machinery, though present, had not moved in weeks.

The gate stood firm, anchored by a heavy chain and unyielding against the world beyond. They placed it there, not to truly seal the area, but to create the illusion of being sealed.

"This is no longer a place of prayer," Ernst said, barely above a whisper. "They are cleansing everything that is truly sacred. Not the paper trail, but the memory in the walls."

They moved with purpose, their eyes sharp, as they approached the church's quiet sanctuary in the back courtyard. Stillness enveloped the heart, like a soft blanket. The world outside faded, and in the silence, one could hear the whispers of thoughts long suppressed. Before the sidewall, a thick stone slab stood, heavy and unyielding, as if no time had passed. The stone lay beneath a layer of white limewash, its surface muted and still. However, time and moisture had taken their toll; the surface had cracked and peeled and knelt away in spots.

Lina knelt and scraped the stone's surface with her gloved fingers, gently and deliberately. Dust fell apart into tiny pieces. In the quiet moments, beneath the surface, two letters appeared, faint but visible against the worn ground.

PM

Ernst moved closer, his eyes fixed on the letters. He muttered, as if only the stone should hear, "Pater Magnus... most likely his mark."

Matteo's fingers brushed against the cold stone wall, a gentle rhythm echoing in the silence. He listened intently to the whispers of the surface beneath his touch. The first few taps were firm and resonant. He paused at a point where the sound was thick and muted, as if it came from a deep, empty void.

"There is a cavity here," he declared, his voice firm and unwavering. He traced the stone's edge with his fingers and felt a slight indentation. It was not a doorway but rather a clue placed with purpose. His gaze met Lina's. "It is a door."

They took their time, hands steady, removing the loose stones from the wall with deliberate and quiet movements. When they removed the final barrier, a gap appeared, barely half the height of a man. They bent low to pass through. Ernst lighted his lantern. The yellow light illuminated the cold, rough stone, revealing its harsh texture. Dust danced in the light in a slow, quiet waltz.

The air inside was dense, pressing down like a weight on the chest. The air was heavy with the scent of dampness, a combination of stone seepage, earth age, and the weight of forgotten years.

The tight passage twisted for about twenty metres before opening into a small chamber with a gentle dome ceiling. In the centre of the room was a massive stone sarcophagus, carved from a single block of granite. It bore the marks of time, with a fissured surface and green edges. Nevertheless, it stood firm—quiet and unyielding.

The sarcophagus lay in front of him, its surface etched with ancient carvings that told stories from a distant past. Ernst drew the lantern closer, the light flickering in the dimness. A faint but visible date appeared in the upper left corner.

1798

Below it, lines etched with care:

"Pater Magnus. Custos Concordium." [1]

Lina knelt in silence, the ground cooling beneath her knees. She allowed her fingers to glide over the cold stone of the sarcophagus, feeling the engravings beneath her

---

[1] Pater Magnus. Guardian of the Concordium.

touch. A hand carefully shaped each line and curve, as if understanding the weight of the world. Concordium's symbols stood out starkly: a shattered cross encircled. Shapes stood at the corners, each distinct and determined.

There was no sign of the Pope. There were no crowns or saintly symbols to be found. Lina whispered; her voice softly echoed against the cold stone. "This place belongs entirely to Concordium. Not to Rome..."

Ernst lowered his head and focused on the words carved into the stone. He murmured, "1798... The year Napoleon invaded Rome. The Vatican fell, but Concordium moved. This... is silent proof of its escape to Vienna."

They didn't have time to pry open the sarcophagus. Each moment carried its own weight. Lina took the notebook from her bag. She began sketching with a steady hand, each line deliberate and precise. She noticed the carvings, inscriptions, and symbols etched into the stone. Every detail mattered.

As Ernst looked around, he noticed a narrow passage in the wall to his right. The stones covered in moss kept the coolness of the damp earth beneath them. A low ceiling hung above, and age had worn the floor. The passage was like a hidden vein beneath the earth. Their path was forming.

The silence had returned, heavy and still. But the silence was not born of fear but of understanding. The silence of a truth buried deep waits in the shadows of a grave, longing for the light of day.

31

"We must go on," Ernst said.

They moved through the narrow passageway. They felt the pressure of the tight walls and low ceiling. At last, the path led to a narrow crevice. Before them stood a small stone room, almost forgotten. The floor showed signs of ageing, with stains and damp spots in various areas. In one corner, a large metal box sat, its surface marred and darkened by age.

A layer of dust, tinged with rust, lay on the box's surface. Yet, at its heart, a dried wax seal remained firm. The shape was circular, with familiar Concordium markings on the outer edges. In the heart of it all, an inscription stood out, clearly carved.

Pater Magnus

Matteo knelt, his movements deliberate and precise. He moved his fingers around the seal before slowly lifting the lid's edge. A soft click echoed through the silence. Lifting the lid brought the past into the room, filling it with long-forgotten memories. The documents inside were in meticulous order. Thick parchment scrolls lay scattered, some tightly bound in leather folders with frayed and worn ribbon ties. The scent of aged paper and ink hung heavy in the air, a testament to stories long kept silent. However, one folder stood out from the rest and immediately drew my attention. Inscribed in a time-worn hand:

"1912–Beobachtungsliste Wien" [1]

Lina knelt, her hands closing around the folder, its weight a quiet burden. She brushed the dust from the letters on the cover and then opened it slowly. The careful arrangement of the pages inside, each in its place, was a testament to order amidst the chaos of life. Notes of

---

[1] 1912 - Vienna Surveillance List.

observation filled each page; some were typed, others were scrawled by hand. The pages lay in their neat rows, each one following the other in the order of the letters, a quiet testament to the simplicity of structure. Lina traced the letters with her fingers, feeling the weight of each stroke beneath her touch. "G... H..."

Then she halted at a line. Her eyes narrowed. Her breath slowed. Despite her steady fingers, a heaviness lingered in her touch.

"Hitler, Adolf."

Stillness settled in the air. The cold that filled the room became palpable, a presence that wrapped around the weary souls within. Ernst knelt beside Lina, his hands steady as they grasped the file. He looked over the words, searching for meaning. He took the book in hand and read, the words flowing quietly in his mind. In the opening of the report, a short description lay waiting.

Name: Adolf Hitler
Year of Birth: 1889
Date of Registration: October 14, 1912
Category: Potential Candidate
Status: Under surveillance—comprehensive development started.

Someone wrote the next section in handwriting. The script was unsteady but understandable, with carefully crafted, interconnected sentences:

"Isolated from officer circles yet fixated on officers. Lacks a strong artistic identity but shows a tendency for symbolic thought. Significant rhetorical capability. Social responses are assessed, yet self-worth evaluation is skewed. It is essential to monitor development.

Social interaction is restricted; nonetheless, he demonstrates a propensity to take on a leadership role within small groups. In spontaneous debates, discussions, and public speaking, a notable persuasive skill and smooth oratory have been evident.

He often asserts his own ideas. Exhibits leadership traits instead of merely following others. Possesses the capacity to generate an immediate effect on audiences. Even with an introverted nature, he displays intense passion and a resolute stance on particular ideological matters.

Attention: Increasing fascination with metaphysical rhetoric. Develops the idea of a 'new order' based on his unique interpretations. In his speeches, terms like 'harmony', 'purity', and 'spiritual duty' are becoming more prevalent. He seeks an identity and stays open and receptive to external guidance.

Suggestion: Opt for redirection instead of persuasion. Must be maintained at a distance, ensuring no evidence remains. Might strengthen alongside alternative structures. Appropriate for use."

Matteo stared at the open lid of the box, the silence stretching before him like a long, empty road. His fingers did not brush the edge of the document, but his gaze remained fixed on it. He inhaled deeply and nodded slowly. "So he's been watched since then. They knew before anyone else did."

Lina said, "They didn't just watch him. They chose him to carry their thoughts and ambitions. They led him purposefully."

Ernst placed the documents one by one into the linen bag, his head bowed slightly in the room's silence. Each page weighed heavily, not in the bag, but on his tired shoulders. He spoke in a low murmur, but every word rang true.

"Hitler... possibly not their direct creation. They saw promise in him. They moulded him in silence. He transformed into a man who mirrored their thoughts, remaining silent but understanding. The danger lies here: They chose him, or rather, guided him. They observed and studied. Then they shaped it into something new, a product, and programmed it to serve the machine."

The room was once more silent. But this silence had gone beyond the ordinary darkness. There was a silence that hinted at beginnings, like a whisper in the darkness.

They all understood. These papers contained more than just history.

They spoke quietly about a future that was yet to be revealed.

32

They carefully placed the documents in the bag. Then they moved on. The space between the stone walls narrowed, and the air thickened around him. Finally, they came across a sturdy iron hatch, its surface weathered by the years. Matteo lingered, his fingers tracing the cold metal of the hatch, feeling the gravity of the situation. He eased the hinges with care. The metal yielded, a tired sound escaping, but it held its ground. Light crept into the tunnel's shadow, dim but unwavering.

As they crossed the threshold, the weight of the Karlskirche lifted off their shoulders. They stood on the outskirts of the worn industrial district. They stood amidst the rusted tracks and soot-darkened factory walls. The streets were bare and silent beneath the weight of the fading light. There was no one there, but the air was thick with the presence of unseen eyes lurking in the shadows around every corner.

They inhaled deeply. The cold air entered their lungs. Tension subsided, if only for a moment, giving way to cautious relief. The dome of Karlskirche loomed far away, a faint outline shrouded in the morning fog.

Lina reached into the inner pocket of her coat and pulled out the chart that Heller had given them. She unfolded the page carefully. There was a handwritten note in the lower corner of the paper that was nearly invisible. She hadn't seen it until now.

"Pater Magnus's trail ends in Prague. Beyond that lies shadow."

She tightened her collar against the biting wind and scanned the horizon.

"Prague", she said, barely audible above the whisper of the wind. "The next stop is ahead."

33

They left the industrial zone as night fell, casting a quiet shroud over the weary landscape. Lina raised the collar of her coat and looked down the street again. Each window and shadow seemed like a trap waiting to be sprung. "We cannot linger in the light," she said.

Ernst nodded, a subtle but meaningful movement. "We'll stay here for the night. In the morning, we'll talk to Heller about Prague. Complete the plan and leave the next night."

Matteo moved forward, his gaze sweeping the length of the street, checking both sides with a quick, practised glance. The industrial district on the western outskirts of Vienna was less crowded than the city centre. The people here remained vigilant. An unfamiliar face would immediately stand out, like a shadow in the sun. "No one knows us here. However, if we continue to move in this manner, we will soon attract attention," he said.

They looked around for a while before discovering it. An abandoned shack stood silently behind the brick workshop, forgotten. The door remained slightly open. They entered without making a sound. Lina opened the door with a light touch of her fingertips. The shack lay in deep silence, as if the rest of the world had forgotten about it. Inside, there were only a few weathered wooden crates, tattered cement bags, and a stack of planks leaning against the wall. The wind whispered through the cracks in the ceiling beams, a soft murmur weaving between the splintered wood. Outside, silence reigned. Inside, it was as if time had stopped.

The three of them settled in among the crates, the world outside fading to a distant hum. Lina opened her bag. She took the chart Heller had given them with steady hands and spread it across her knees. "The trail of Pater Magnus fades into the shadows of Prague," she said. "But how do we get there?"

Ernst took a small, creased map from the dark recesses of his coat pocket. He knelt and laid it out in front of Lina, the fabric unfolding, a story poised on the brink of silence. "We have two paths before us: one leads north through Znaim, the other east into the Moravian woods, where we might find our way to Prague through Brno." Matteo nodded, his eyes following the lines on the map with quiet concentration. "Znaim is brief, but it leaves us vulnerable. There are no forests and nowhere to hide. Brno stretches out before us, but the mountain passes and dense forests will obscure our path."

Ernst raised his eyes, a determined expression on his face. "Then we take the road to Brno. The road is longer but safer. We will stay here for another night. If there is a shadow behind us, it may appear before we take our next step."

The shack was cold and secure. They took turns keeping watch. Lina made brief notes in her notebook. Ernst reviewed the documents. He counted them and acknowledged their existence. The only sound all night was the wind murmuring between the rafters.

They slipped out of the shack as quietly as shadows as dawn broke. They moved quietly, taking care not to leave a trace in the world's dust. A stack of newspapers lay before a roadside kiosk, drawing their attention. The headline in the top paper stood out as bold and unyielding.

"A fire raged in Berlin, consuming the archive building. It fell to ash, a ghost of what once stood. The cause lay shrouded in mystery, a matter still under scrutiny."

Matteo took the paper in his hands, his gaze quickly moving over the words. "They're covering their tracks... or had to destroy documents that fell into the wrong hands."

"Elias!" Lina said. "I hope it didn't catch him."

34

By midday, they had returned to Heller's house, passing through the cool, shaded streets of Josefstadt. They took deliberate steps forward, toward the dark green door bearing the number 23.

Lina surveyed the surroundings before rapping her knuckles against the door. The sound of the metal bolt being withdrawn emerged with a familiar echo in the silence. Then the door creaked open slightly. Heller looked down the street, his eyes narrowing behind the lenses of his glasses. He caught her gaze for a moment before nodding and pushing the door open wider. "Enter," he said.

They rushed in, closing the door behind them with a soft thud. Heller firmly closed the door, drew the curtain tight, and beckoned them into the sitting room with a quick motion. The room remained a tangle of chaos, with fountain pens strewn across the table, notebooks open, and a collection of old dictionaries. "I did not expect to find you here again," Heller said. "I assumed you'd have left by now. Did something happen?"

Ernst took off his coat and placed it on the rack, the fabric whispering against the wood. "No, there is no problem. We're headed for Prague. We felt it was necessary to speak with you once more before we leave."

Lina opened her bag, her fingers brushing against the worn fabric, and drew out the cipher chart Heller had given them earlier. She pointed to a small, scrawled note tucked in the lower corner of the parchment. "We saw it last night," she explained. *"The path of Pater Magnus leads to Prague. Beyond that, there is only shadow.* This note sealed our decision. The next stop is Prague, I believe."

He took a deep breath, steadied himself, and replied, "Yes... Prague is one of Europe's ancient crossroads. It is often forgotten, but despite lacking the might of Rome or the heart of Berlin, it contains profound remnants." He fixed his gaze on the walls, which bore the weight of the past. "Until the late nineteenth century, many documents, particularly manuscripts, made their way to Prague. Not to be preserved, but to fade away. Concordium's presence there does not follow an open plan. It is in shadow."

Matteo enquired, his eyes fixed on Heller's face. "So we do not know what awaits us there?"

Heller shook his head slowly and deliberately. "No. Pater Magnus' path concludes at that point. When a man's path ends, it is by the hand of another or by his own choice to fade into the shadows."

"What exactly are we supposed to look for?" Matteo asked.

Heller paused, the weight of the world resting on his shoulders. He slid the drawer open; the wood creaked softly beneath his touch. He produced a yellowed pamphlet. He set it down on the table and lightly tapped the title. "We are fortunate," he admitted quietly. "In Prague, the Academic Language Society will hold a two-day seminar that will begin in ten days. Professor Karel Melnik stood before them."

Lina held the pamphlet in her hands, her gaze moving over the words, looking for meaning within the printed lines. "Melnik…"

"He is a researcher, one of the few mentioned in attempts to decipher the ancient documents. He is a mysterious figure in Prague's academic circles. Nobody can tell what his true allegiance is. So it would be wise to stay cautious."

Lina folded the brochure, the paper crisp against her fingers, and placed it in the pocket of her coat. She looked up and enquired, "Do we need permission or an invitation to attend the event?"

"No," Heller replied, his voice firm. "The seminar welcomes everyone. It will take place on Karlova Street, inside the old stone walls of the university building in the heart of town."

Ernst placed the map flat on the table. His fingers moved rhythmically between Brno and Znaim. "We plan to travel to Prague via Brno. Although the northern route is more direct, it can be dangerous. The path through the Moravian forest is more secure."

Heller gave the map careful consideration. He nodded slowly. "This is a wise decision. Recently, there has been an increase in checkpoints along the Znaim route. Civil matters in rural areas continue to be underreported. It is easier to lose a trail in Brno."

He turned and reached for a small black leather notebook sitting in the corner of his desk. He meticulously turned the pages before revealing a slip of paper hidden between the lines and presenting it to Lina. The note was in his handwriting. "I know little about Melnik. This note may provide you with a useful address. If you mention I referred you, they will assist you in finding accommodation and some important contacts."

Lina took the note and tucked it carefully into her pocket. She then looked into Heller's eyes. "I appreciate all that you have done."

Heller smiled lightly. "Remember the chart I gave you," he instructed. "The papers you seek in Prague will remain silent without that guide. They will only speak to those with the right eyes." He took slow, weighted steps until he reached the door. He raised the bolt with a steady hand. He slowly opened the door, gazing into the world beyond. "Good luck," he said as his gaze shifted to the vast expanse above. "I wish for our paths to cross again... But I am confident that you are on the right track."

They stepped out onto the street with the sun high in the sky. Three shadows blended into Vienna's familiar bustle before disappearing. Their path lay before them, clear and unwavering.

Prague.

35

The preparations were done quietly, with each task completed with a steady hand and a logical mind. They would leave from the eastern edge of Vienna, travel through the Moravian forests, and arrive in Prague via Brno. They contemplated each step as if the world depended on it.

They left the western part of Vienna around 3:00 a.m. As they left the city, the stone walls and narrow streets said a soft goodbye before fading into the distance.

They spent the first night in an abandoned stable near Wiener Neustadt. It was a place long abandoned by creatures, where the scent of hay mixed with the chill of dampness. They moved in the dark for three nights. By day, they sought refuge among the thick leaves and jagged stones.

On the fourth day, they arrived at the Moravian woods' boundary. The cold was an unkind companion, creeping into their bones as the wind howled through the trees, sharp and unyielding, cutting deep into their flesh. The wind howled through the limbs rather than the branches. To avoid the cold, they had to walk during the day. They huddled together all night, seeking warmth and regaining strength. Their feet were aching, swollen, and tired. Their shoes' seams were frayed and gaping, and their heels cracked like old leather. Earth's weight burdened their clothes, colours merging with the shadows of trees.

Lina came to an abrupt halt as they approached a small village on the edge of the woods. Her thoughts shifted away from the road, consumed by the signals from her own body. "We won't make it to Brno like this," she said softly and steadily. Her voice carried the weight of exhaustion.

Matteo and Ernst moved quietly, their eyes scanning the landscape. They approached a lonely farmhouse on the outskirts of a village, hidden from the outside world. When darkness fell, they moved quietly toward the barn behind the house. The door remained open, unbarred, and waiting. They entered quietly. Three dark coats hung on the wall, with a few pairs of old trousers dangling from rusted nails. They were simple, worn but durable. Clothes made for the field, abandoned as if lost in the dust of labour. It felt as if an unseen hand had expected their arrival, leaving the clothes for them to find on this night of all nights.

"We are fortunate," Matteo said softly. "Fortune smiles upon us."

They laid their old clothes to rest among the stones in the peaceful forest. When they set off again, they looked different. They walked down the street unnoticed, like ordinary farmhands, their presence blending into the dust and silence of the day.

On the sixth day, as dawn broke and light crept over the stone walls, they reached the outskirts of Brno. They walked silently, their feet falling in time, through the narrow lanes that led to the station. Avoiding the gaze of others, they walked past the shop windows. They moved on, attempting to vanish and blend into the very air around them.

They arrived at the Brno Train Station with the sun blazing overhead. Inside those walls, life pulsed with a strength that the city outside could not comprehend. The crowd moved restlessly and unyieldingly, a tide of souls pushing and pulling in the low light. Farmers and coal miners worked under the relentless sun. Soldiers maintained their vigil. The vendors shouted their offerings into the air. Women moved intently, their steps sure. Children danced in the dust, their laughter mixed with the day.

Buying a ticket, giving a name, and showing identification were too risky. Matteo examined the freight cars, his gaze wandering over the rusted metal and shadows they cast. He raised a finger, a quiet gesture that communicated volumes. The darkness was heavy within. There were only a few rotting wooden crates and coiled ropes lying in disarray, and the stench of years past hung heavy in the atmosphere.

They climbed into the car without speaking, settling into the shadows and waiting in silence. The air inside was cold, cutting at the skin like a sharp knife. Darkness had fallen, and the night was still. The pale glow of the station lamps flickered in the mist. When the time came to leave, the train lurched forward with a sudden, powerful jolt. The wheels clattered against the rails, creating a steady hum in the evening quiet.

Lina's voice was barely audible against the silence. "All the shadows…it's as if they're coming with us," she said, and the words hung like a distant memory.

36

November 26, 1935
Prague

The constant sound of the tracks beneath them marked their journey. The sound fell like a heavy curtain, suffocating their thoughts and casting their fears into the shadows. Matteo looked through the narrow opening in the door. Thick darkness lay beyond, offering no promise of discovery. It felt like a cleansing, leaving only the silence of what had once been.

As the morning light brushed against the car's metal, the train rolled into Prague's main station. They were exhausted; the tiredness that seeps into the bones and lasts long after the day is over. Their clothes were clean, but their boots were heavy with earth, and their bodies hadn't touched water in days. Yet they went unnoticed.

Lina removed the small piece of paper from the pocket of her coat, where Heller had placed it. It had only an address and a few words scrawled below.

"Prague may not have the same level of control as Berlin or Rome, yet it also doesn't guarantee complete safety. Please proceed to this address. Rap on the door and mention my name. They will offer a secure environment." Heller.

The address led to a stone three-storey building in the Josefov district, just behind the Old Jewish Cemetery. The building stood silent, its windows draped and its walls strong against time.

They knocked on the door. After a brief pause, the door slowly opened, revealing an old woman, her eyes sharp and wary. She surveyed their faces. Lina took the note from her pocket, her fingers brushing against its surface, a silent moment suspended in the air.

"Dr Heller?" the woman asked quietly, her voice barely breaking the silence. She nodded, made a slight gesture, and moved aside. "You may enter. Go upstairs," she instructed.

The room above was modest but clean. A desk stood firm in the corner, and shelves along the wall supported many books. A clean cloth rested on the desk, its edges crisp and straight. In the centre of the room, a stove stood firm, flanked by piles of firewood and coal, waiting for a spark of life.

Silence reigned supreme in this place; finally, after many days, they felt the air filling their lungs with a freedom long lost.

Matteo approached the window, the light spilling in like a promise for the day ahead. He looked into the street, which was framed by stone walls and shrouded in mist. His voice carried a distant sound from his mind: "Kraków, Vienna…and now Prague."

37

This city was more than just another location on the map. It was a threshold, allowing for the shadowy investigation of what had come before. Lina rose from her bed, the sheets slipping away in whispers. She drew aside the curtain, allowing light to enter the room. Frost flowers clung to the windowpanes. Winter was approaching, and nature had left its own message on the glass.

Matteo crouched in the centre of the room. The door of the old stove was ajar. He carefully crumpled the newspapers, placing pieces of coal between them, each movement deliberate and measured. A match ignited, casting a dim light into the stove. "I do not recall ever feeling warmth since Berlin," he said, his voice tired.

Ernst rose silently. He spoke without raising his gaze. "Today, we must move as whispers. We will hear and mark the words, but we will not reveal ourselves."

Lina sat silently as dawn broke, the world outside moving on without her. She placed her bag on her lap, her hands moving purposefully as she sorted through its contents, each item finding its place quickly. The parchment folder lay open, revealing Heller's encryption chart. A small notebook, a pen, and a flask of water sat beside it, waiting in the quiet stillness. Everything settled into place, bringing a sense of calm certainty. "We will not speak until the conference ends," she said, her gaze fixed on the bag. "We shall not reach out to anyone."

Matteo raised his gaze away from the fire. "Heller spoke plainly: *'You will be nothing but observers.'*"

Ernst gave a small nod, a quiet acknowledgement of the moment. He moved closer to the stove. His hands remained cold, with palms turned to the warmth of the fire. A faint red hue had touched the tips of his fingers. He lifted a log from the pile and placed it in the stove, the wood rough and heavy in his hands. The fire danced briefly before roaring back to life. "It is cold out there," he said. "Let us warm ourselves before we depart."

Lina spread the plain clothes the old woman had left on the bed. The fabric was heavy and woven from dark wool. The colours were pale and plain.

She wore her dark brown coat, lifted the collar and tucked her hair inside, seeking protection from the cold. Matteo draped the grey-brown overcoat over his shoulders, its fabric heavy and familiar. He placed a fedora on top of his head as a subtle nod to the world outside. Ernst followed suit. Common enough to blend in with the crowd while remaining perfectly appropriate when needed.

He looked at his wristwatch, the hands moving steadily to show the passage of time. The sun had just risen. It was half past seven in the morning. He did not raise his gaze as he stated, "We must be inside the building by 8:30 a.m. Arriving early means slipping into the shadows, unnoticed and unremarked upon. However, the latecomers always catch the eye."

They stepped onto the narrow cobblestone street. The frosty morning in Josefov hit them hard and fast. A tram called out in the distance, leaving a lingering sound in the air. A boy's footsteps were steady and sure as he delivered the morning newspapers. The first sign of Prague waking from its slumber emerged.

They arrived at the Old Town Square. The Astronomical Clock Tower stood out as a dark silhouette. It was nearing eight o'clock. The sky brightened a little, but the sun remained hidden. Lina paused and turned her head slightly. "Keep going," she whispered. "Karlova Street is nearby."

They continued walking, the silence between them thick, unbroken and heavy.

38

Lina came to a halt when they reached Karlova Street. "This is it," she mumbled. The structure in front of them was the conference hall of Old Town University. It was a restrained yet noble interpretation of Baroque architecture, typical of Prague—not flashy, but confident. The weathered stones of the façade had deepened in colour over the years. Rain, wind, and time had left their marks on the walls. The stone columns supported more than just the structure; they bore the weight of centuries.

The statue near the towering wooden door was impressive. A woman, blindfolded, holds a scale, evaluating yet oblivious. The other—a man with his head lowered and lips closed—silent and expressionless, as if to observe, saying nothing.

Matteo took a few steps backward. He looked at the statues, squinting slightly. He said softly, "This can't be a coincidence."

Ernst studied the figures flanking the door with great interest. He examined the fissures in the stone and the intricately carved features on their faces. He gave a subtle nod. "An appropriate detail for a seminar on silence and symbols."

A simple poster had been discreetly placed to the left of the door. The paper moved gently in the breeze. The text was in both Czech and German.

18th Century Symbolism and Writings of Secret Societies
Prof. Karel Melnik
European Academic Language Society Conference
Open to All

Lina stood motionless, her gaze fixed on the sign, the words hanging in the surrounding air. She examined the date and time written beneath the lines. She shifted the strap of her bag on her shoulder, a slight movement that conveyed purpose. "This is the right place," she explained.

Matteo grasped the iron knocker, its cold weight resting in his palm, and pulled it steadily against the door's wood. The stone walls absorbed the sharp metallic sound as it turned, leaving no trace. The door creaked open, a weight hanging in the air, unsettling and thick. They entered, and the scent of the place hit them like a wave. The air was thick with the scent of a worn-down memory. It carried the echoes of countless conversations, the weight of silences, and the whispered secrets of the walls and floors.

The corridor was in shadow. Voices drifted from the lofty hall ahead, sometimes whispering, sometimes murmuring softly. The marble flooring underfoot felt alive, as if it drew in the surrounding air. At the entrance to the hall, two young attendants stood. They wore dark grey jackets and black fedora hats, their faces set in quiet determination. They were not looking for proof of his identity or a welcome. Their eyes held no scrutiny, only the simple grace of a nod welcoming one to pass.

Matteo stepped through the door, making a subtle shift toward Lina. He whispered, "We don't attract attention in here. We will watch from the sidelines; nothing else."

The hall stretched out before them. It stood tall and unyielding, a testament to a bygone era's artistry. The ceilings rose high, supported by sturdy arches. In every corner, the frescoes, worn by time, whispered stories from the past. Light filtered through stained glass windows, casting faint shadows on the floor and transforming into something almost tangible. The dark oak benches were arranged in solemn rows, a testament to the art of the stage. The wooden seats bore the marks of time, each telling a story of what had happened.

Almost fifty people filled the hall, creating a quiet murmur in the air. Their clothing conveyed restraint: dark wool coats wrapped tightly, buttoned overcoats that concealed, bowler hats perched firmly, and linen satchels slung over shoulders. A small group of men in military uniforms stood apart, their faces hard, their eyes sharp and watchful. Some in the room stared down at their small notebooks, while others murmured. They sat, each engrossed in thought, their gazes fixed and unwavering.

They took their intended positions near the back of the hall, in one of the dimly lit side rows. Matteo drew an old notebook from the depths of his coat and placed it on his knee with quiet deliberation. Ernst maintained a steady and deliberate gaze as he scanned the hall. Lina sat straight, hands deep in her pockets, her gaze fixed on the horizon ahead. They moved with a grace that appeared common, but it took a keen eye to see the truth in their simplicity.

Contrary to all expectations, a deep, abiding silence filled the hall instead of voices. Before the words were spoken, everyone present, meeting simply to confirm the validity of their shared ideas, seemed already to understand.

The bronze clock next to the door read 8:55 a.m. The seminar was about to start, and the air was thick with anticipation.

The whispers in the room faded, silenced by a force that needed no words. At 9:00 a.m., when the clock's wooden hands met, the heavy door on the right groaned open. The man who entered walked with caution, each footfall a quiet calculation in the space's stillness. He stood tall and slender. His beard was short and greying, a perfect complement to his sharp yet tired expression. He wore a black wool suit that fit snugly across his shoulders, a reflection of the man he had become. The collar of his shirt pressed hard against his neck, and the tie was a deep, unadorned shade that stood silent witness to the day ahead. His right hand remained buried in his trouser pocket, while his left held a thick notebook.

His footsteps echoed on the stone floor, bouncing off the hall's high, arched ceilings. The sound was soft, but each echo pressed against him, a heavy reminder of his presence. The sound of his footsteps broke the stillness. He approached the lectern and paused. Carefully, he placed the notebook on the table. He raised his head, made a slight movement, and let his gaze wander around the room, never settling on a single face, glancing over each with a brief, deliberate pause.

Lina's throat felt dry as those eyes moved across her. Matteo wore a distant expression, as if his thoughts extended far beyond the room. Ernst leaned in and whispered to Lina. "Karel Melnik", he said.

Lina's gaze remained fixed on the professor, and a subtle nod left her lips.

39

His hand is hovering over the notebook. He nodded in a slight gesture before turning the pages. Each movement was deliberate, and each pause held great significance.

Before he said anything, his presence spoke volumes — not of facts, but of intent.

Finally, the first words appeared. He spoke calmly, but with a sharp edge: "Esteemed colleagues, researchers, historians, and thinkers... Today we meet to discuss Europe's complex and often hidden legacy. It is the symbolism of the eighteenth century, the written words of societies that thrived in the dark."

His thumb lingered briefly at the edge of a page. The yellowed paper rustled softly, as if it contained the memory of hands long gone. He continued, "The eighteenth century in Europe was not just about armies, kings, dynasties, and borders. It was a period of intense conflict, a clash of ideas that swirled like smoke in the air. Thoughts wrapped in symbols and hidden behind the walls of exclusive circles shaped national destinies, leaving the average person adrift in a sea of uncertainty."

Lina focused intently on Melnik's hands. Every gesture carried the weight of a ritual, rich in meaning and silence. These documents were not simply papers. They served as a quiet challenge to what had gone before. This was not merely a story; it was a trial. Melnik shared information, but it was more than that. He measured them, determining who could bear the weight of it all.

Melnik removed an old parchment from his satchel and set it on the lectern, the weight of history resting on the wood. Time had worn away at the edges, leaving a faded yellow in the centre, a ghost of what once was. He handled it with care, as if it were more than just paper, a piece of history that demanded respect. "This document", he said in a deep voice, "was kept in a private collection from the days before the revolution in France, in the late 1780s; the other copies vanished in Paris in 1794... or, more likely, were brought to ruin on purpose." Melnik's voice was tight, like a taut string about to snap, as if it contained a warning in its tremor. "This text is not just about politics," he said. "It is the vessel of a doctrine—one that, from the outside, appears chaotic, even coincidental. But when approached with the right understanding, it reveals the path to a profoundly interconnected truth."

He slowly turned the parchment and carefully presented it to the audience. The dim lighting at the front of the hall cast shadows on the paper. There were two interlocking circles with a broken cross in the centre and a Latin phrase untouched by time — *'Initium veritas silentii'*.

Melnik raised his gaze from the page to meet the crowd's expectant expressions. This time, his voice rang out, steady and measured, almost sacred: *"Truth begins with silence."*

Melnik continued, "This is more than just a statement of symbols. This saying expresses the essence of many confined systems. The truth is naked, revealed only in the quiet moments that occur between words, for knowledge is a burden that not everyone can bear. Wisdom comes to those who are prepared."

"This kind of text", he said, his voice dropping, "says nothing on the surface." The pattern before him was intricate and silent. The writings whispered secrets, their meanings hidden deep. Symbols standing like sentinels guarded unspoken truths. "To the untrained eye, they appear to be mere adornments, but for those granted access, they reveal a path. Silence writes where the turns are, which paths are open to whom."

Lina sat straight, her back firm against the chair's embrace. She looked at the void where Melnik's words took shape, rather than at his hands. She didn't pay attention to his voice. *This man was more than just an observer; he was integral to everything.*

In the hall, the academics sat, their heads bobbing slightly as they scribbled in their notebooks, hoping to capture the words that filled the air. In the front row, an old man with a white collar removed his glasses and stared intently at the symbol. A low murmur sounded in the distance. Young students huddled close, heads bent, carefully tracing the design lines into their notebooks.

Matteo drew the shape with a steady hand, pressing his left wrist against the table and moving the pencil purposefully across the page. He meticulously documented every detail, as if he were charting a new territory.

Melnik's hand slipped beneath the lectern at that moment, and he pulled out a small velvet pouch, the weight of which remained hidden in his palm. The fabric lay in shadows, dark red and worn, and its texture bore witness to the passing of time. His fingers loosened the string, revealing something hidden and long forgotten. From within, he fashioned small dark metal seals. Each was unique, but all shared the same quiet grace. Their lustre was gone, and their contours had softened with time, but they still stood as symbols of power: quiet but unyielding.

He placed the seals on the lectern with a steady hand, each one with intention and thought. He raised his head to survey the hall and articulated; his words cut through the air. "These seal specimens are tied to a structure thought to have existed in Prague from 1770 to 1815, though no official record has ever confirmed it." His fingertips brush against the seal. Symbols carved into its surface reflected the light, revealing them rather than hiding them. "In certain old records, this group is called *Societas Concordium Occulta — the Secret Society of Concordium*."

A young scholar sat in the front row, his head gently bobbing as he scribbled notes on the page before him. Matteo cast a quick glance at Lina, a flicker of intent fire dancing in his eyes. Lina lowered her eyelids in a subtle gesture, a nod that could have gone unnoticed. Melnik's voice became slightly softer. Now, he spoke not as a researcher but as a witness to history: "Most of the documents of this structure vanished during the Revolution of 1789, the Napoleonic Wars that followed, and the uprisings of 1848 — or rather, they were methodically destroyed."

"In the quiet corners of Prague, there are private collections. *Lingua Symbolica Manuscripta*, a collection of texts, remains uncatalogued. Here, the faint echoes of this structure remain."

Ernst wrote a single line along the edge of his notebook.

Lingua Symbolica Manuscripta → Prague connection → verification required.

Melnik turned to face the wooden board next to the lectern. He held a heavy sheet of drawing paper, the edges carefully creased. He carefully opened it and placed it on the board with a steady hand. The drawing depicted an abstract map. He sketched geometric shapes in pencil. Thin lines crossed, circles merged, angles broke, and loops spiralled. It appeared not only beautiful but also functional—a design with purpose.

He lifted his head slightly. Behind the lenses of his glasses, his gaze moved across the room, taking in the shadows and light. His voice returned, softer than before but with a deeper meaning: "You see... Chains that curve round and round, triangles that meet and separate, loops that twist and turn indefinitely..." His finger moved to the centre of the shapes and remained there. "These are not part of Catholic iconography or Church-sanctioned art. These are drawings of buildings where the ties that bind are loyalty, allegiance, and the silence of unspoken words. Each stands as a door, understood only by those who live within."

The listeners sat differently now; pens traced the page with deliberate slowness, and eyes remained fixed on the figures, as if looking for meaning in the lines.

"Only those who know understand these symbols," he explained. Each figure represents a doctrine or a step in the initiation process. Outsiders see them as scattered and unconnected sketches. However, to the astute observer, they unveil the contours of a more expansive structure.

Lina focused her attention on the drawings pinned to the board, the lines and shadows telling their own stories. She held her breath, hoping to imprint each line on her memory. Matteo sat quietly, his pencil moving quickly but carefully, capturing the essence of a fleeting moment in his notebook. His fingers moved with practised grace, not just tracing the shapes in front of him but also searching for the hidden meaning woven into their forms.

Melnik closed his notebook after a long pause. Questions lingered in the air, unspoken but weighty. And then, once more, he broke the silence: "Those who triumph—emperors, kings, and conquering armies—weave the story of history... But 'they' maintain their existence not through words, but through the silence that surrounds them."

The words lingered, suspended in the room's silence. He closed the notebook, its pages whispering secrets now held in silence. He raised his hand briefly, a silent nod to the world around him. "I appreciate your ear," he said.

40

For a moment, the hall was still, enveloped in a heavy silence. Then there was a brief, deliberate clap that filled the air. Here, knowledge was more of a burden than a source of wonder. The participants rose one by one from their seats. Their footsteps echoed softly across the wooden floor. There was no rush and no loud words to break the silence. The silence had settled deep within the room's walls.

Matteo said quietly, "The very tone of the speech carried the weight of a ritual."

Lina leaned in, letting out a whisper as soft as the wind through the trees. "We need to talk to him, but not in this place. Someone might be watching."

Matteo nodded, a slight movement, barely noticeable. "We go after him when he departs."

Ernst spoke quickly and decisively, his gaze fixed on the hall's shadows. "We will go our separate ways. We must create the impression that we are not going after."

The crowd thinned in the hall, and each person rose from his or her seat to tiptoe into the night. Their eyes fell to the ground, and their steps were deliberate, as if they were any other student wandering around campus. They averted their gaze, each absorbed in his or her own thoughts.

Melnik emerged from the side door approximately ten minutes later, his worn leather satchel cradled beneath his arm. His grey coat collar stood high, and his head dipped just enough to hide his eyes. He walked quickly down Karlova Street. He walked with purpose, each step unwavering, his gaze fixed ahead, unconcerned about the world around him.

Ernst followed at a distance, measured and calm, his movements deliberate but unforced. He kept his eyes down, but his mind caught every detail: Melnik's shoulder movement, stride length, and head tilt. Lina walked on the opposite side of the street, her steps steady and sure, reflecting the rhythm of the world around her. Matteo stood at the end of the street, his gaze searching for exits and routes.

Melnik confronted Josefov. The crowds had thinned, and the streets were silent, a hush falling over the city. The night air, heavy with the scent of smoke from old house chimneys, hung over glistening cobblestones. Along the path, shadows danced as the streetlamps flickered dimly. Ernst moved into the narrow passage and quickened his pace. Melnik's shadow flickered against the wall, a fleeting presence in the night's stillness, illuminated by a dim lamplight.

Ernst approached, his voice steady and measured: "Professor Melnik?"

The old man drew his satchel closer, a subtle shift in his appearance, as if the world around him had become heavy with unspoken realities. He looked at Ernst through his glasses, his eyes steady, unflinching, neither startled nor afraid. It was a reckoning, a weighing of old truths, and the silent doubt of years past lingered in his eyes.

Lina and Matteo moved quietly, keeping their distance on purpose. Nobody stirred. The air was thick with tension; each breath counted, each heartbeat a quiet drum in the silence. They wanted to keep the professor at ease.

Ernst raised his hand, making a slight gesture. His voice remained low and steady. "We listened to your lecture, Professor. We do not want to impose. Across Europe, we toil over scattered papers. We seek your wisdom and guidance."

Melnik stayed silent. His eyes, framed by the glasses, moved over each of them individually. Three figures, worn by long journeys: sweat dried on their coat collars, mud coated on the edges of their boots, and faces etched by sleepless nights. They were real, unmasked in their essence. They sought the truth, something tangible in a shadowy world.

Finally, he grabbed the strap of his satchel and looked over his glasses with a steady gaze.

His voice was low and clear. "We can't speak here. The walls have ears. They hear the whispers of the night, the secrets carried by the wind. Meet me in St Salvator Church's rear courtyard in thirty minutes. It is safer there."

Ernst nodded; a small sign of agreement.

41

Half an hour later, they arrived at St Salvator Church's rear courtyard. Melnik stood there waiting. He leaned against the eastern wall, his silhouette lost in the shadow of a column. He kept his gaze low, but the sound of footsteps approached. Even with his back turned, he felt it: they had arrived, and he could sense their purpose and presence. They came to a halt a short distance away. Nobody moved. Silence hung in the air, heavy and unwavering, as if it were the first rule of this gathering. Finally, Melnik turned his gaze. He looked at them through his glasses. His voice rang out, clear and soft. "Were you followed?"

Ernst replied, his voice steady and confident. "No. We are alone."

Melnik shifted his glasses. "Certainty is a fleeting shadow during these times," he said. "This is a quiet city. And silence is a mask worn in this place. One can detect the scent of a stranger from two blocks away." He took a step forward. His voice was now lower but more resolute: "Why did you follow me?"

This time it was Lina who answered. Her words were direct: "The Lingua Symbolica Manuscripta you mentioned during the seminar… we need to access it."

Melnik held his breath for a moment. His eyes turned instinctively — scanning the surroundings out of habit. Then he turned back to them. Before he spoke, he lowered his head slightly, and his voice grew faintly husky: "Normally, I wouldn't help anyone with this, especially strangers. But your silence... it says everything. It's not your questions that speak — it's what you haven't asked. It wasn't academic curiosity that brought you here."

Matteo said, "We are following the thread from Prague to the Concordium archive." His tone conveyed the weight of a secret, a whisper capable of opening a long-closed door.

Melnik's expression changed as a shadow passed over his features. The lines on his face deepened, and his pupils narrowed slightly. His lips moved, but silence lingered. Finally, he looked into Matteo's eyes, his voice low and almost breathless: "Concordium... It's been a long time since I heard someone say that name out loud."

The words hung in the air, not a confession or a simple warning. They were something more, a door left open, inviting but foreboding. A threshold stood in front of them, a line drawn in the dust. Only the brave would dare to go through, and only they could cross.

Melnik turned and walked in silence. The trio followed, keeping their distance, eyes alert, and hearts steady. The short walk ended at the edge of the rear courtyard of St Salvator Church, next to a weathered stone bench covered in moss. He dabbed his glasses and slowly turned his head toward them. "I don't have the original document," he said. His voice was no longer as formal as at the podium, nor as guarded as it had been in the street. The distance between them seemed to have narrowed. "I never did. But I saw a copy. In 1923... here, in the rear section of the Klementinum Library. Back then, no one knew what it really was. Today, it doesn't appear in any official catalogue. But someone from the inside whispered that it's still there. Under 'Sonderbestand' — the special access collection. They said it's archived under the name *Codex Fragmenta*."

Ernst leaned forward: "What does this document hold?"

"The first clear sign of Concordium's internal structure. Like the many stories of a noble building, each symbol in the system carries its meaning and weight in the world, creating a layered and structured whole. The method employed by the cipher is significant. Most importantly, there were the first whispers about a core circle known as *Ex electis*."

Lina repeated the last words spoken quietly and determinedly. Her voice was low but clear. "Ex electis... The Chosen."

Melnik nodded slowly and deliberately, as if weighing the weight of the world in one simple gesture. "Yes. It is Concordium's tightest circle. There, knowledge is no longer just information; it has developed into something owned. For those who stand apart, only silence remains. The transmission of knowledge is a deliberate act that is not left to chance. A bloodline, a chain of loyalty, or a verified allegiance from the past—sometimes all three are required. They prefer blood relations. But not always necessary."

Matteo pulled his small notebook from inside his coat. He held his pencil but did not take his eyes off Melnik. "How can we get to this document?" he asked.

Melnik looked over the rim of his glasses. His voice had softened to a whisper in the stillness. "Through the means...? It is impossible. The Sonderbestand is accessible only to high-level researchers with academic credentials. And you... are not such individuals."

A moment of silence hung in the air. A tram moved slowly in the distance, its sound fading into the daytime silence. The sound echoed off the ancient stone walls, filling the night with its presence.

Melnik lowered his head slightly. His lips moved just enough to let the words escape: "But there is another way. Beneath the old laundry building in the rear garden of the Klementinum... there's a maintenance tunnel from 1919 that still holds. No one uses it, and most don't even know it exists. You could enter through there—unnoticed."

He paused for a moment. He looked at each of them, his gaze lingering on a few. "You must go at night. During the day... eyes are everywhere. But at night, the city is only stone and wind. No one asks. No one responds."

As Matteo quickly scribbled notes into his notebook, Lina and Ernst remained silent. Melnik stepped back a few paces. The weariness he carried had now seeped into his voice. "My role ends here," he said. "I cannot go any further. I must leave you on your own."

He looked at them one by one. In his eyes was not a warning but the burden of a foreseeing witness. "Following the Concordium is not about pursuing papers. When the trail finds you, understand that you are already being watched by unseen eyes. Remember that when the Concordium finds you, it is not just silence but complete erasure."

His last words hung in the air like a heavy echo. He bowed his head, turned, and walked away. With each step on the stone pavement, he left behind not only traces of the past but the looming shadow of danger.

They stood still for a while, their eyes fixed on Melnik's silhouette shrinking into the darkness. The wind swept through the church's stone arches with a hollow whisper.

Ernst spoke quietly: "We need to plan."

There was resolve in Matteo's voice. "We're one step closer to the heart of the Concordium."

Lina slowly nodded. "We can't stay here any longer. Let's go back."

They began walking in silence. In the flickering light of the streetlamps, their shadows blended together, melting into the city streets with the wind. None of them spoke again until they returned to the house in Josefov, which the old woman had opened for them.

42

What lay ahead in the darkness of the next night was more than just a search; it was the crossing of another threshold. And now the path lay before them, unwavering and clear.

The Gothic towers of Prague rose against the night, their shapes obscured by the deep shadows that enveloped the city. On the surface of the Vltava, the moon's light trembled like a silver whisper in the night, hanging low. The city slept peacefully. The wind swept through the stone streets, carrying dry leaves in its wake.

They walked softly down Karlova Street, pausing at each corner to avoid the light from the streetlamps. Klementinum stood tall against the fading light, a stone fortress at dusk. The massive Baroque structure loomed large in the fading light. Built in the name of science, faith, and control in the 18th century, it stood, bathed in the pale glow of the moon, not as a temple of worship but as a testament to the stillness of confinement. The large windows looked out like watchful eyes, and the stone walls, worn by time, bore silent reliefs that spoke of meanings lost to the ages.

Ernst glanced down at his wristwatch. "We must find the tunnel swiftly."

Lina nodded, a slight movement that barely registered. She drew her hood close against the cold. She kept her gaze fixed on the details lost in the shadow of the massive stone structure, as if she were afraid to meet its gaze.

Matteo moved forward, determined in his purpose. He tiptoed down the stone path that led to the courtyard. In the courtyard's shadow wall, a rusted iron grate stood, worn by time and neglect. It looked different from the others—set a few centimetres inward, as though it didn't quite belong to the surrounding masonry. He knelt down, probing the rusty joints with his fingertips. He discovered a loose part of the locking mechanism. The crease in his brow deepened, casting a shadow of concern across his face. He took the end of his jacket, wrapped it around his hand, and turned slowly, pulling the rod free.

They entered the courtyard quietly, passing through the half-open gate. The inner courtyard of the Klementinum remained silent, a place where sound faded and time lost its meaning. In the far right corner of the courtyard, a small, worn structure leaned against the wall. Hidden from view, neglected, and tucked between the stones—it was the old laundry room Melnik had described: a portal into the heart of silence.

The door hung on rusted hinges, open but unguarded. Lina moved forward and pressed it gently, her hand steady and deliberate. The hinges creaked, and their rusted jaws slowly opened, emitting a deep, guttural sound into the still air. Then, the smell from inside struck their faces. It wasn't merely physical; it felt as if the rot of a bygone era, along with everything it had concealed, had been sealed inside.

The room was dim. Cracks ran through the walls; in places, the plaster had bubbled, exposing patches of bare stone beneath. On the north wall stood a stone slab. To the untrained eye, it looked like an ordinary section of the wall—but to those who knew how to look, it was a gateway.

Matteo immediately crouched down. He ran his finger along the edge of the stone. On the icy surface, he discovered a hollow, a small respite in the harsh expanse. Ernst knelt beside him, quiet and steady, and offered his hand. They moved the stone slowly and deliberately, each hand steady in its task.

Ernst spoke softly, barely rising above the silence. "This is a tunnel. We entered the shadow of the Klementinum."

Matteo pulled a thin, long candle from his pocket. With trembling fingers, he lit it. As the faint yellow light illuminated the narrow opening, stone steps descending into darkness appeared. They entered the tunnel one by one—Lina first, followed by Ernst, and finally Matteo. They slid down the steps. The stairs were narrow and damp. The heavy, persistent scent of moisture rose from every corner of the stone surface.

They walked a hundred metres and came across a heavy, unyielding door. It was made of sturdy wood. The door opened, its hinges creaking softly in the silence. Beyond it lay a narrow and long corridor that served as an archive for old memories. Shelves stood along the walls, shaped by the slow passage of time rather than being placed by human hands. In the dim light, surrounded by leather-bound books and linen-wrapped scrolls, the air was heavy with the weight of sealed crates. It wasn't just information that vanished into the shadows; it was a quiet whisper of secrets.

There was a small open space at the beginning of the corridor. The room contained a worn and faded desk. A cabinet toppled in the corner, spilling its contents. An old ladder lay forgotten and motionless among the shelves.

Ernst spoke softly, a breath barely escaping his lips. "This must be it. Sonderbestand: The section for special collections."

Lina proceeded without hesitation. She reached into the inner pocket of her coat and drew out the small list of symbols that Heller had given her. She raised the yellowed paper to the flickering candlelight. The ancient symbols breathed once more. She traced her fingers over the shelf labels, feeling the embossed letters on the book spines and the symbols that represented untold stories. Every line, circle, and letter contributed to the creation of a map. Heller's pattern was intricate and unyielding, like a language woven through a maze. Lina had progressed beyond being a mere reader. She was a translator, deciphering the quiet threads of history that Concordium had woven in the shadows.

Matteo looked at the side shelf. He drew out a heavy, worn scroll, its surface thick with dust. Lifting the leather cover, he skimmed the words inside. He whispered, "No..." with disappointment in his voice. "The Tübingen collection: Medical manuscripts from Germany." He carefully closed the pages and returned the scroll to its proper place. His gaze moved to the shadowed corner of another shelf.

Ernst leaned in close to the tattered book. His fingers brushed against the dusty label, feeling the roughness beneath the skin, a reminder of something long forgotten. "No..." he whispered, leaving a shadowy impression. "Documents of Ancient Egypt".

Time was drifting. They calculated every step and every breath. Minutes passed between the shelves, deepening in silence like a test of patience.

Lina then turned toward the shadowed shelf in the corner, her eyes slitting in the fading light. One book stood out among the others, its presence undeniable. It lay there, wrapped in dark brown leather, the corners worn smooth by the years, the spine showing the signs of ageing. The weathered seal kept its meaning for those who knew. A broken cross lay between two circles, intertwined like fate itself. Concordium's quiet symbol. A history buried in darkness.

Lina's voice came out as nothing more than a breath: "I found it."

She extended her hand cautiously. Her hands brushed the book's cover, a gesture of quiet respect. She wiped the dust off with steady fingers. But within her, a weight was growing, heavy and unyielding. She lifted it with both hands, carefully and deliberately. The words on the book's spine were barely discernible, written in nearly faded handwriting:

Codex Fragmenta—Ex Electis Manuscripta
1784

She lifted the book's cover. The first page was empty, like a blank canvas waiting for words to fill it. Then the second page arrived: *"Initium est in silentio."*

"The beginning is in silence." This phrase stood firm, guarding the entrance to the depths of all that was hidden. In the absence of silence, the truth remained hidden, masked by the noise of the world.

Lina turned the pages slowly. Intricate tables, interlocking geometric figures, and whispers of partially encrypted genealogies filled each leaf, all drawn in fine ink. Some lines were erased by time, others faded—but each line stood firm, holding a secret.

Matteo approached the book, his hands steady and deliberate. As if on a path through the wilderness, he knelt and traced his finger along the diagram. He appeared to be etching the words into his memory. He whispered, "This reveals the internal structure of the order, the rites of initiation, and the chains of authority... Concordium's main plan lay before them, stark and unyielding."

As she turned the page, she noticed a hurriedly scrawled cautionary note between the heavy lines: *"Qui non pertinet, interit."*

Lina carefully translated: "Who does not belong, perishes."

As her words faded, the book weighed heavily on the room's stillness, heightening the silence that surrounded them. Ernst spoke softly. "They created this book specifically for members of the *Ex electis*. Others perceive it as a maelstrom of uncertainty. But to those who have the right key, it's a map drawn in the dark."

Matteo offered a solemn nod. "Only for the chosen few... To others, it is just the cold, steady thrum of a gear in motion."

Lina closed the book and softly placed her hand on its cover. Her fingers rested on the cold leather, heavy and still. "This book lays bare the framework of Concordium... it may also uncover those who dwell within that framework."

Ernst glanced at his watch. His troubled eyes focused not on the words but on the silent passage of time. "We cannot stay here any longer. We must leave this place."

The book lay wrapped in linen, a quiet promise, and was gently placed in the bag.

Matteo took one last glance around the room. Each shadow and speck of dust served as a reminder of what had come before. They were no longer relics of the past but symbols of the weight that now hung over him.

43

Lina walked ahead, her steps sure and steady, breaking through the morning's silence. She moved with purpose, each step deliberate, as if she understood the significance of a single misstep. Ernst and Matteo followed a few steps behind in silence.

At the end of the tunnel, a large stone block lay dislodged and stubbornly blocking their way. Matteo knelt down on the floor. His hands traced the stone's rough edges. The dampness and passage of time had taken their toll, and what had eroded over the years had now become their means of escape. He inhaled deeply before leaning in with a measured effort and pressing his weight forward. As the stone shifted, it let out a low groan. They emerged from the dark tunnel onto the narrow street, the cobblestones rough under their feet. The morning was still a whisper, but a soft light crept from the east, illuminating the buildings' windows.

Lina took a quick look around and spoke without moving her gaze. "We must leave. We can't stay on this street for long."

They wandered the narrow streets of Josefov. Their footsteps echoed against the cobblestones, creating a steady rhythm in the evening's quiet. They arrived at the old woman's house ten minutes later. They opened the door carefully and entered the house.

Ernst placed his bag on the small table. He carefully opened it and examined the files and scrolls one by one. "The Codex Fragmenta remains here. We cannot take these documents outside again," he said, his voice steady, the weight of the words hanging in the air like a storm cloud about to burst.

Matteo sat by the narrow window, his gaze fixed on the street beneath. In the soft morning light, his eyes were sharp and alert. "Yes. Just in case, we've been lucky so far. We can't afford any mistakes from now on."

Lina removed her heavy coat and draped it across the back of an old chair, the fabric whispering against the wood. She paused and then knelt to remove her boots. Her fingers rubbed together, and her chilly hands brushed against her face. "We leave at dawn," she said, weary but determined.

Ernst glanced at his watch. "At most, we have four hours of sleep. We must arrive before the seminar begins."

No more words were required. They felt exhaustion creep in, heavy and unyielding, pressing down on them.

Lina stretched out on the bed, the weight of the day settling over her like a heavy blanket. Ernst reclined in his chair, his eyes closing against the weight of the world. Matteo spread a blanket in the quiet corner and settled in.

The room smelt of old wood; the wind whispered against the stone walls, and they felt a tenseness in their bones.

In the quiet of their last moments, one thought stood out: *"The codex is in our hands. Now, we will discover ourselves—and the things we can change."*

Then there was silence, and they fell into a deep sleep.

44

They were already awake and had quietly gotten ready. The weight of the day had settled on their shoulders even now. Ernst adjusted his hat in the mirror by the wall, took a step back, and glanced at Lina, his lips barely moving as he said, "Let's not be late."

They arrived at Karlova Street around eight o'clock. The stone façade of Old Town University stood tall as a silent testament to time. The poster near the entrance hung on, its edges curling like the leaves of an old book, but the words remained clear.

18th Century Symbolism and Writings of Secret Societies
Prof. Karel Melnik

They took their seats in the dim back row of the hall. At nine o'clock, the side door creaked open. Melnik approached the lectern with steady steps, dressed in the same black wool suit he had worn before. His face remained motionless, a mask of quiet determination. He moved forward as if the past had not faded away but lingered behind him, waiting to be picked up again. He stood at the front of the podium, breathing steadily, and carefully opened his notebook. His voice rang out again, as clear as ever, but with a deeper weight.

The lecture ended at 11:00 a.m. Melnik descended from the stage, greeting a few academics with polite nods that faded as quickly as the light in the room. He tucked the leather bag under his arm and exited through the side door.

Lina trailed behind him, her eyes fixed and unwavering. When the time came, she called out, "Professor Melnik."

Melnik paused and turned back. He kept a close eye on Lina, his glasses perched on the bridge of his nose. Her voice remained steady, but beneath it was a tight urgency. "We went into the Klementinum last night... We discovered the codex."

His face tightened for a moment. His eyes narrowed, and his voice became colder. "We cannot speak of this in the open."

Lina took a small folded paper from her pocket and extended it forward. Melnik accepted it, but his hand trembled slightly.

"When night fell. Our place in Josefov. Still and safe."

Melnik nodded slightly. "Understood," he replied, then continued on his way.

Lina remained motionless. Ernst and Matteo joined her shortly after. They stood silently as the world around them faded into the background. Finally, Ernst murmured, "This night holds weight."

45

The door knocked softly, a timid tap breaking the night's silence. Lina stood up immediately and moved toward it. Ernst lifted his gaze from the pages of his notebook. Matteo emerged from the shadows near the stove, his senses sharp. Lina approached the window, her fingers brushing the fabric of the curtain as she drew it aside to gaze out at the world beyond. In a hushed voice, she said, "Melnik."

She hastened to the door, silently drew back the heavy bolt, and cracked it. Under the dim glow of the streetlamp, an old man appeared, gripping his hat tightly in both hands. With his head bowed, he slipped inside. The door closed swiftly behind him, thickening the air in the room.

"There is no one," he replied quietly. "I looked down the street before I arrived. No one followed me."

He strode to the stove with purpose. As he removed his gloves, it was clear his hands were trembling. "Time is short," he stated with conviction. "We shall start at once."

Ernst carefully lifted the lid of the chest, the wood creaking softly beneath his touch. He reached deep inside and pulled out the codex. He placed the book on the table with the same care and weight as a vow rising from within the silence. The flickering candlelight danced across its cracked surface, revealing the faded lines of ancient ink.

Melnik gripped the book tightly at its edges. "I cannot believe you have truly found this," he whispered, his fingers brushing the cover as he adjusted his glasses.

Lina moved forward, her resolve unwavering. "We've looked through everything. Cipher sequences and symbols, bloodlines intertwined. Everything aligns with the Concordium's structure."

Matteo added, "We've decoded some constructs. But the full connections are still unclear. Especially the directions..."

Melnik slowly turned the pages, holding each one in his hands for a moment. His fingertips traced the worn letters, each one bearing witness to time. At one point, his fingers stopped moving. He leaned in, his voice barely audible: "Here it is..."

They drew closer. Lina focused on the worn markings in the lower-left corner of the page. Two small circles intertwined, with a broken cross in the middle. Just below the figure, a faint Latin phrase remained, nearly erased but still legible: *"Ad initium Florentiae."*

"At the beginning of Florence," Lina said, her voice low and steady. "It starts in that place."

Ernst furrowed his brow, the lines on his forehead deepening. "What's there?" he asked. "A document? A hidden room? Or a name?"

Melnik nodded, his finger moving slowly over the words, as if looking for meaning in the text. "This is Concordium's timeless encryption, a path designed with purpose. It provides no guidance. Just a path... a hint of what could be. It does not take you to your destination; it directs your attention to what is truly important." He pointed to the words with his fingers: *"Lilium, Sanctus Spiritus, Archivum, Custodia."*

After a pause, Matteo said softly, "Lilium—the lily is the emblem of Florence."

Melnik nuzzled his glasses up and turned the page. Under the flickering candlelight, a nearly erased line appeared along the edge of the next leaf. It was handwritten in German; faded in colour and cracked in form, but still legible. All three leaned in quietly.

Wenn du den Ursprung suchst, dann führt dich der Weg zuerst nach München, dann nach Florenz.

Ernst squinted, his voice low and measured. "If you seek the origin, the path takes you first to Munich, then to Florence."

Lina furrowed her brow. "What does that mean?" she asked, her voice heavy with uncertainty. "We thought the beginning was in Florence."

Melnik carefully opened the notebook, its pages whispering secrets from the past. He turned the pages, holding the symbol templates that Heller had given him. He matched the symbols to the hidden marks woven throughout the text. His eyes darted across the page, his fingers skimming the lines, searching for order in the chaos of symbols.

"Look here..." he said, his voice measured, pointing to the line of symbols in front of them. A title stands alone: *"Academia Augusta - 1919"*.

Ernst spoke again, his tone steady but tinged with sharp awareness: "Academia Augusta... I have never heard of it before."

Melnik made a slight nod. "You wouldn't have. It's not an official organisation. This is Concordium's concealed framework in Munich. In 1919, as the Weimar Republic gained traction, they unceremoniously moved some archives and documents from Berlin to Munich."

Ernst bowed his head, his voice calm and thoughtful. "Hitler first stepped onto the political stage in Munich…"

Matteo's gaze lingered on the open page of the codex: "And the years when Mussolini established his party in Milan and began his march to Rome. Europe was changing form."

Melnik ran his fingers over the page, feeling the roughness beneath them. "The codex does not issue direct commands; it only points. But the arrangement of symbols, the layers of script… they all lead to the same conclusion.

Academia Augusta in Munich is the first link in Concordium's restructured chain."

"And Florence", Lina said, "may not be an archive, but it may serve as a centre of knowledge."

"If we can uncover who Hitler was in contact with in Munich, the circles that supported him, and which structures Concordium used to guide him... we can reach the centre in Florence." Lina's gaze wandered deep into the pages of the codex. "Then we'll know not only why they chose him but also how they guided him."

Melnik slowly removed his glasses. He drew a cotton fabric from his pocket and carefully wiped the lenses clean. He raised his head slightly and spoke clearly: "Munich is under Nazi control. They watch every move there. Every face could be a threat. Florence... lies under Mussolini's shadow. Both carry their own kind of hell."

He gently placed his hand on the weathered cover of the codex. His fingers rested gently on the documents, hoping to touch the pages one last time. "The codex must remain here," he insisted with conviction. "Take only the symbols and the guiding key phrases. Keeping this book will ruin you if you're caught. It wouldn't just be your end."

Matteo worked, his hand moving quickly across the page. He recorded the code sequences, encrypted phrases, and directional symbols, each one a piece of the puzzle, a hint of something bigger. Lina closed the codex with a deliberate motion, the weight of its pages hanging in the air. The cracked leather cover lay motionless, a sentinel of time, keeping its secrets close as if it had watched the world change for centuries. She softly placed it into the chest and took a deep breath.

Melnik placed his hat on his head. He approached the door, looking back. His gaze swept across their faces. "Once you leave Prague, you'll be alone. Trust no one... except each other." He opened the door and walked into the courtyard, as silent as a shadow, leaving the hum of emptiness behind him.

"Our journey to the Concordium's core begins now," Matteo said, his voice low but filled with solemn awareness.

They sat at the table, silence hanging in the air as they reviewed their notes. They had no guide now. Their only guide was the bond they shared, an unwavering loyalty that kept them together in the vast unknown.

46

The soft, pale morning light crept into the room, casting shadows that danced across the walls. They sat silently at the small table. Ernst was the one who broke the silence first. His voice cut through the tired spirits that lingered from our night together.

"The codex will remain here," he stated. His tone was not hesitant; it bore the weight of responsibility. "This is too much for us to bear. If we continue on this path, we will not be the only ones who suffer. We will expose everything." He nodded slightly, his gaze focused on the bag. He said quietly, "We will only take what is necessary."

Lina placed the codex in a linen pouch, carefully tying the drawstring. Each movement felt like a step in a solemn ritual, deliberate and loaded with significance. She placed the pouch at the bottom of the chest and draped an old, nearly worn blanket over it. Her fingers brushed the fabric as if to say goodbye.

She took a deep breath, filling her lungs with the weight of the situation. "Once we leave this place, there is no turning back," she said. Her voice was heavy with weariness, but beneath it was a deeper current—the unwavering determination of a chosen path.

47

They had carefully planned their train journey. To use the main station was a substantial risk. It was a place of spies, collaborators, and men who wore suspicion as a cloak. Instead, they chose Zličín Station in the west. It was small, inconspicuous, and hidden from the world.

When they arrived in Zličín, the city was still quiet and asleep. Only a few workers remained at the edges of the platforms, silent and with heads bowed low.

Matteo led them down a narrow side alley before they arrived at the station. They stood at the base of a wall, shrouded in the shadow of a column.

"We will not enter the station together," he declared, his voice filled with a firm resolve. "I will take the lead. I'll buy the ticket and head to the platform. Ernst will arrive in five minutes, and Lina will be the last." Then he added, "We'll act like we're complete strangers. We will board separate cars. We wouldn't exchange a single glance until we arrived at our final destination."

Lina and Ernst exchanged a quick glance before nodding their acceptance of Matteo's suggestion.

Matteo made the first move. He walked at a steady pace, like the rising sun on the horizon. He moved slowly, each stride controlled and sure. From the ticket booth, he averted his gaze. After a brief nod, he replied, "Furth im Wald via Pilsen. Third class." The ticket clerk fixed his gaze on the counter, his hands working in their usual cadence. He stamped and slid the ticket without speaking.

Matteo accepted it quietly and entered, taking a solitary seat on a bench at the edge of the platform near the rails.

Five minutes later, Ernst arrived. He buried his hands in the pockets of his heavy coat, and the brim of his hat shadowed his brow. He moved to the booth slowly and deliberately. His soft words blew away in the wind. With no concern, he bought a ticket for the same trip and headed to the platform. He ignored the benches and tracks. He stood unmoving, crushed against the wall in the silence of a forgotten corner.

Lina was the last to arrive. She appeared to be lost in her own world, with a remote and hard posture. With her hands in her pockets, she stared at the rails disappearing into the distance. She stayed motionless, but her gaze wandered incessantly, searching.

Matteo raised his head, a moment of stillness and fixed his gaze on Lina. Their eyes remained apart, distant as the horizon at dusk. He shifted his gaze away, as if the weight of the situation was too much to bear. They behaved as if they were strangers, each lost in their own thoughts, the silence thick between them. Their strategy relied heavily on silence. They would take their seats in separate cars and, if questioned, would pretend they had never met.

The metallic hum of the tracks broke through the morning silence. A figure emerged from the mist, its outline becoming clearer with each passing moment as it approached. The steel wheels clattered against the rails, filling the air with purpose. The steam locomotive approached the station, moving slowly and purposefully, like a beast of burden bearing the weight of the world.

Matteo rose with quiet resolve, his bag resting on his shoulder. He approached the second-class car, which loomed near the front. Ernst bowed slightly and moved forward, stepping into the cramped third-class car at the heart of the train. Lina was the last to leave, slipping quietly toward the compact passenger car at the back of the train.

They avoided looking back. They sat quietly, the weight of unspoken thoughts hanging in the air.

Ernst looked out the window of his carriage, his gaze fixed on the mist that had crept over the Vltava, engulfing Josefov as the city clung to the remnants of morning. His lips parted, and words emerged into the quiet air. His voice was just a breath. "We are starting now."

The train left Zličín Station and headed north along the Vltava Valley. A thick layer of morning fog covered the bare plains and sleeping trees. The cold had seeped into the carriage's very bones, leaving a quiet, persistent presence in the air. Inside, silence reigned, broken only by the steady, metallic chime of the iron wheels. With each kilometre, the path led deeper into the shadows of the unknown.

Lina sat by the window of the last carriage, watching the world pass by. She focused her gaze on the unseen rather than the scene. Lina's gaze darted from the window to the corridor and finally to the carriage door. She sat still, her ears tuned to the silence that surrounded her. Her bag lay between her knees, and her feet remained steady beneath the seat.

When the train arrived in Pilsen, they disembarked, each finding their own place to stand standalone once more. There was a pause, a stillness in the air, until the voice broke the silence. It mentioned the train to Munich, which was waiting at Platform Two, ready to carry souls across the land. The three proceeded as they had planned. Matteo led the way with steadiness and confidence. Ernst followed at a safe distance, while Lina took up the rear, monitoring the trail behind them. The carriages of the German steam train were bright and new, in stark contrast to the worn and tired Czech train. Their blue-grey bodies featured the Reichsbahn's embroidered eagle emblem, a symbol of discipline and severity that conveyed order and purpose. The rigid precision of the Gothic German script on the carriage doors captured the eye with unwavering clarity.

At 10:00 a.m., the train arrived at Furth im Wald station, close to the German border. The clatter of the rails faded, leaving an uneasy silence in its place. Each breath inside the carriages was full of quiet longing. This was the most important crossing on the journey. The border was no longer just a line on a map. The border served as a lethal barrier, stripping identities bare, removing masks, and revealing the strength of the spirit.

Matteo leaned forward, his eyes sweeping through the window. Two German customs officers stood as sentinels on the platform, their forms rigid in the morning chill. A man dressed in plain clothes stood there quietly, watching. A single glance revealed his true identity: the Gestapo. He wore a long, dark overcoat that fit him perfectly, and he tucked his hands into leather gloves. His eyes remained sharp and still beneath the brim of his hat, as if a hunter were waiting silently. He exhaled softly, barely audible. "Keep calm," he reminded himself.

The inspection began in the last carriage, where Lina sat alone. Standing in the doorway, the customs officer in the black coat surveyed the passengers. The travellers presented their papers one by one, each offering a small surrender to the waiting hands of authority. Lina carefully took out her forged Swiss passport. She held it out with firm hands, despite the tremor that threatened to shake her resolve. The customs officer collected the document. He cast a brief glance at Lina's face. She held his gaze steady, a faint smile on her lips. Neither brimming with confidence nor shrinking back in fear, just the look of a common traveller. The officer bowed his head before returning the passport. Lina took a deep breath, unseen.

Then came Ernst's carriage. The inspection proceeded quickly and steadily. Ernst passed the document, his gaze drawn to the window, where the world sat waiting, uninterested. The customs officer glanced down at his ledger, then up at Ernst's passport, and finally into his eyes.

The officer nodded briefly before returning the passport. "Thank you," he said, his tone firm.

As they approached Matteo's carriage, the air thickened. The Gestapo agent, a shadow beside the customs officer, leaned in close and whispered into his ear. The brief silence hung in the air, echoing throughout Matteo's entire being. He extended his hand and presented the passport. The Gestapo agent's gaze shifted to Matteo's face. The look was brief, but it went deep into Matteo's flesh. "Business trip?" he enquired, his voice carrying an unusual weight.

Matteo furrowed his brow, a calm confusion settling over him like a morning fog. "Yes... coming back to Munich from Prague," he said. He spoke calmly, carefully choosing each word; neither too formal nor too casual. The two men examined the passport, their attention drawn to the worn edges and smudged ink. Furrowing his brow, the Gestapo agent remained silent. The officer gave a brief nod before returning the document with a terse "Safe travel." Matteo lowered his head in silent gratitude.

As the inspectors stepped off the train and onto the platform, they breathed out together, unaware that the others were present. They had held their breath for too long. Life had returned to their lungs, filling them with the warmth of being once more. The train whistle broke the silence, a sharp sound that showed movement. The carriage moved slowly and gracefully. As the border slipped away, the compartments became filled with peaceful freedom. Although tension remained, they had passed the first threshold.

48

December 1, 1935
Munich

The train arrived at Munich Hauptbahnhof around 11:30 a.m., its wheels groaning against the iron rails. The steam locomotive whistled sharply, cutting through the air before disappearing beneath the station's massive dome. With a loud creak, the iron doors swung open wide. The cold air blew in, striking the passengers' faces like a slap.

They exited the platform as planned, passing through separate doors and becoming one with the crowd's pulse. Ernst lingered beneath the great clock that hung from the station's lofty iron arches, his body still for a moment, trapped by the weight of time. Lina walked confidently to the far end of the platform. Matteo walked away from the train, raising his collar to shield himself from the biting cold. They spoke only with quick, deliberate glances as they stepped out of the station and into the street.

When they reconnected, Lina spoke first. She looked around and said quietly, "No one is on our trail right now."

Ernst nodded, his gaze fixed on the Nazi emblems above the station's entrance. "It seems so."

Matteo cupped his hands in front of his face, looking for warmth in the breath he expelled. "So, where are we going to rest?" he asked.

Ernst paused, his gaze scanning the crowd for something just out of reach between the faces. "I've had a long-standing friendship. Franz. He lives in Schwabing. He has no desire to join the Nazis, but he has learnt the importance of staying silent in order to survive. I have faith in him."

Matteo gave a slight smile and tilted his head. "If there remains a soul in this city who has kept his silence, I would like to meet him."

49

They proceeded cautiously down Karlstrasse, the sidewalks slick with ice and glinting in the low light. Men in uniform walked purposefully around the street corners, their eyes sharp and alert. The youth wearing swastika armbands stood vigilant, scanning their surroundings with a fierce intensity.

They arrived in Schwabing, where the street stretched out in front of them, lined with art galleries, dimly lit bookshops, and cafes nestled against the ancient stone walls. They paused in front of a three-storey building with ivy-draped walls that appeared to have been long forgotten. Ernst tapped the old iron knocker twice. Moments later, the old wooden door creaked as it opened. A man in his fifties stood of average height, his face marked by the fine lines of age. He looked through the crack cautiously.

"Ernst?"

"Franz".

Their gazes locked for a moment, and a silent understanding spread between them. The door swung wide, revealing what lay beyond.

"Enter. Quickly," Franz said in a steady whisper, full of urgency.

When the door closed, he slid the bolt in place and quietly closed the curtains. He turned, scanning them with a wary expression. "To come here is to invite danger. Three strangers, especially in this neighbourhood, caught many eyes," he explained.

"I know," Ernst said; his voice was steady and unwavering. "We will not stay long."

Franz nodded and turned to lead them into the dim interior. They walked into a room with a low ceiling and a narrow layout, but it was comfortable and welcoming. A stove glowed in the corner; bookshelves stood as sentinels along the walls, and an old bicycle leaned against the plaster, worn from years of use. Newspapers, ink bottles, and a typewriter were on the table.

Ernst looked around the room, his voice low. "This still feels like a place where thinkers gather."

Franz smiled slightly, just touching the corners of his mouth. "It happened once. Nowadays, only those who understand the value of silence remain in this place." He took a brief pause before continuing his speech. "I will not question why you came. The city has gone silent, and questions remain unanswered. Trust is a delicate thing that is easily lost in the shadows of doubt. And I would rather not find out."

Ernst nodded. "That is why we will remain silent and unseen."

Franz approached the stove, his hands reaching for warmth in the cold air. "I don't want to know why you came here. Remember, though: do whatever you plan at night, if possible. The city comes alive in the light of day, its eyes sharp and its senses acute. And I choose to remain within these walls."

The room held its breath, creating a stillness that reflected the weight of unspoken words. Then broken words from days gone by, familiar faces, and the sharp outlines of a faded past appeared. Each person brought with them stories that had faded into silence.

As midnight approached, Franz got to his feet. "The night has ended for me." He said, "You should rest as well," and then slipped out of the room, leaving the silence behind him.

They gathered around the table as the sound of his footsteps faded. Heller's drawings and Melnik's notes lay scattered among the opened maps, awaiting understanding.

Lina spoke quietly, scratching her pencil against the paper: "Melnik remarked it was *'architecturally plain, yet there was a hidden order within.'*"

Ernst studied the map, his brow furrowed in thought. "The Glyptothek's exposure is excessive. Could this be The Propyläen?"

Matteo shook his head. "That is not true. Look at this." He pointed to a mark on the map's edge. "A small service gate is on the northwest side of the Glyptothek. It's mentioned in the plans."

Lina nodded; her gaze was steady and determined. "The mark of two circles... it is as appears in Melnik's sketch. However, to be sure, we must examine the entire area."

Ernst folded the map with care, each crease bearing witness to the journey ahead. "Tomorrow, we will part ways. We will all do our part to investigate. Our plan is to observe, take notes, and return here in the evening."

Lina stood quietly and moved to the worn chair next to the stove. "We must leave at dawn," she said, her voice low and determined. "We should find some rest now."

50

In the morning, they walked down Franz's wooden steps. Franz was waiting for them in the narrow foyer, beneath cold stone walls. His eyes were heavy with fatigue but bright with acute awareness. "Remember", he said, "don't speak. Don't attract attention. You should not be remembered."

The door creaked open, and a sharp cold flooded in from outside, chilling the room. They walked into the morning with soft steps and split up to take different routes to Königsplatz.

Ernst remained at a safe distance as he watched the patrols move around Königsplatz. The SS units moved steadily, and the junior members of the Hitler Youth, despite their youth, surveyed the area with cold, unwavering focus. Men in plain clothes stood with their hands deep in their pockets, but their eyes were alert. Ernst's expression remained motionless, a mask of silence and determination. In his notebook, he recorded their numbers, paths, and moments.

Matteo walked through the Propyläen's grand stone columns, feeling the weight of history all around him. He looked for symbols carved into the granite stones' edges and cracks in the floor. But there was nothing to be discovered. It is just a stone relic with no mystery.

Lina walked the path around the Glyptothek, her feet steady and sure on the stone. The air was cool, and the columns' shadows hung long in the dim light. She kept her hands in her pockets, and she fixed her gaze on the wall patterns, studying them with a slight tilt of her head and a flicker of her eyes. She recalls vividly the symmetry and details of the front façade. Finally, she made her way to the back of the building, where she found a rusted and heavy iron door. A plaque hung above it, its surface worn and faded from age. The plaque shows two entwined circles, weathered but still in shape. Lina squinted, her eyes clear and unwavering. She turned and walked away from the scene, her steps quick and determined.

As the light faded and the street lamps flickered, they gathered in Franz's small apartment. The room felt warm, and the stove crackled softly. The map was once again open on the table.

"Not the Propyläen," Matteo said, still wearing his coat, which was heavy on his shoulders. "It was too much of a display that sought attention rather than anything."

Lina placed her glasses firmly on her nose. Her voice was heavy with tiredness but undeniably direct. "There's a service door behind the Glyptothek. Two circles intertwined above the door, just as Melnik suggested."

Ernst nodded slowly and deliberately. "It should be there. We leave tomorrow night. But until then, we're staying here. There is no reason to be in danger."

Franz entered the room, his voice barely audible in the silence. They swiftly closed the map. He examined them one by one, his gaze fixed on Lina. "How did it go?" he asked. His voice was gentle, but there was a sense of doubt about it.

Matteo smiled faintly, his chin lowered. He said, "We just went for a walk."

Franz shrugged, and a low grunt came from his lips. "I hope it stays that way."

51

As midnight approached, three people remained awake in Franz's apartment. Lina, Matteo, and Ernst knelt around the large map spread out on the table. The flickering candlelight created shadows along the edges, revealing the drawn routes, symbols, and fingerprints. Franz had already withdrawn to his room.

Ernst spoke quietly and clearly: "The entry point is the northwest service door of the Glyptothek. Security conducts hourly patrols. The best time frame is between 1:10 and 2:00 a.m. That's when the gap appears."

Matteo said softly, "The door will be locked," without taking her eyes off the map. "To be silent is necessary. Every sound is more audible in the night's silence. There were unlimited possibilities of what could happen inside those walls. We do not have a floor plan. We need to be cautious."

Ernst pointed to the highlighted areas on the map and said, "If anyone follows us, I've meticulously planned two separate escape routes. If something goes wrong inside, we will proceed to the northeast gate."

The others nodded but said nothing.

Lina's gaze shifted to Franz's door as she threw her bag over her shoulder. It was slightly open, but no sound came from inside. He could've been sleeping or listening. But he knows how to keep himself quiet.

The air was still foggy when they arrived at Königsplatz. The wind died down, and the city seemed to hold its breath. Matteo paused in the centre of the square. He tilted his head slightly to the left. "On our left is the Propyläen, and on our right is the Glyptothek."

Ernst softly pointed to the northwest corner of the building and stated, "The service door is there. Let's go."

All three hastened to the darkest part of the wall, out of reach of the streetlamp. They came to a stop in front of the door. Matteo leaned against the wall and looked around. "There are no patrols; no one is waiting. Now is the time."

Ernst went down on his knees. He pulled a thin steel wire and a short screwdriver from his coat. He put his left hand on the door hinge and started working on the lock with his right hand. Time seemed to go on forever. Matteo and Lina were on guard. There was no sound or movement. They could hear only Ernst breathing. Finally, they heard a faint but clear click. The door moved slightly. For a moment, the silence was broken.

Lina and Ernst gazed at each other. "Quick," she whispered, opening her lips. They walked in and discovered a completely dark hallway. Their footsteps resonated gently and ominously in the darkness. Every echo of a step indicated how far they had travelled.

The hallway started straight and then veered right onto a narrow stairway. Matteo paused in front of the steps. The lamp lit his face as he looked around in the darkness. He murmured, "Upstairs or down?" It was hard to hear.

Lina did not think twice before responding. "Melnik stated that the private archives were in the basement. There is nothing up there for us. We go down."

The stairs were slippery. They walked at a regular pace, not too fast or too sluggish. They found an old door at the bottom. Ernst pushed lightly, and it creaked open. There were old cleaning rags, rusty buckets, and fading brushes inside. Matteo entered and inspected the walls and floor stones. He shook his head. "This isn't it."

They approached another door about fifteen metres later. That door was metal. Ernst knelt down to study the lock. It opened with a quiet click. There was a small archive room inside, with wooden shelves along the walls. Some brought scrolls; others, leather-bound books. The middle had precisely arranged crates and sealed boxes. A heavy layer of dust had accumulated over everything.

Matteo came in first, took up the candle, and said, "We begin."

For what felt like hours, the three of them stared at papers, saying nothing. Latin legislation, diplomatic correspondence, family records, old campaign maps, aristocratic seals... but none of them refer to the Concordium. Lina quickly closed her notebook and murmured, "There's nothing. These are only plans concerning the old city. This is not the correct location."

Ernst's tone was low but firm. "There has to be another room."

They returned to the hallway, inspecting every shadow and gap in the walls. Lina's fingertips came to rest on a wall protrusion as she prepared to gaze back. She felt it with her fingertips and realised it was circular. She stepped closer, carrying the candle with her. "Two circles that fit together..."

Ernst swiftly caught up with her. He removed a little screwdriver from his pocket. He pushed for the first round of relief. A tiny click, followed by another. The wall gently shifted aside, accompanied by a mechanical sound from within. A tiny spiral staircase emerged into view. Lina's eyes grew brighter. "This is it."

They did not hesitate before taking the spiral stone stairs. It seemed like the plunge would never end; the walls got closer together, and the air became heavier. Finally, they stepped through a low arch and into a big, domed room. The ceiling was very high. In the centre stood a large stone table with intricate carvings. The surface was granite with small fissures, but the artistry remained obvious. There were dusty bookcases along the walls that went all the way to the ceiling. They held hundreds of books, all silent, as if communicating from the past.

There was a closed metal chest on top of the table. Ernst walked up gently. He contacted the edge of the chest. His fingertips shook. "This..." he spoke gently. "This is the Concordium archive."

52

Ernst cautiously raised the lid of the metal chest. There were several sealed files and neatly knotted bundles of documents within. Some of the yellowed pages had breaks around the edges, and a thin film of dust had collected on them.

Lina extended her hands slowly. She picked up the top document and carefully unfolded it, touching the edges with her fingertips. She froze as her eyes moved over the lines. Her pupils got bigger. She handed Ernst the page and said, "Look at this..." with a shocked expression. Ernst brought the candle closer to the page and started reading.

SECRET!
GERMANY HIGH-LEVEL STRUCTURE SCHEMA
Date: 14.04.1933   File No: 1933-017
Subject: German Structure—Current Task Allocation

It continued with an explanation section below:

Himmler, H.
Role in the Nazi System: SS leader. Responsible for the creation of secret structures, symbols, and ceremonial sites.
Role in Concordium: Regional leader of Germany. Oversees ritual systems and organisational structure. Maintains contact with internal cults.

Ernst's voice quivers slightly. As he read the next lines, his face turned to stone.

Goebbels, J.
Role in the Nazi System: Minister of Propaganda. Mass manipulation, information control.
Role in Concordium: Berlin cell leader. Full control over the media, publications, and communication channels.

Hitler, H.
Role in the Nazi System: Chancellor of Germany. Figurehead leader.
Role in Concordium: External representative. Acts according to directives hold no independent decision-

making authority. Primarily reports to the regional leader of Germany and secondarily follows directives from the Berlin cell leader.

Pater Magnus.

A distinctive seal appears beneath this: *a broken cross surrounded by two overlapping rings.*

"So, this is real..." Matteo got closer to the paper. "The task list... from within the Concordium... Himmler is the region's leader and maestro of ritual. Goebbels, the head of Berlin, employed propaganda and manipulation. It states that Hitler is merely a symbol."

Lina's voice shook. "Hitler was not the decision-maker... *He's just a puppet.* He is under the control of a genuine group operating behind the scenes. The Concordium tells him what to do."

Matteo swallowed without making a sound. "We've always looked at the actors on stage. We never saw who was really in command behind the curtain."

For a minute, there was silence. Ernst reviewed the top line of the page before returning the paper. "1933. That was the first year under Hitler's leadership." He stated in a low, authoritative tone, "Everything was planned to be under control from the very beginning. This may not be happening only in Germany. If the Vatican, universities, monarchies, and other institutions accepted the Concordium, history would be altered forever."

Lina knelt next to the chest and placed her hands on the papers. "This is the best evidence we have of how the Concordium is organised in Germany. If this comes out, the world will know who truly holds the strings."

Ernst positioned the candle slightly away from the paper so that the flame would not destroy it. "Not yet. We can't take that chance until we see more." He continued carefully to review the materials. He suddenly realised there was a second scroll lodged in the chest's bottom. It was tied with a leather strap and had a detailed drawing. He carefully rolled it out.

He said the first phrase aloud, "Wewelsburg..."

Matteo instantly leaned close to him. His gaze searched the map. "This is not a normal blueprint."

The map depicted more than simply the outside of the castle. It went into considerable detail regarding the internal arrangement, including the circular ceremonial hall, the star-patterned stone flooring, the underground corridors, and the secret doors that only opened when certain symbols were employed. Each detail was drawn with careful attention.

Lina concentrated on the round symbol at the centre of the drawing. It appeared she was breathing. "That is the core. Not merely a place for ceremonies. It could be the Concordium's centre."

Matteo nodded. "There will be a nucleus there if we look for it." He delicately wrapped the papers with his fingers. "Now we need to get them out."

Loud footsteps suddenly echoed from the outer passage onto the stone floor.

Ernst got up immediately. "Don't move," he whispered. "Someone is coming."

Matteo snuffed the candle without thinking. The room was immediately shrouded in total darkness. The stone walls, which were laden with dust and moisture, amplified and reflected the echo. Every step was resolute.

Lina leaned against the stone wall, holding her bag close to her chest with one hand. Ernst hurriedly grabbed the documents from the chest and tucked them into his coat to keep them secure. Matteo discreetly crawled up the spiral staircase and lay flat on the ground to view the higher level.

One shadow arrived, then another: a long leather coat, a densely woven fedora, and heavy footsteps along the walls. He could hear Matteo's heartbeat in his ears: the Gestapo.

Ernst leaned toward Lina. He mumbled, scarcely moving his lips. "We can't go back up. We can either pray and wait or seek another solution."

Matteo crept back toward them through the darkness. "There are two of them waiting right outside. It might be a routine check, but if they catch us, nothing can help us."

Time halted. Not an hour yet; the minutes seemed to go on forever. Then, from outside, came a muffled cough. "Come on, let's go." A rough voice said, "No one's down here."

Another sighed. "You must have misheard. I warned you against drinking, but... I don't even see why we come here every damn night."

The other person laughed. "Let's have another glass."

They moved one, two, three steps before fading into the silence. Lina leaned her head against the wall while still on her knees. Her long inhale was hushed. "That was close."

Ernst lowers his head. "But we're still here."

"We have to go back," Matteo remarked. "In the same way... Quietly."

53

After carefully rolling and fastening the documents, they stealthily climbed the spiral stone stairway. In the last step, Ernst hesitated and gazed back, as if the blackness of that stone hall had left an impression on him. Then, without speaking, he turned and reset the mechanism on the wall. With a slight stone click, the door closed and vanished into solid brick.

Along the corridor, they moved like shadows. They remained silent and held their breath. They closed the exterior door without making a sound. Königsplatz was empty. Only a few streetlamps created weak, flickering reflections on the stone pavement.

When they arrived at Franz's home, they knocked gently. A few seconds later, the wooden door creaked open. Franz, drowsy yet aware, cast them a watchful glance.

He tiredly said, "Mein Gott…at this hour? What happened?"

Ernst stepped in, lowering the collar of his coat. He was weary, but his gaze stayed sharp. "Franz, prepare some coffee. We have a lot to tell you."

Lina silently sank into a chair as Franz placed the old kettle on the kitchen stove. She opened her bag, gently removing the documents and placing them on the table.

As Franz laid down his coffee, he observed the first heading. His lips parted, but no sound came out. "Himmler… Goebbels… Hitler…" The words escaped in a whisper.

Ernst nodded and kept his gaze fixed on the documents. "This reveals Concordium's structure in Germany. Behind the curtain lies Himmler's ceremonial system, which serves as a framework for protecting the inner circle. Goebbels was concerned with media, propaganda, and mind control. Hitler was only a symbolic figurehead. Concordium adopted a face as its symbol to guide the masses."

Matteo's fingers traced the edges of the sheets. His eyes wandered not over the words but across the delicate ghosts of the past. "We always felt Hitler was at the centre. However, he was really a mask for the true process.

Concordium turned him into a vessel, nothing more than hatred and charisma armed."

Franz couldn't keep his eyes off the documents. "Nobody will believe it. It extends beyond reality itself."

Lina tilted her head slightly. Her finger pointed to a line. "There is a small but important note here. *'Wenn du den Ursprung suchst...'* [1] The rest is clear: *Wewelsburg.*"

Ernst abruptly straightened. He adjusted the table and took a step back. "Wewelsburg: Himmler's Castle, the symbolic heart of the SS. They have convened there since 1934 for training and celebrations. If Concordium's real ritual papers exist, they are there."

Franz frowned and wrinkled his face. "That area is under particular protection. Himmler deemed it sacred ground. Infiltrating it is crazy."

Matteo gave a slight smile. His eyes still conveyed a subtle defiance. "So were Prague, Vienna, Berlin, and Munich. All impossible, but here we are."

Ernst spoke in a firmer tone this time. "The plan is obvious. Wewelsburg. If we get inside, we can take down the system."

Franz gave a heavy sigh. He ran his hands through his hair. "Alright... But how do you plan to get there?"

Matteo removed the map from his pocket. Despite its worn folds, the paper continued to direct the path. "We will take the train to Paderborn, then to Büren. If we depart at night, we will arrive in the morning. The rest are forest pathways. Woods heavily surround the castle region. This is the most effective strategy to approach quietly and unobserved."

Lina nodded in agreement. "It'd be stupid to approach during the day. At night, we could approach the castle."

---

[1] If you are looking for the origin...

Matteo checked his watch. "The first train runs at 6:00 a.m. We've got three hours. We need some sleep, no matter how brief."

Franz said nothing. He simply nodded. They took the maps and paperwork from the table without saying a word. The stove was still gently blazing, providing the room with warmth. However, no amount of warmth could ease the brutal reality of the voyage ahead.

Wewelsburg was waiting.

54

Franz waited at the door. He has turned up his coat collar; he was wearing worn but neat boots, and his eyes were cautiously dark because of habit. The farewell did not last long.

"The train from Münich to Paderborn," he stated gently. "Via Würzburg and Kassel. There is a country rail to Büren. From there, you can walk to Wewelsburg or follow the agricultural roads."

Hours passed quietly. Around noon, they arrived at the Kassel station. The platform remained silent, but the buildings yelled. Every wall and poster features the Führer's portrait, as well as large red flags, swastikas, and the bold words **"Ein Volk, Ein Reich, Ein Führer."**

When they got to Paderborn, night had fallen. They waited for the Büren train in a dark, secluded spot near the station. The surroundings were empty. Ernst removed the map from his pocket and spread it on the ground. "There are no more trains beyond Büren. We'll have to walk." He inspected the map. "We'll turn off the road at Alte Mühle and take the forest trail. There should be a maintenance trail along Wewelsburg's northern wall."

Lina spoke quietly. "Infiltrating an SS headquarters... This is completely another level. The smallest mistake ends everything."

55

Wewelsburg

They landed at Büren around 10:00 p.m. They discreetly slipped away from the station and headed north down the forest path. Snow enveloped everything like a thick blanket. After double-checking the map, they started moving silently and cautiously. With each step, their boots slid into the snow, and the winter wind cracked the dry trees in the woods.

In the distance, the silhouette of Wewelsburg loomed. Its conical top and massive stone walls stood out like a ghost in the shadows.

Ernst pointed with his finger. "There."

They approached the wire barrier carefully. Except for the screaming wind, there was silence. They gently lifted the fence. They heard a slight rustle above the snow. Ernst walked first, followed by Lina and Matteo, who entered softly.

Matteo took a quick stop as they approached the castle's cold stone walls. His gaze examined the tower's shadows and window recesses. "No one in sight," he mumbled.

Lina pointed to a little projecting grate among the stones at the bottom of the wall. "Look. There's an old canal. No water flow. The entrance seems to be open."

Ernst quickly nodded. "If we wait, we'll get caught. Let us move."

They squatted and slid through the tight gap, one by one. The moist stink in the air permeated their lungs. With each step, little creaks erupted from the stone floor, echoing faintly before dying away. At the end of the tunnel, they discovered an old door. The hinges remained intact, although the surface had rusted with time. Ernst slowly turned the handle. The door moaned from the inside as it slowly opened.

He took a tiny step back before turning to face the others. "We're entering the heart of Wewelsburg," he added gently.

They slipped in like shadows. The tunnel narrowed considerably inside. The ceiling had fallen, requiring them to squat at points in order to walk forward. With every step, the flickering light from Lina's small lantern bounced across the stone walls in a yellowish shimmer, creating unfamiliar shadows. Matteo led the way, carefully testing the ground with each step. "This passage... It's not on any official plans," he stated quietly. "It's definitely a concealed access route."

Ernst nodded slowly. "It appeared in the Concordium archival drawing. Without it, we would not be here."

After roughly ten minutes, the tunnel broadened. In front of them was a gigantic, monolithic stone door. The entire surface displayed symbols, including embossed images, faded Latin inscriptions, and the well-known Concordium symbol: two interlaced circles with a broken cross in the centre.

Lina guided the lantern's light up to the symbol. Her eyes glittered.

Matteo cautiously grabbed the lever to the right of the door. He turned it quietly. A deep mechanical scraping reverberated along the stone passageway. The door then opened slowly and heavily.

What they saw inside stunned them for a few seconds. In the centre of the gloomy cavern sprawled a massive round figure lined with rich green-black stones. Twelve spiral lines extended forth like a vortex, aiming toward the centre. *It was the Schwarze Sonne.*

Lina stepped back from the core of *the Black Sun*. She held her breath. "I never imagined it would be this big," she grumbled.

Her knees trembled slightly as her gaze followed the spiral patterns on the black stone tiles. The ceiling was so high that the dim illumination of her lantern could only reach the outer edges of darkness. Darkness cloaked everything beyond, crushing them like an invisible but palpable weight.

Columns and arches adorned the surrounding walls, etched with intricate writings in dozens of languages, including Germanic runes, Latin, Greek, and Etruscan scripts. Paintings surrounded the inscriptions in crimson, black, and gold that had faded over time but were still distinct. There were individuals holding torches, spiral stairs rising into the sky and human faces encircled by symbols.

Ernst verged his sight along the wall. "Himmler's obsession with a *'cosmic centre'*," he claimed. "This is where Concordium's darkest ideology became apparent. Wewelsburg is more than just a stone construction; it serves as a physical and spiritual focus. To them, the strength of Aryan existence is supposed to come together here."

Matteo went slowly towards the dark stone columns. As he lifted the wavering lantern light, he observed the carved figures on the surface. His eyes become instantly sharper.

"The swastika."

Lina stepped forward. "There's an inscription here..." she replied almost breathlessly. They all gathered at the largest column on the south-eastern side of the hall. At the top, a Latin line drew their attention.

"Symbolum Antiquissimum Ordinis Concordium" [1]

Ernst's voice was hardly audible. "This is incredible." The swastika is not just an Aryan racial symbol, as is believed; Concordium's symbolism goes back much further. "The Nazis simply turned it into a national emblem."

Lina's gaze wandered to the second line beneath the stone slab. Dust had collected between the letters. She carefully swept it away with her fingertips as she read aloud.

"Solis et Lunae unitas. Veritas silentio regit." [2]

Matteo took a deep breath. The Black Sun design in the centre of the hall caught his attention. "So Hitler's swastika had more than just a political purpose; this symbol embodied the essence of Concordium's philosophy. The Sun and Moon represent unity and opposition, as well as night and day. Silence is their version of doctrine."

At the northern end of the hall, an enormous oak table parallel to the wall attracted them. It contained three sealed chests, rows of wax-sealed scrolls, and paperwork neatly organised in the corners. The Concordium symbol appeared frequently on parchment, seals, and wax stamps.

Ernst gently opened the little chest. The interior housed parchment. He gently removed the top document.

---

[1] The oldest symbol of the Concordium Order.

[2] The unity of the Sun and the Moon. Truth is governed through silence.

He lifted it up to the light. The title, printed in bold black ink, sprang out against the weathered surface like a wound.

"Metaphysische Reinigung"

Ernst focused his gaze on the lines. His eyes froze, his forehead furrowed, and the corners of his lips compressed. The only sound to break the silence was the muted power of his breathing. He muttered, *"Metaphysical cleansing...* I feel I know where this will go. Nothing I knew would have prepared us for this."

Lina went gently beside him, leaning over the parchment with him. With her left hand, she smoothed the edge and moved on to the next page. She began reading the words in a low, rational tone.

"The Jewish people, as bearers of undesirable cultural and metaphysical influences, must be permanently removed from the organic structure of the new order."

The air in the room got noticeably thicker. The stone walls darkened, and the Black Sun emblem became more frightening. A deep, silent strain fell over them.

Ernst's voice was rougher and drier this time. "This isn't just a cry for racial eradication. It is a spiritual genocide—the destruction of religion, identity, and life in the name of metaphysical purity."

Lina's fingers trembled as she reached into the chest for another document. The parchment shook slightly in her palms. Her breathing increased as she scanned the lines. She said, "There's an addendum here," and started reading.

"The Final Solution is not to be understood as a racial extermination but as a metaphysical purification."

Ernst gently shook his head. "Therefore, Himmler shaped the SS as a cult rather than just a military force. The system developed beneath the Black Sun was spiritual rather than biological. This text academically explains the craziness."

Matteo discovered a folder while browsing through the neighbouring boxes. The dossier was dark brown with a thick cover. He brushed off the title with his fingertips and murmured:

"Der geheime Krieg gegen das Papsttum" [1]

The first page started with one sentence:

"The Pope is a worldly deceiver. Concordium must reclaim the ultimate truth of light and shadow."

Lina swallowed quietly. "This reflects their hatred of the Vatican. To them, the Pope is more of a worldly symbol than a spiritual leader, standing in the way of Concordium's total authority."

Matteo removed his glasses and put them on his forehead. His voice was almost a sigh. "Concordium regards the Pope as a misleading source of illumination, not a threat to the soul. This institution claims it has the only actual light."

Ernst unlocked the bottom chest. A dark, leather-bound book drew his eye. The thick, simple cover bore a single engraved phrase.

"Mithras-Kult Operation"

He opened the book. The first page contained the following lines:

---

[1] The Secret War against the Papacy.

"Concordium must return to the original source of the pre-Christian mysteries. The Mithras cult is to be purified, renewed, and used as the foundation for the path to ultimate enlightenment."

Lina exhaled deeply. "Mithras is a belief system used by secret societies in the Roman Empire. Concordium aims to resurrect rituals honouring the Sun God."

Ernst took the folder again. The pages contained redesigned versions of Mithras' rituals, as well as symbols called *'phases of illumination'*.

Matteo spoke through clenched lips. "SS rituals, Himmler's ceremonies, even the Black Sun floor... they're all variations of this belief system."

Lina lifted her attention to the dimness above. "They are establishing a new religion that is godless, popeless, and ruthless. Based entirely on control, symbolism, and complete obedience."

56

Ernst carefully gathered the documents in front of him. Despite his quivering hands, his voice was firm and commanding: "We know everything now," he declared. "We need to get out alive and provide the evidence. We cannot allow these evil ideas to be carried out. This would be the end of civilisation."

His words resonated off the stone columns, the Black Sun's interwoven spirals, and the etched seals on the pillars. It was as if they had expected the occasion and were waiting for the trio.

Matteo slowly rose to his feet. He took a last look around. His eyes glimmered with a mix of caution and the serenity that comes from steady determination. "Let's go," he whispered. "If we don't leave before sunrise... they will silence us here forever."

Lina murmured nothing as she delicately placed the final parchment scroll in her bag. She gripped the leather strap hanging over her shoulder hard. Her eyes went outward, through the darkness, toward a more distant target. She muttered, "Florence", as if speaking to herself. "The last clue will be there."

They needed no more words. They approached the massive stone door. The grinding sound as they twisted the handle sounded like the groan of a being that refused to wake up. Behind them, the chamber, governed by the haunting circular Black Sun, plunged into a deep and terrifying silence.

57

The lantern's flickering light rushed across the walls, passing over cracks, reliefs, and traces of a past that had yet to be erased.

Ernst grasped the old chart tightly in his palms, counting his steps and whispering the turns in a low voice. Matteo, at the back, kept gazing over his shoulder into the darkness, walking on edge as if a shadow could appear at any time. Each drop of water falling from the ceiling generated a sound resembling footsteps, as if someone were following them. The tension had reached deep into their bones.

Matteo suddenly paused. He tilted his head slightly, listening to the darkness. "Something," he murmured quietly. "Something's wrong." And at the moment, the footfalls were far and repetitive; the rhythmic sound of boots striking stone, quick and trained.

Lina's mumble was barely more than a breath. "Someone…is coming down."

Ernst quickly leaned forward. "We go to the alternate exit," he said. "The map shows a second hidden door to the western passage." He passed his hands along the tunnel's stone walls. Then his fingertips brushed against a rusty, circular metal ring. He pulled in one motion. The wall gradually but steadily shifted open. The air that came out smelt like dust and rotten mould; it was like being in a lifeless room.

Lina swiftly ducked into the tight corridor. "Quick!" she exclaimed, whispered. Ernst followed closely, holding the map tight to his chest. Matteo groaned under his breath with each snag of his pack; his shoulders scraped against the stones as he crawled forward, keeping his elbows from hitting the wall.

Footsteps echoing down the rear passage were now clearly audible. Matteo held his breath. "They're getting closer," he muttered.

Suddenly, a faint light shone ahead. The tunnel widened. They emerged into a circular chamber. Ernst, hands trembling, unfolded the map. "Left corridor, then the eastern canal exit," he said. "Let's go."

They hastened. Ernst approached a rusting iron grate set into the stone wall. He tested the bars, which were both resistant and breakable. He used a rusty rod from the floor below as a lever. When the rod snapped, a piercing metallic crack sounded through the tunnel like a scream. He gave the command without hesitation. "You go first, Matteo, then Lina. I will go last."

Matteo pulled himself through the tight gap. His shoulders scraped against jagged stone edges, but he wiggled free. Lina removed her backpack and crawled through with difficulty. Ernst pushed the bag of paperwork through before pulling himself behind it.

Just suddenly, there was a sound: heavy footsteps. A lantern beam, a blinding shaft of light, penetrated the darkness. Matteo crouched down swiftly. He gently pulled the grate back into place. Lina took a loose stone from the ground and laid it over the grate. The lantern's beam flashed on the wall, but it saw no traces where it expected them.

A tense hush followed. It was as if the air within could betray them. A gruff voice said, "Nothing here... Go to the next corridor!" A grunt and the sound of footsteps faded rapidly.

They exhaled deeply. Kneeling with their backs to the wall, their heartbeats echoed in their ears.

Lina closed her eyes. She muttered, "That was almost the end."

Ernst nodded. "But it wasn't."

Matteo stood up. "No," he responded. "Not yet."

Snow had fallen again. They needed to leave as soon as possible. Saying nothing further, they slipped onto the snow-covered wooded trail. Each step left faint imprints in the delicate white layer, and their breath ascended like wispy clouds in the cold air.

Lina, chin deep in her scarf, hurried breathlessly beside Ernst. "Which way?" she whispered.

Ernst raised his hand without hesitation. "South"

They maintained silence. The snow occasionally reached their ankles and wrapped around their heels. Their breaths, like spirits ripped from their bodies, mingled in the night's darkness. Far behind, faint dog barking continued to reverberate, occasionally interrupted by a loud whistle. However, the sounds became more distant. Perhaps they had lost the trail.

Twenty minutes later, the silhouette of an ageing farmhouse emerged ahead. Lina slipped through a cracked wall in the darkness, and the others followed close behind. The interior air smelt moist. The wind blowing through the wooden surface created a sound like hushed whispering in the abyss.

Nobody spoke. For a few seconds, the only sound was their frantic, uncontrollable breathing. Each tumbled to the ground. Lina leaned against the wall. She brushed her fingers against her boots, seeking to warm up her hands.

Matteo threw his head back and closed his eyes. "That was close," he muttered. "We escaped by seconds."

Lina approached the window and listened from the outside. She turned to face the night. The darkness was silent but terrifying. "It's quiet now," she finally said. "But we can't stay. We need to get to Paderborn by train. The walk lasts two hours."

They rose promptly, as if on cue. With care, they opened the door and slid out. Stealthily, they walked northward toward Paderborn. The moon shone dimly behind the dense clouds. Snow had fallen again, as if the sky was attempting to conceal the footprints they had made.

58

The walk took two hours, and they arrived in Paderborn. The station was silent. In the waiting hall's gloomy yellow light, an old coal stove spewed flickering smoke, while the wall clock ticked away with each second.

Lina pulled her hood tight about her face as she approached the ticket window. "Three tickets to Munich, third class." The cashier gave her a quick glance before handing her the tickets, saying nothing.

Half an hour later, they heard the steam locomotive's first low rumbling. They boarded the train through different doors, as three strangers acting their roles. As the train left Paderborn, the early morning light created pale shadows across the snow-covered fields. During hours of strain, the song's repetitive clatter served as the lone companion. They stopped in Bielefeld, Gütersloh, and Hamm, each time holding their breath silently. The possibility of meeting the Gestapo or SS weighed on them like a hand crushed against their chests. However, they were fortunate that day.

At 3:00 p.m., the train approached Munich Hauptbahnhof. The crowd on the platform moved in time, with the steam rising from between the tracks. They slipped rapidly through the station's chaos. After about an hour, they reunited on a quiet backstreet and entered Franz's apartment's rear patio. They stood motionless in front of the old wooden door. It opened gently.

Franz muttered, "You're alive... I was almost certain I would not see you again."

Ernst embraced him. "There's much to discuss... but let us go inside first."

They entered the room, where the stove was lit, and the aroma of coffee filled the air. They pulled the curtains.

Lina was the first one at the table to speak. "Wewelsburg was real. The Black Sun chamber, the Concordium archives, hatred toward the Vatican, the Mithras cult... we found it all, with documentation."

Franz's expression turned serious.

Matteo shook his head. "The war against the Pope... a *'new world religion'* constructed through the Mithras doctrine..."

"What will you do now?" Franz asked.

"All the documents we've followed since Prague, the symbols in Wewelsburg... It all points to one place." Ernst said.

Lina gently concluded her idea with, "Florence."

"The lily crest, the Basilica of the Holy Spirit, the Archivium Custodia... The last major Concordium archive is there." Matteo said.

Ernst talked firmly and without looking away. "We will leave tomorrow night."

Matteo nodded. "We will meet someone there."

Lina's attention turned towards him. "Who?" She asked.

Matteo responded gently. "Anna Di Lorenzi... She is trustworthy."

Franz averted his gaze to the ground. "On this journey, you can only trust each other now and the truth."

That night's sleep was brief but profound, as the voyage into the final black layer of history would begin the next night.

59

December 10, 1935
Florence

By the time they arrived in Bolzano, they had crossed into Italy. The cold iron grip of the German Reich was no longer with them, and Mussolini's shadow stretched ahead of them. The silence within the train had not changed, but all three were alert. They had passed the brief but thorough inspection conducted by Italian border guards.

The journey had been slow, winding through the mountainous terrain of northern Italy. After passing through the harsh, windy slopes of the Brenner Pass, South Tyrol's snowy valleys gave way to milder plains. When they arrived in Verona, the morning light was shining through the windows like a pale curtain.

Matteo looked out the window as the train approached Florence. The Arno River moved silently, like a serpent. The river's surface was nearly still. Along the banks, the bare trunks of the poplar trees stretched like silhouettes. The mist obscured the arched structure of the Ponte Vecchio with its shops on top. The distance barely allowed the reddish dome of the Duomo to be seen. Matteo held his breath for a moment. The scene conveyed both the comfort of returning home and the weight of the unknown ahead. He whispered to himself, "Florence... here lie the first answers and possibly the last questions too."

When the train arrived at Santa Maria Novella Station, passengers quietly dispersed through the narrow streets. They quickly exited the crowded station and walked toward the city's historic district. Matteo took the lead, softly saying, "Follow me. Anna lives near Santa Croce, on Via delle Pinzochere."

Stone-paved streets echoed faintly beneath them. The towering stone buildings, wrought-iron balconies, hanging lamps, and faded frescoed walls silently told the city's story. Some doorways still bear the Medici crest or carved marble family emblems. The muffled sound of distant church bells brought back memories of Florence's ancient soul.

They arrived in front of a small building with wooden doors and stone walls. Matteo pressed the small metal bell by the door. Inside, they could hear the creaking of the old wooden floors. A few seconds later, the door opened. A slender woman with brown hair emerged. The deep lines beneath her eyes showed fatigue, but her gaze remained sharp and instinctive. She tilted her head slightly and briefly focused on them.

"Matteo?" she asked, surprised.

"Anna".

Anna di Lorenzi opened the door a little wider. "What would bring you back here after all these years?"

Matteo smiled faintly, but his tone was serious. "It's extremely important, but we can't talk outside. Please let us in."

Anna didn't hesitate. She gave a slight nod before fully opening the door. "Come in."

60

They entered quietly. Oil paintings and old shelves piled high with centuries-old books lined the narrow stone hallway. A stone staircase led up from the end of the hall. When they reached the top, they entered a small but elegantly decorated sitting room. The dark wooden furniture, antique table, bookcases, and heavy embroidered curtains at the windows created the atmosphere of one of Florence's hidden sanctuaries steeped in history.

Anna leaned back. "Let's hear it," she said.

Matteo took a deep breath and rested his hands on the edge of the heavy wooden table, gazing at Anna. "The documents are after us, Anna."

Anna's expression turned serious. "What documents?"

Matteo gave a slight nod. "We first discovered traces of them in Berlin. We initially assumed they were just strange coincidences and inconsistent reports. However, our research showed that this was only the tip of the iceberg. Secret documents, symbols, and maps point to a structure called *Concordium*".

Ernst took charge, his voice clearer and more determined. "In Munich and later in Wewelsburg, we discovered definitive proof. Concordium is one of Europe's oldest secret societies. For centuries, they have quietly infiltrated monarchies, churches, universities, and armies."

Anna frowned, her eyes moving between the three. "I had never heard of them before. What do they want?"

Lina lowered her head slightly. "Their only goal is to reshape human history in their own vision; to exert indirect control over belief systems, governments, and cultural structures. They are ultimately responsible for any chaos, war, or revolution."

Ernst continued. "Even the Nazis were pawns in their scheme. At Wewelsburg, we discovered documents that revealed Himmler, Goebbels, and Hitler's roles within Concordium."

Anna remained silent, her gaze fixed in the distance. She asked, "What about Italy?"

Matteo directed his gaze at her. "Mussolini. He represents Concordium's branch in Italy. But more importantly, we must look into their influence within the Vatican."

Lina replied quietly, "That's why we came here. We don't know what we'll discover, but if there are Concordium traces in Italy, we'll find them here."

Anna kept quiet for a while. Her fingers crept along the table's edge. Finally, she took a deep breath, slowly raised her head, and gazed at the three of them. "All right," she replied in a soft but firm voice. "Then we'll follow this secret together."

61

As the first rays of morning light illuminated the Arno, the streets around Santa Croce awakened. Baker boys darted around, dropping off breakfast loaves beneath windows, while elderly women waited with woven net bags in hand for the church bell to ring.

A breeze blew along Via delle Pinzochere, gently nudging the heavy iron flowerpots on balconies, and a muffled chime from the distant bell tower of the Basilica of Santa Croce heralded the start of another day in Florence.

Anna wore a dark blue dress and a light brown cape. The sound of her low heels echoed down the quiet street. She shot Matteo, who had grabbed her arm, a brief but meaningful glance. "This city enchants me all over again every morning, Matteo," she mumbled. "But today... there's a restlessness I can't explain inside me."

Matteo tipped his hat slightly lower over his brow and looked down the street as they walked. "Nothing in Florence is ever exactly what it seems," he said. "Today we'll take a careful look around Palazzo Medici Riccardi."

Lina and Ernst had already reached the corner of Palazzo Medici Riccardi. They sat at a small cafe just across from the Palazzo. The many half-opened books and scattered papers on their table led passers-by to regard them as two scholars reviewing Florentine Renaissance research notes. Both wore dark, vintage-inspired coats. Ernst wore a dark brown fedora, and Lina had thin, round reading glasses that had fallen to the tip of her nose. Lina would occasionally lean over the books to take notes, while Ernst observed his surroundings with measured interest. Their silence and natural demeanour were so finely tuned that even the slightest movement would go unnoticed by an untrained eye.

Ernst leaned slightly over the table and started writing lines in a tiny notebook. The scratch of his fountain pen blended almost imperceptibly into the cafe's serene background. "We need to find where the entrance might be," he said, staring sideways at the Palazzo's massive stone walls.

Lina nodded quietly over her glasses, slowly flipping through an old history book. "Matteo and Anna are scanning the outside perimeter." She whispered, "We'll try to get information from inside. If we act like two historians, no one will suspect anything."

Ernst nuzzled his coffee cup aside before returning to his notebook. "We'll be careful," he whispered. "There are always eyes watching."

They stepped inside and gazed up at the massive stone walls of Palazzo Medici Riccardi. The frescoes on the high ceilings depicted Medici crests, classical Greek gods, and mythological scenes, providing a silent reminder of Florence's rich history. To avoid drawing attention, they quietly joined a small group of visitors and walked down the corridor. In the hall, an elderly man walked slowly between the columns. A large ring of keys swung in his hand. He dressed exactly like a Florentine academic, with a dark grey coat, a neatly tied thin tie, gold-rimmed round glasses, and a well-groomed beard.

Lina gently nudged Ernst's arm, whispering, "I think that man... he's the one."

Ernst paused briefly before taking a few steps towards the elderly man and speaking politely but reservedly. "Excuse me, signore. My name is Dr Adler, and I'm an architectural history researcher. This is my wife, Dr Berger," he introduced them gracefully. "We are researching the hidden passages and structural secrets of the Palazzo Medici Riccardi. If you have a moment, we would appreciate a brief discussion."

The elderly man examined them carefully through his gold-framed glasses. He remained silent for a few seconds, studying their expressions, before nodding slightly with his thin head. "Dr Berger... Dr Adler," he said quietly but authoritatively. "I am Professor Montalbano. I retired from the Florence Historical Institute, but I still provide academic advice to the Palazzo."

Lina exchanged a polite smile and nod. "It's truly fortunate we met you."

Montalbano turned the heavy ring of keys between his fingers, smiling faintly. He said, "Come," with caution. "You've only got a few minutes. There's a special programme at the Palazzo this morning."

The elderly academic led them down a narrow, low-ceilinged passageway that diverged from the main corridor. As they walked silently along the stone walls, his fingers whisked across the century-old marble. "Palazzo Medici Riccardi", he stated, "concealed Cosimo de Medici's wealth and political power. It once served as a gathering place for bankers, artists, and diplomats. There have long been rumours of hidden rooms or passages beneath the floor... However, no one officially documented them."

Ernst cocked his head slightly and asked, "What about the so-called *'camera segreta'* mentioned in old documents?"

Montalbano paused, turned his head slightly, and checked his glasses. "Ah, so you've heard that tale too?" he asked quietly. "Yes, people believe Cosimo de Medici built a secret vault to house private books and documents. People know it only as a legend. There is no evidence of this in any official documents. However, in Florence, legends are frequently half-true. Legend claims an old wall door is beneath the small service stair on the north side. Some believe it was a secret tunnel built to help the Medici flee in the event of a siege or an unexpected attack." He adjusted his glasses and lowered his voice until it was almost a whisper. "Many knew of Cosimo's fear of Vatican agents and political rivals. Perhaps that explains why he was so cautious. However, people believe someone completely sealed it in the nineteenth century."

Lina shifted slightly forward, her voice soft but clear. "Which section?"

Montalbano smiled softly, excitement in his eyes. "On the Via Cavour side, slightly north of the rear courtyard. A stone block on the wall differs only slightly from the others. Only a keen eye would notice. If you find that stone, you might be lucky."

Ernst gave a small bow of gratitude. "You've been of great help to us, signore."

Montalbano walked away, calling over his shoulder until his voice echoed against the stone walls. "Remember... the Medici do not surrender their secrets easily."

62

By late afternoon, night had fallen, and the dim glow of street lamps illuminated Florence's narrow streets. They'd regrouped at Anna's house. Silence reigned in the old stone-walled room. The flickering flames of thick candles in brass candlesticks danced across the bookshelves, casting shifting shadows on the wall. The candles cast a pale yellow glow across the maps and notebooks spread out on the wooden table.

Ernst pointed to an open city diagram with his finger. "Lina and I scouted the area," he stated quietly, but clearly. "On the northern courtyard wall of Via Cavour, there is a stone block with a different surface than the others. There is also a noticeable structural gap in the northern façade. Florentine craftsmen in the 15th century would not have made such a mistake." He slid his finger to the edge of the map, his eyes fixed on the sketches. "It appears to have been untouched for a long time. If the hidden passage Montalbano mentioned exists, it must be located here."

Lina opened her notebook and carefully pointed to a particular spot on the thick pages. "Professor Montalbano marked the same location," she said quietly but firmly. "We must act tomorrow night."

Anna placed her hands on her knees and leaned slightly forward. Her eyes appeared unusually firm. "During the day, crowds constantly fill the Palazzo, but at night, it's completely silent. There are only two guards patrolling. The outer courtyard houses that section of the wall, and it receives infrequent inspections. If we time it right, we might have a chance."

Matteo looked at the map one more time before slowly nodding. "Then the plan is clear," he said, his voice low but firm. "We move at 1:00 a.m. tomorrow."

63

Footsteps echoed down Florence's narrow stone alleyways. The moon appeared and disappeared at brief intervals between clouds in the sky. They crept silently into the Palazzo Medici Riccardi's back courtyard. They paused for a few seconds, their backs against the cold stone wall, listening to the surrounding sounds.

Ernst pointed with his finger at a dark grey stone block on the northern façade of the wall along Via Cavour that protruded slightly more than the others. "Here," he whispered, taking out a small, thin metal crowbar. Matteo carefully felt along the wall, running his fingers through the small cracks. When he found a small indentation, they started working with the crowbar. The stone block slid slowly outwards. Behind it, a dark, narrow passage opened.

They exchanged quiet glances. Lina whispered quietly, "*Medici's Camera Segreta...*"

Matteo took the lead. He pointed the lantern's flickering light at the ground, temporarily softening the darkness of the passage. Lina and Ernst followed silently behind him. The corridor became wider about ten metres later, and they entered a room. On the left wall, a rusted iron ring was hanging. Beside it, faded remnants of old frescoes stretched across the surface.

A large oak table sat in the centre of the room. Leaning and tossed, chairs surrounded it. The shelves appeared to hang from time itself, with small scrolls of parchment, wax-sealed bundles, and cracked leather-bound notebooks hidden beneath a layer of dust.

Everything was calm, but the silence screamed.

Ernst held the heavy ledger in the centre of the table with both hands. The front-cover title was written in faded gold letters.

"Operatio Italiae" [1]

Each letter glowed in the candlelight. Ernst slowly placed the ledger on the table, his hands still resting on its edges, and whispered, "This could be what we're looking for."

Lina approached him right away, quickly but carefully, flipping through the pages with her fingers. Even the texture of the paper communicated historical

---

[1] Italy Operation.

significance. The first entries were from the late 1920s. Every line was meticulously written. The text revealed evidence of a shadow organisation that grew alongside Mussolini's rise. Lina read aloud without looking away from the pages.

"Imperium Control"
"Aim: To create a figure from within the Kingdom of Italy. Systematically weaken papal authority. Construct an environment of absolute control aligned with the doctrines of Concordium."

Matteo, meanwhile, took a small box from a nearby shelf. He carefully opened it and took out a roll of documents. The words on the parchment seemed to cut through the air with their force.

"Operazione Cattolica" [1]
Rome, 10 June 1924
Figure: Benito Mussolini
Mission: Undermine papal influence. Direct the Catholic population to vote in favour of Concordium.
Implement censorship, propaganda, violence, and isolation.

His voice grew hoarse as he read the lines: "If the Pope resists... if he stands against the plans... uprisings will be incited among the public. Revolts, forged declarations, and internal chaos... The goal is to dismantle the Vatican. Remove Rome's designation as the spiritual capital."

Lina's voice rose. Her anger was contained, but it trembled with each word. "Even the Lateran Treaty was a fraud: a fictitious peace. The script aimed to transform the Pope into a Concordium puppet."

---

[1] Catholic Operation.

Ernst bowed his head quietly, the shadows emphasising the lines in his face. His lips moved, but he spoke after a pause: "Mussolini did more than just lead political revolutions. This was a spiritual war. Concordium planned it gradually and step by step."

While looking through more documents on the nearby shelf, Matteo noticed another box. The lid almost popped off on its own. He found more sealed documents inside, their wax stamps intact and neatly arranged.

Lina selected the topmost document. The parchment bore a single line of bold, handwritten Latin at the top.

"Conventus pro Duce [1]*–4 Julii 1912"*

She gently unrolled the parchment. She noticed her hands trembling, but she continued reading.

"Meeting Date: July 4, 1912
Location: Vatican Observatory
Participants:
– B. Mussolini (Representative of the newspaper Avanti)
– A. Drexler (Founder of the German National Workers' Society)
– Pater Magnus
Purpose: To covertly steer European workers' movements; to identify and gain control over potential future leader figures."

Matteo's voice barely left his lips. He looked at the document and stated, "Drexler, the founder of Hitler's party."

Lina nodded and kept reading, her voice filled with wonder and unease.

---

[1] Meeting for the Leader.

*"Pater Magnus spoke to Drexler about a young Austrian artist: poor, angry, yet passionate. Marginalised by society but possessed of extraordinary oratory power.
Name: Adolf Hitler."*

Ernst's face became pale. He leaned against the table's edge to stay steady. In 1912, he was still painting on the streets of Vienna. This document... confirms the list of names we discovered in Vienna.

Ernst slowly turned on the parchment. He noticed a phrase written in bold ink at the top of the reverse side. He pointed at it in a cold, sharp tone.

"The Führer will be an independent leader but a controlled figure under the Concordium protocol."

Lina lowered her head slightly, her gaze fixed on the parchment. "The image of Hitler presented to Europe... orchestrated by Mussolini."

Matteo was scanning another document from a dusty shelf when he halted. He spoke with suppressed anger, saying, "There are more names here... These are cardinals. They all served on the Vatican's highest councils. This is a list of infiltrations—Concordium's shadowy extensions within the Vatican."

Lina nodded, trembling, her gaze drawn to the rusted seals in the shelf's corner. Her voice carried a tinge of disgust. "So they wove their way into the Vatican step by step, covered in silence, rituals, ceremonies, and internal politics. Mussolini could not have established himself so thoroughly without their help."

Matteo took a deep breath and carefully folded the documents before putting them into his bag. His eyes conveyed both calm precision and the gravity of the impending confrontation: "We have a plan. We will make duplicates of these documents. We must send copies to

Geneva through a neutral channel. It must get to the international media and diplomatic circles. But... we're heading to Rome. We are going to contact the Pope directly."

Ernst's eyes darkened with determination. His voice was unwavering. "The original documents must be placed on his desk. Concordium's roots in the Vatican must be burnt out from the inside. No one from outside can do this."

Lina glanced around the dimly lit room. Her gaze swept across the embedded books, sealed scrolls, and symbols etched into the stone floor. She articulated. "The Pope can only see Concordium's true face in the documents. If he is convinced, the Vatican will purify itself from within. This war will be fought internally."

Matteo's gaze shifted to the doorway. The dim candlelight behind them flickered softly as the tunnel ahead stretched into darkness. He spoke quietly but clearly: "We're leaving on the first train at dawn... to Rome."

64

Darkness shrouded the ancient stone walls of Florence. The trio emerged from the Palazzo Medici Riccardi's secret room, bearing the weight of a great secret. The city was silent; only the echo of their footsteps on the cobblestone streets broke it.

When they arrived home, Matteo knocked on the door. As soon as it opened, they slipped inside. Anna's eyes were tired, and her expression was concerned.

She replied, "You're back. Were you followed?"

Matteo gently shook his head. "No. We left no shadows behind."

Lina placed the bag on the table. The documents inside were not only damning for Mussolini and Hitler; they could spell the end of Concordium's structure throughout Europe.

"We have the documents," she said quietly but firmly. "We now have actual evidence."

Ernst slowly sat in the old chair next to the stove, taking off his jacket. His face expressed relief. "We have to go to Rome," he said.

Anna entered the small kitchen and set a water-filled pot on the old stove. She turned her head as she spoke. "At least stay until the morning. Going out at this time would be insane."

Matteo paused briefly before nodding. Despite his tired eyes, he remained focused on the journey ahead. "Alright, a few hours' sleep, then we left before sunrise."

65

In the early morning light, three silhouettes cast shadows on the walls beneath the lamplight, one last time going over the documents on the table. They carefully wrapped the papers, powerful enough to bring down Mussolini and Hitler, into small parchment scrolls; each fold held the potential to change the course of history.

Anna would secretly send the copies to Switzerland, while they would show the original documents to the Pope.

Matteo slung the bag over his shoulders. A faint smile appeared on his lips. "We'll either be the ones who change the course of European history," he says, his voice cracking but firm. "Or three ghosts who never existed."

Lina stood by the window, her gaze fixed outside, and she said, "Both are equally likely."

Their farewell to Anna was quiet, with concern in their eyes and unspoken wishes on their lips. Then they descended the stone steps and disappeared into the Florence streets. When they arrived at Santa Maria Novella Station, there was an uncomfortable silence. Fascist propaganda adorned the platforms. Mussolini's shadow lingered around every corner.

Ernst lowered his head slightly. "We're walking in Mussolini's shadow until we reach Rome."

Lina focused her attention on the locomotive at the far end of the platform. "But that shadow doesn't know we're carrying its downfall." She approached the ticket window, speaking in a calm but refined tone. "Tre biglietti per Roma Termini. Terza classe." [1] The woman behind the window gave Lina a quick, hollow look before handing over the tickets indifferently.

The locomotive loomed over the tracks like a massive shadow. They quickly made their way to the third-class cars. The train's whistle echoed through the sky like a sharp scream. Matteo took a last look at the station. "If we succeed, Mussolini will fall. And he might take Hitler with him. Concordium will unravel from within."

Ernst gave the rails one last look. "If we fail... our names, faces, and bodies will vanish with this city."

The train started moving. With the journey's start, the cars swayed. The bare plains of Tuscany passed by the window, slowly. Slender bell towers appeared on the horizon occasionally, while wind-bent poplars and withered vineyard rows spread across the landscape like rippling waves.

Throughout the journey, passengers were half asleep or deep in thought. Lina looked out the window. For a

---

[1] Three tickets to Roma Termini. Third class.

moment, the stone pavement of the Appian Way appeared from the mist. It felt as if ancient Rome was still whispering from beneath the ground. Her gaze remained fixed in the distance. "Rome..." she whispered, barely moving her lips.

The train slowly approached Roma Termini. When they arrived at the platform, they noticed an unusual crowd at the station. Fascist militias dressed in black scanned the passengers, while grey-coated plainclothes agents pretended to read newspapers while monitoring the crowd.

Matteo lowered his head slightly and whispered, "We're now in the heart of fascism."

Part 6

Sanctuary to Resistance

66

December 17, 1935
Rome

The sky over Rome stripped the stately stone façade of St Peter's Basilica of its sanctity, revealing it as a mute warning from centuries past. Along Via della Conciliazione, wind-whipped propaganda posters with Mussolini's face floated through the air, each ripped corner invoking past lies.

Lina sought safety in the shadow of the columns on the left. She stayed still but awake. Then, at the basilica's side entrance, a man in a grey coat and fedora emerged. Lina gave a small nod when their gazes met. Ernst responded with a short tilt of his head. Everything was silent and planned.

Another individual separated from the crowd. His steps were rapid but measured, slow and purposeful. He wore a brown jacket and a plain hat. He was Matteo. His gaze briefly met Lina's. His lips moved, but his words remained scarcely audible: "Clear?" Lina gave a subtle nod. Matteo responded with the same tone: "No tail, at least until this point."

Ernst took a little step closer and stated without breaking eye contact, "Ten minutes. Caffe San Pietro."

Lina offered a small nod.

Matteo scanned his surroundings once more. "If we linger, we'll draw attention."

Neither of them said anything more. Each took a different path, slipping into the crowd like shadows. They dispersed amid praying elderly people, anxious clerks carrying documents, and troops with intense gazes. Rome quietly devoured them whole.

67

The iron sign for Caffè San Pietro waved softly in the breeze, and the yellow light that filtered through the glass left hazy streaks on the cobblestone pavement. The decor was outdated; wooden chairs groaned, and picture frames on the walls concealed years of dust. The aroma of coffee lingered in the air.

They gathered at a back corner table, whose marble top had broken with age. As they sat down, an elderly waiter approached. He did not take orders or ask questions; instead, he quietly placed three simple coffees on the table, bowed, and walked away.

No one spoke for a while. Matteo gently took a folded piece of paper out of his pocket. The plan was simple: lines, corridors, a time window, and a door circled in red ink.

"This is our only chance before morning," he replied gently. "There's identity verification, but merely a name list."

Ernst leaned over the diagram. His eyes moved with the accuracy of a fighter accustomed to reading battlefield maps. He lowered his head slightly. "We have no uniforms, no identities."

Matteo smiled faintly, with a proud expression. He opened his luggage and took out three basic smocks made of cotton. "These are backup smocks from the San Frediano Laundry, supplied to the Vatican cleaning service. Nobody will notice." He then pulled out a document and three identification cards. "This is the morning shift schedule. Three teams take part. We'll pretend to be the fourth. Entry at 6:00 a.m. The main corridor cleaning begins around 6:30 a.m. And these are our identities."

"Reaching the Pope is still impossible," he explained. "We will leave the documents on Cardinal di Forlì's desk, an old friend of Anna's father and a trustworthy individual. If anyone within is plotting against Concordium, it may be him."

Ernst nodded. "Let's hope he's still trustworthy."

Lina's stare seems to spread far beyond the room. "What if someone else finds them?"

"We act like nothing happened," Matteo remarked. "We're just cleaners."

Following the remarks, silence fell. They reached for their cups almost simultaneously. They set them down without taking a sip from the now-cold coffee.

"Tomorrow, we will either face the Pope…" she quipped, "…or history will forget us."

Matteo checked his watch and stood up. "Let's return to the pension. We will pack the uniforms and review the documents one more time. Departure is at five o'clock. We must be inside by six o'clock."

68

The streets were silent. Three silhouettes went down Via Borgo Pio in basic cleaning smocks. After travelling past Piazza Risorgimento, they turn onto Via Sant'Anna. The Vatican's northern service entrance looked like a black mouth beneath a frigid stone wall. The sign above trembled slightly in the wind: Servizio Pulizie—Ingresso del Personale.

There was only one Swiss Guard in the sentry box. Matteo went forward, gave a modest nod, and took the morning shift schedule and personnel card from his inner pocket. The guard attentively reviewed the documents. His gaze was fixed on Matteo's face for a brief while before returning to the papers. After checking the other two documents, the gate opened. The squeak of the massive hinges was soft and cautious.

"Second corridor," Matteo muttered. "Cardinal di Forlì's office is on the right."

Footsteps echoed at the far end of the corridor. Metallic, solid, and with a beat gained through training: a Swiss guard. They froze instantly. Lina slid into a dim alcove. Matteo slipped inside the arched wall recess. Ernst paused with only his eyes moving. The footsteps neared and then retreated. "We have two minutes," Matteo explained.

When they reached the door, Ernst bent down to test the lock. He pulled out a thin metal instrument. On the second try, the lock turned. The door quietly opened. They stepped inside.

The chamber was enormous, with high ceilings and sturdy stone walls. Books filled the shelves. The curtains over the window have been drawn. In the dimness, there stood an enormous desk and an attractive high-backed chair. They had created a small prayer nook in one area.

They approached the desk. There was an open journal on it. It is bound in leather and has age-worn corners. Lina gently flipped the pages. Fine handwritten notes filled the lines.

Some files are locked in the Archivio Segreto. Access is granted only with papal authority. However, the Concordium could have gotten confidential papal correspondence.
I suspect a few people, but none of them came forward. They're hazardous.
But I'm not alone. Some people are still holding out.

I need to collect more evidence before bringing this to the Pope's attention. Unfortunately, what I have won't be enough to persuade him.
Everything must move silently.

Ernst stayed concentrated on the journal. "He's aware of Concordium. He opposes it. Look... he openly suspects them."

Lina leaned in closer. "This handwriting is recent. He is still working, searching for something from within."

Matteo took out a tiny envelope from his bag. Inside was an impressive replica of the documents they were carrying. A small message was attached to the mail.

Your Excellency. Cardinal Di Forlì,

We came into your office tonight without your knowledge. We understand you do not know us. But we don't mean you any harm. We want to work together against a common enemy.

The included example shows Concordium's function within the Vatican. If you are the man we think you are, please read this message carefully.

We want to meet you in person. We propose:
Location: Santa Maria Sopra Minerva
Date: December 18, 10:00 p.m.
Sign: A woman holding an orange notebook and a grey scarf.
Please come alone.
You'll find us. And we believe that collectively we can bring light into the darkness.

They concealed the envelope beneath the cardinal's diary, ensuring it would be visible but not prematurely revealed.

"Ready?" Ernst questioned.

"Yes," Lina replied.

"And now", Matteo added, "we will wait for Rome to awaken."

The door closed silently. The stone corridor enveloped them once more. Behind them, only a note, an envelope, and documents with the ability to change history remained.

It was still dark outside when they went out. However, nothing in the Vatican had altered from only hours earlier. In one office, a cardinal was about to awaken and confront history.

69

Santa Maria sopra Minerva seems to have disappeared throughout the night. The obelisk in front of the church casts a single shadow in the moonlight, falling across the stones like a sinister warning.

Lina fastened her grey scarf over her neck. She held an orange notebook. She was sitting on an iron bench in the churchyard. Ernst waited directly across from her, hiding in the shadows behind the archway, while Matteo positioned himself to the left, near the tomb entrance, monitoring the street for movement.

At precisely 10:00 p.m., a black shape emerged from the church's north side. He had a broad-brimmed hat and a pitch-black robe draped over his shoulders. Although he used a cane, his steps displayed controlled strength, a product of habit, rather than weakness. He was all alone.

Lina got up and approached him.

The cardinal's gaze fixed on her. "So, it's you," he said. His speech was calm, but with a slight tension. "The note in the envelope was clear but highly risky."

"Time is running out," Lina replied. Her voice sounded forceful. "As you've probably discovered, Concordium is deep inside. If you are the man we think you are, they may already be watching you."

Cardinal di Forlì bent his head slightly. His gaze moved across the church's stone walls, as if he were reading an invisible inscription. "You saw the notes in my office," he explained.

"Yes," Matteo responded, emerging from the shadows. "We entered without permission. But that wasn't a threat; it was intentional. We sought the truth. And we realised you were fighting for the truth."

The cardinal took a deep breath. The cloak over his shoulders appeared to become heavier as the night progressed. "What do you expect from me?"

Ernst stepped forward gently. He drew a document sealed with wax from the inside of his coat. The light gently touched it, yet the seal was obvious. "This is only the beginning," he stated. "We have various records, including names, assignments, and dated notes. All of this is real. Evidence of the structure spread like a malignancy throughout the current system."

"And?" the cardinal asked. His gaze remained fixed, but a sharper spark glinted in his eyes, showing that he had gotten accustomed to opposition.

"We want a one-on-one meeting with the Pope," Lina said unequivocally. "There are no intermediaries. Direct."

"That", the cardinal continued, gently dropping his voice, "is both bold and potentially dangerous."

"If it's not the time for boldness," observed Ernst, "then it must be the time of their victory."

The cardinal became silent. He focused his sight on the church's closed doors. He then turned back to Lina. "Prayers, diplomatic rituals, and false promises fill the Pope's schedule. But..." His gaze narrowed and focused upon Lina's. "If what you hold is more than I imagine, I may prepare the ground for such a meeting."

"How much time do we have?" Matteo queried, his gaze wandering around the square.

"Two days", the cardinal replied. "It's December 20. That morning, the Pope will have only a few visitors in his private audience hall. He has no other plans later. I cannot supply you with credentials. But I can provide you with a valid excuse to be there. I will be there as well." He paused. His face had a fine, powerful aspect. "But...you promise you will not use these documents to scare the Pope but to awaken him. To achieve a positive outcome, avoid being destructive."

"Our goal is not exposure," Lina clarified. "It is about regaining the Vatican, to release it from its own shadow."

The cardinal grabbed for the internal pocket of his cloak. In his palm was a simple wooden cross. He handed it to Lina. With a brief nod, he turned and began strolling to the far end of the square. His shadow mingled with the obelisk and spread across the street.

Lina looked down at the cross in her palm. "December 20," she said.

"And on that day", Ernst said, "the first crack in the Vatican will be born of silence."

70

December 20, 1935
Vatican

Cardinal di Forlì greeted them in his dark robe. His eyes looked tired, but his speech was clearer. "You are taking significant risks."

"We can't get anywhere without taking risks," Matteo remarked.

The cardinal nodded. "Then follow me."

They proceeded across the inner courtyard, past the marble columns. As they moved down the corridor, the cardinal spoke. "Contacting the Pope wasn't easy. His closest circle is being scrutinised. But now he is alone."

When the enormous wooden doors opened, the inside was simple. The ceiling was high, and the walls were almost bare. There was only a desk, a crucifix, and a chair. The man sitting near the window, clad in white, had his back turned to Rome.

The Pope turned around. His basic clothing was nearly colourless. His eyes were ancient but clear. He examined each one at a time.

"Cardinal di Forlì, do you vouch for these people?"

The cardinal bowed his head. "I cannot vouch for them. But I believed them. This is not the same."

The Pope smiled slightly. "That answer is more honest."

Lina opened her bag. She took out a brown leather folder and walked up to the desk. "Your Excellency", she said, "These are sentences written in shadows. Now is their chance to see the light of day."

71

The Pope sat beneath the high ceiling of the private audience hall. The only sound in the room was the rustling of paper as he slowly took the first file from its wax-sealed envelope and opened it on the oak desk in front of him.

Cardinal di Forlì stood quietly beside him. Lina, Ernst, and Matteo took a few steps back, enveloped in shadow. The Pope bent over the first page. A title with big red letters stood out:

"Altamente Riservato–Sacra Congregazione" [1]

His cheeks paled as his gaze went across the lines. He read silently. His fingers stroked the unsteady Latin notes down the page's margin. He adjusted his spectacles slightly before raising his head to inspect the three individuals in the darkness. "The cardinals listed above are still active. They are still near me."

Ernst stepped forward. "They're all embedded within the inner structure of the Concordium."

Cardinal di Forlì presented the following set of documents.

"Operatio Italiae"
"Operazione Cattolica"

The Pope flipped through the pages swiftly. Each one revealed a long-term strategy: Mussolini's ascension, the Lateran Treaty, manipulation of Catholic public opinion, and internal erosion through censorship and propaganda.

---

[1] Highly Confidential – Sacred Congregation.

*"Lower papal influence.
Turn public opinion in Concordium's favour.
Encourage a revolt.
Discredit the papal office.
The spiritual framework must be directed from within.
A new doctrine of authority must be developed."*

The Pope took a long pause after these words. "This is not only about politics. This is a declaration of war—a fight from inside."

Ernst bowed his head. "The formula for the spiritual occupation of the Vatican."

Lina went further: "Mussolini, with Concordium's support, purchased not just loyalty, but the people's spiritual allegiance… and that plan left the Papacy alone."

"If the Pope resists… internal uprisings will be started." When the Pope read that line, his voice broke for the first time. "Uprisings…" Then he leaned back. The light highlighted the lines under his eyes.

A long hush ensued.

Then Ernst presented the final dossier.

"Germany High-Level Structure Schema"

The Pope took the document. His hands were now noticeably trembling. He read the lines slowly.

*– Himmler – ritual control, in charge of Concordium's internal structures.
– Goebbels – Berlin cell leader. Media manipulation.
– Hitler – external figurehead. No independent decision-making power.*

The Pope lifted his head. His gaze went into space. "So the Führer was merely a figure…"

"Yes," Matteo responded. "The hands behind the system belonged to Concordium."

The Pope stood and began pacing around the room. He turned his head slowly. "Is there more?" he asked.

Ernst took the final paperwork out of his suitcase. Symbolic marks sealed the pages.

"Conventus pro Duce–4 Julii 1912"

Participants:
– B. Mussolini (representative of the Avanti *newspaper)*
– A. Drexler (German National Workers' Society)
– Pater Magnus
Purpose: To covertly guide European labour movements and to identify and control future leadership figures.

The Pope's hands shook. "Drexler? Hitler's precursor..."

"Hitler's name appears here for the first time," Lina mumbled. "Mussolini was the first; Hitler was the second."

The pope's voice was gruff. "So both men were just... representatives? Concordium's public front."

"They're puppets," Matteo explained. "Figures presented to the masses."

Cardinal di Forlì nodded silently. "And they became what they are."

The room sank into a deep hush. The Pope's gaze perused the documents on the desk once more. Then he slowly lifted his head. "If these are true, the world needs to be rewritten. But I can't make this decision alone."

Lina stepped forward. "But if you remain silent, you will lose alone."

The Pope approached the window. Rome persisted outdoors. "Whoever is inside this structure must be purged; but from a light that came from within the Vatican, not from outside."

Then he turned to face the trio. "Are you the first spark of that light?"

Ernst responded. "No. We simply point to the darkness. The light must come from you."

After a long quiet, the Pope nodded. "December 21, 1935. I will sign the first document filed against Concordium, but first, I will pray."

Cardinal di Forlì gave a bow. "Then we will wait outside. The Vatican will speak after the prayer ends."

The Pope gently took his seat. Before raising his gaze, he meticulously rearranged the documents on the table.

72

There was no sleep in the Vatican the night the Pope prayed. Footsteps did not resound down the palace's stone hallways, but the lights remained on till daybreak. Every chamber was dimly lit—not from insomnia, but from the weight of decision.

Cardinal di Forlì retrieved the sealed files from the Pope's desk. Nothing was any longer hidden. Silence would no longer be used to defend one's religion but to conceal treachery. The Vatican could no longer shoulder such a burden.

They issued the initial order late at night. The cardinal directed that five journalists from the Papal Communications Office be called immediately. Rome, Paris, Munich, London, and Zurich were each assigned one task: to make officially certified versions of the documents available to the public with Vatican consent.

The cardinal would handwrite the news stories and stamp them with the Pope's seal.

Before morning, a courier delivered identical news templates to the headquarters of L'Osservatore Romano, La Croix, Stimmen der Zeit, The Catholic Herald, and Neue Zürcher Zeitung. The headlines were fixed.

"The Vatican Breaks Its Silence – Concordium Officially Rejected"

They arranged the subheadings according to nationality to preserve linguistic differences. But the essence has never changed:

"The internal structure of Concordium has been exposed."
"It is documented that Mussolini and Hitler were controlled by Concordium."
"The infiltration within the papacy has collapsed."
"The Pope signed the documents on December 21, 1935."
"Peace shall begin with the acknowledgement of truth."

This was not simply a Vatican decree. It was the demise of an old order from within. Each country would react differently, and each city would interpret the news uniquely.

However, all of Europe would realise the same thing that day: the cornerstone of terror was silence. The stillness had suddenly been broken.

In the morning, Cardinal di Forlì issued a second order. He called Lina, Ernst, and Matteo to his side. They were no longer just document couriers; they were the papacy's official representatives. The Pope handwrote a reference letter and created Vatican identification cards. Their purpose was to represent, not simply transmit, information. They carried not light, but the truth. And the truth needed to move forward.

Their destination was clear: Paris. The mission's definition was explicit. France's intellectual centres, including universities, archives, and journalists, were to receive the records. The purpose was more than just revelation; it was to start the building of a European consciousness free of Concordium's influence. The task wasn't public relations; it was a cognitive intervention.

They wouldn't spend much time in Paris. They only had two days. Concordium was adept at hiding its tracks, and any delay might develop into a trap. Cardinal di Forlì would accompany them to Paris to activate ties and facilitate transitions. His aim was to get the documents into the hands of and alert France's long-silent journalists. No more.

What followed was clear. The next destination was Berlin. They would travel there alone.

The journey would start at 6:15 a.m. on January 2nd, leaving from Rome's Termini Station. They would board quietly. But the three passengers on that train were no longer just people; they were shadows, symbolising the end of an era.

Concordium would collapse if exposed.

Words, not silence, would carry the future.

Part 7

Fall from the Shadows

73

January 4, 1936
Paris

It was past five in the morning. Paris had not yet awakened. The streetlights were still on, creating long, immobile shadows across the cobblestones. Light shone from a solitary window on the third floor of Quai Voltaire's narrow-faced flat. A single yellow lamp lit three people huddled over a table inside. Damp finger traces wrinkled and stained the materials on the table.

Cardinal di Forlì stood by a window. He clasped his hands behind his back. He buttoned his jacket from top to bottom, demonstrating self-discipline. "The printing has been approved," he added. His voice remained consistent and forceful, neither harsh nor gentle. "La Croix begins distribution at eight in the morning."

Lina spoke without moving her gaze away from the pages. "Is the text complete? Not a single line removed?"

"The document includes everything," the cardinal stated. "With papal approval, we generated the stuff, but his name is not on it. We are not the source of the news."

Ernst took his glasses off and fetched a handkerchief from his inner pocket. He began carefully cleaning the lenses. "So there's no turning back now," he added gently.

Matteo sat at the table, carefully folding the map in front of him. His fingers were powerful, like someone who had learnt to survive on the streets: calm and watchful. "There never was," he said. "We were just waiting for the right moment."

The cardinal began pacing slowly around the table. His footsteps resonated lightly over the parquet flooring. "It's being released simultaneously from three centres:

Paris, Lyon, and Marseille," stated the official. "All from publishers affiliated with the Vatican."

Lina took a slight turn and held one document. "What about Germany?"

The cardinal nodded slightly. "Berlin is different; underground printing is unofficial. We have assigned the distribution chain directly to contacts there."

"Illegal?" Ernst asked, putting his spectacles back on.

"Yes, at least on paper. We cannot seek authorisation there. Silence would signal capitulation. We can't afford that luxury."

Matteo got up and checked his watch in his coat pocket. "Are the guards ready?"

"Yes," the cardinal replied. "Léon and Anton will leave with you in the morning; from Gare de l'Est to Strasbourg, and then on to Berlin."

Lina gazed at the cardinal. "Are they armed?"

"Yes, trained and loyal."

After a brief quiet, Ernst asked, "What about Mussolini? Has the last message from Rome arrived?"

The cardinal's posture shifted slightly. His voice became colder and more distant. "He has asked the Pope for forgiveness in writing."

Lina turned to face him. Her eyes narrowed with suspicion. "He asked the Pope, but not the people."

"He's trying to save himself," the cardinal explained. "But it is too late. The balance in Italy has shifted."

Matteo moved to the window. Without lifting his gaze from the outside, he enquired, "What about the King? What will he do?"

The cardinal hesitated for a time. "Mussolini will be dismissed soon. The decree is ready; it will not take long."

"Will they exile him?" Ernst asked, twirling a pen in his hand.

"Most probable; according to what we've heard within the palace, even his own guards aren't following his commands."

Lina gently rose. She appeared to be in deep contemplation as she put on her coat. "Is our target in Berlin clear?"

The cardinal caught her gaze. This time, his expression was harsh. "Goebbels and Himmler; Hitler's name is not mentioned in the texts. But everyone will know he is a puppet."

Lina halted for a few seconds. "Why is he still silent?"

The cardinal sat in his chair after unbuttoning his jacket. He appeared exhausted. "Because he is afraid of his own shadow."

Ernst transferred the documents on the table into his bag. The cardinal's red seal appeared multiple times between the pages. "Is our first stop in Berlin the printing press?" he asked.

"No," the cardinal replied. "First, Friedrichstrasse: a kiosk. The person who will meet you will be there. He'll recognise you."

"When will the radio broadcast start?"

"We will make the documents available at the nine o'clock briefing. The Vatican will not make a direct statement. After La Croix's headline, the quake will begin."

"Will we be able to reach you directly?"

"No. However, the Geneva line will stay operational. Use it only in emergencies." The cardinal rose again. He clasped his hands behind his back and looked at each one separately. "From this point on, the eyes watching you will change," he said. "It's no longer only Concordium; governments, intelligence agencies, and ordinary folks will all be able to track your movements. But remember that the word is no longer ours. The truth will speak for itself."

For a brief while, the hush in the room ceased. There is no ticking clock or noise from outside... Lina finally offered a tiny nod before opening the door. "Let's move out."

74

"Car six, compartment eight," Matteo explained.

There were very few passengers. A few staff walked around the platform, one of whom checked tickets at the train's entrance. The attendant examined them and gave a small nod. He asked for no identification and no enquiries.

Anton had moved to the back of the carriage, while Léon had gone to the front. The compartment was old. The worn seat upholstery showed its age. Lina took the window seat. Ernst sat in the centre. Matteo sat beside the door. The bag rested at his feet.

The train started going slowly. As the carriage swung, the metallic sound of the rails mixed with their peaceful departure from Paris.

Ernst peered outdoors. "Paris is behind us," he mumbled.

The train headed north. The first hour passed without a word. As they passed the Marne River, the first glimpses of the countryside arrived through the window. The pale morning light showed the silhouettes of the fog-covered fields and sparse trees. Even the horizon appeared to disappear in the distance.

They landed in Strasbourg at about 9:00 a.m. Customs officers boarded the train. Their uniforms were excellent. Their expressions were expressionless; they were simply men performing their jobs.

Lina removed a diplomatic transit paper from her bag, bearing the Pontificium Consilium seal. The official seal appeared to be newly imprinted. One cop took a brief look at it before going to Ernst and Matteo. He bent his head slightly and carried on in silence. Nobody asked questions. Nobody took notes.

After the officers had left, Matteo mumbled, "The next checkpoint is at the German border. Offenburg."

At 11:00 a.m., the train slowed in Offenburg. Four German officials waited on the platform. Their uniforms were dark green. Two of them boarded. One door after another opened. Each rush of frigid air that entered emphasised the quiet.

They pounded on the compartment door twice. Ernst stood and opened it. The two men standing there peered around the room with piercing eyes. They demanded passports. Ernst handed them over. The police examined the stamps, verifying the birth dates and names. When they observed the Vatican affiliation, one of them gave a brief nod. There was nothing left to question.

Lina muttered, "They aren't looking for us."

Matteo closed his eyes briefly. "Not yet."

The train has moved again. The scene beyond the window was suddenly that of Germany: disciplined, rigorous, and exact. Symmetrical street signs lined the way. People were quieter. Even their steps were rhythmic.

January 4, 1936
Berlin

They landed in Berlin at around 10:00 p.m. Crowds have filled the Hauptbahnhof. However, an intangible pressure loomed over the gathering. Men dressed in civilian clothing roamed around the station. Some young people wore Hitler Youth pins on their lapels. Uniformed soldiers and plainclothes police officers walked together. Their footsteps concealed authority.

Léon and Anton left the train from the back and took places throughout the group. The goal had everyone's attention. Friedrichstrasse: a little kiosk. A man is inside, wearing a black trench coat and a fedora hat and clutching an English-language newspaper.

"Is this the signal?" Matteo asked.

Lina nodded. "Yes, an English newspaper. Who else would carry one in Berlin?"

They approached the kiosk cautiously. He gave them a nod. "The press is ready. The printing will happen tonight. If we do not act now, we will attract notice."

"Where will we stay?" Lina asked.

The man wrapped up the newspaper and handed it to Lina. "The address is on the inside page; safe house." Then he turned away and returned to the kiosk. He didn't look again.

76

The door was made of steel and coated with wood. It was on the second floor of a historic three-storey terraced structure on a peaceful backstreet in Friedrichshain. There were no lights in the neighbourhood.

Lina handed Ernst the newspaper, with the key carefully wrapped inside its pages. He turned the key to open the door. They entered stealthily. The hallway was short and narrow. There were no marks, nails, or artwork on the walls. There's no shoe rack or coat hanger. Someone intended that there would be no evidence of life. The door to the living room was open. Inside, a small stove burnt, casting a flickering orange light across the ground. The corner held a basic table, three chairs, and a blanket tossed there haphazardly. There is nothing more.

Matteo approached the window. He carefully studied the curtains. The cloth was thick, and no light could escape from within.

Lina placed her purse on the table. She quietly opened it and pulled out the folder. The cardinal's red wax seal remains on the inside of the cover. She unfurled each document individually and spread them across the table.

Ernst removed his jacket and leaned over the table. "When do you think we'll hear from the print shop?"

"Soon", Léon said.

Matteo went into the back room. When he returned, he said, "Two beds and an old wardrobe. I also checked the windows."

Ernst gave a slight nod. "They don't know about us. But they may have felt something in this building."

"Berlin is quiet for now," Lina replied. "But it won't stay quiet much longer."

The door opened, and Léon walked inside. He had gone to check around the print shop. He discreetly closed the door and spoke directly: "I have approached no one. However, two plainclothesmen are circling the building where the press is located. They have walked the perimeter multiple times. They have not gone inside."

Lina stood up instantly. "So they're watching the press."

"When the printing starts, their first motion will be evident. That is clear," Léon said.

"Is there any chance we can move the location?" Matteo asked.

"No," replied Léon. "The installation is fixed; we cannot move it."

Lina returned to the table. She reviewed the paperwork from the beginning. She shifted one of the three folders forward. One last glance inside followed as she opened the cover. "The press will receive this first batch. The others will wait," she clarified.

Ernst moved closer. His gaze examined the documents. "Anything missing?"

"No," Lina responded. "I checked anyway, three times. There can be no mistakes tonight."

The phone rings at 1:40 a.m. Léon swiftly approached and snatched the receiver. He said nothing but listened. His expression didn't change. His eyes moved between the documents and Lina. He then hung up the phone. "It's time," he said.

They approached the door. As Matteo reached for the handle, he paused. "Tonight will be a long one," he remarked.

77

They sneaked down the tiny tunnel between Schillingstrasse and Rochstrasse in eastern Berlin. While strolling, Matteo asked quietly, "Where exactly is the print shop?"

Léon responded without removing her focus from the road ahead, "Below an old tailor's store. We'll use the back entrance."

"Is someone waiting for us?"

"There will only be one person inside. The door will be unlocked. We will enter discreetly."

Matteo paused and looked around for a moment. "Too exposed; perfect for a trap."

"In this city, everything's perfect for a trap," Ernst told me. "But we can't turn back now."

When they reached the street at the end of the corridor, it was absolutely vacant. The little building in front of them was silent. No light came from within. The tailor's sign had faded, with the letters practically worn away.

Léon stepped forward. He reached into his coat to touch the grip of his revolver but did not draw it. He approached the door and put his hand on it. Then he slowly pushed it, and it opened silently. In the dimly lit room, there was an ancient sewing table. Behind the table was a man in his fifties. He didn't rise. He gave a tiny nod, showing recognition rather than greeting.

"Do you have the documents?" he asked. His voice was low yet clear.

Lina cautiously placed her backpack on the table. As she opened it, her attention remained fixed on the man. "Yes. The first batch is here."

"How many copies?" the man asked, pushing the bag nearer to him.

"Three hundred. Distribution will begin at 4:00 a.m. in the Kreuzberg area," Lina said.

The man opened the file. He swiftly turned the pages, concentrating on the formatting rather than the content.

Ernst leaned in gently. "There are no names; only content. The paper will speak, not we."

The man nodded. "When no one claims something, people question it more."

Matteo studied the shelves, walls, and the machine. Everything was old, yet it appeared to be in decent condition. The printing press was put up against the wall behind the table.

"Will this little machine print all of it?" He asked; his tone was harsh.

Without looking up, the man replied, "Yes. It's modest, but quiet and speedy."

78

At 2:30 a.m., the first page appeared. The ink left a crisp, strong imprint on the white paper. There was no headline, just basic phrases with little emphasis—no quotation marks or signatures. However, each sentence concluded with a date or location:

Vatican Archives, Rome.
Concordium Meeting Notes, Berlin.
Himmler Directive, November 17, 1935.
Goebbels Memo, December 3, 1935.

Ernst took the first copy and examined it. His brow furrowed, but his gaze remained calm. "Clear enough," he said. "Anyone asking questions will understand what they're facing."

Matteo stepped near the window. He carefully pulled the curtain aside. "A vehicle stopped at the end of the street," he said. "The headlights are on, but the engine is off."

Léon walked fast toward the door. His eyes went forth, and he said quietly yet firmly. "If we stay inside, we will be stuck. They're cutting off the exit line."

Lina turned to face the window. "Is there any movement in the vehicle?"

Léon shook his head. "Not yet. However, they look to be waiting for the door to open."

The printer was setting up the second set of pages. His hands moved quickly and did not tremble. "The second batch will be ready in five minutes."

There was a faint knock at the door. Anton entered. He said, "Two men exited the vehicle. I see nothing in their hands, but they are galloping. They're coming straight this way."

Matteo asked, "Police?"

Anton shook his head. "I don't know. They wear simple clothes, yet their gait seems trained, as if they were obeying commands."

Lina removed the bag from the table and carefully placed the copies off.

The printer nodded. "Staying here is no longer an option. You must leave right now."

Léon gave the room a last glance. They left nothing behind. "We will leave via two separate routes. But we aren't going back to the safe house tonight. We are moving to a new place."

Lina asked, "Where?" without turning her head.

"Wartenberg Street", replied Léon. "An old bakery; the entrance is through the back alley."

As they neared the entrance, the automobile remained present. The headlights remained on, but the two men were no longer visible. Anton went along the sidewalk, crouching against the wall. He used a shorthand signal. "They're waiting at the corner. They'll try to break us up."

Léon shook his head sharply. "We go out together. Nobody divides."

Ernst grabbed the packet containing the printed documents and gripped it closely against his chest. "If we can escape this street, Berlin will read these papers before sunrise."

Matteo bowed his head slightly. "And after that?"

Lina replied without hesitation. "After that... Berlin will no longer stay silent."

79

The first light of the morning illuminated the Berlin sidewalks. Three couriers had discreetly moved through the streets of Kreuzberg, Mitte, and Prenzlauer Berg. Each carried documents in his or her luggage. Concordium was no longer a rumour. They had documented it. The printed truth proved more difficult to deny.

At 6:30 a.m., a sleepy radio presenter announced, "The materials distributed on the streets were reproduced without permission, and an official investigation has begun."

After listening, Ernst turned the radio knob. Silence, which once again filled the room, followed the click. "The news has reached them," he stated simply.

"Those who read it understand," Lina claimed. "And now, everyone will have to make his or her own decision."

Matteo was standing by the door. He was wearing a vest, and his coat was on the chair. "This silence won't last long," he said.

Three bangs echoed on the door at that moment. The quiet broke. Anton instantly rose from his seat. He did not draw his firearm, instead reaching for the handle. A familiar voice came from behind the door. "It's me, Léon." The door was instantly open. Léon raced in, his steps rapid and his expression tense. Before locking the door, he glanced outside and announced, "They issued an emergency order this morning. They have ordered raids on homes in the areas where the documents were located."

Lina asked, "Can they find this address?"

Léon shook his head. "I don't think so... However, certainty is impossible to get."

Ernst approached the table. He unfurled the map and smoothed its corners. He swept his fingertips along the distribution zones. "How many zones have they completed?"

Léon showed up on the map quickly. "Kreuzberg and Prenzlauer Berg are complete. However, they detained the courier in Mitte before the delivery was complete."

Matteo crossed his arms. His gaze shifted away from the map and toward the window. "So the documents are out, but the couriers are in danger."

Léon nodded. "Yes, and someone is moving quickly."

Just suddenly, sounds came from outside. Anton approached the window. He opened the curtain slightly and glanced out at the street corner. A vehicle had stopped. The front doors were open. Two men had gone outside. Their hands were in their coat pockets. Their stride was solid.

"They're coming this way," Anton stated. "We're going out the back door."

Lina packed her bag without hesitation.

Anton turned to face the window. He closed the curtain. "Once out the door, we turn right after the second building. There is a passage there."

Léon wedged a chair against the door. "We need to buy some time."

Lina asked, "How much time do we have?"

"Almost none," explained Léon.

Anton approached the back door. He opened it and slid out. After a cursory look, he gestured with his hand. "Clear."

Lina went out first, followed by Ernst. Léon went rapidly, yet in deliberate steps. Anton stayed at the back, monitoring the exit route. As he stepped out, he pulled a small wire from his side pocket and hooked it to the door lock.

Matteo asked. "Explosive?"

"No," Anton responded. "Just smoke. It will scare them away and impede their line of sight."

Two streets away, they discovered an empty tram stop. The morning fog obscured anyone. They crouched beneath the shelter. The street was silent, yet the silence itself seemed ominous.

Lina knelt and looked back. "Are they coming?"

Anton gave a quick nod. "Not yet. But they're on us."

80

After a few minutes at the tram stop, the group continued on. They moved east, toward streets with fewer buildings and more audible footsteps. Rain had started. Thin but steady. The paving stones gleamed, and with each step, the sound of shoes splashing in the water became more distinct. Matteo walked up front, silent but alert, like a tracking dog. Léon and Anton followed, moving in a staggered formation. Both remained steady and willing to change course if necessary.

"Where's the next safe house?" Lina asked; her voice was low.

Léon replied without turning his head. "At Greifswalder, an abandoned bakery near the station. We have the key."

Lina asked briefly. "Has it been checked?"

"Yes," said Léon. "They checked it last night."

As they rounded the next corner, a car appeared across the street. The yellow paint had faded, and the license plate was dirty and unreadable. The driver wore glasses and lowered his head, but he did not move.

Anton instinctively paused. He leaned against the wall and gave a quick glance. "They stopped," he said clearly.

Ernst stepped forward, his eyes fixed on the vehicle. "They're not moving? The rear door just opened; one man exited. He is carrying a backpack. I can't see any weapons, but he walks with discipline."

"Is he alone?" Lina asked.

Anton gave a small shake of his head. "No. The others stayed in the car."

Léon bent down on one knee, lowering himself to the ground. As he looked down the side street, he said firmly, "We're turning left. We'll follow the wall."

Just as they turned off the main road, they heard a metallic clatter behind them. An object struck the pavement and bounced off the stones.

Anton immediately exclaimed, "Grenade!"

Léon reacted immediately: "Get down!"

The entire group fell to the ground at once. The grenade came to a halt just a few metres away and exploded in seconds. With a violent blast, pressure waves spread. The pavement shook with fire. Shrapnel hit the walls and garbage cans. Smoke rose. For a moment, the noise took over everything.

Léon had protected Lina with his body.

"Lina!" Léon called out.

"I'm fine!" Lina responded. "Only my ears are ringing."

Anton drew his weapon, crouched, and surveyed the surroundings. At that moment, a man in a black coat appeared in the far left corner. He carried a pistol. He began firing indiscriminately. Bullets struck the pavement and the building's wall.

Anton knelt and aimed. He fired twice. The second shot hit the target. The man stumbled and grabbed his left shoulder. Then he quickly pulled back. He turned right at the corner and ran. He limped slightly with each step but did not fall.

"He's wounded," Ernst said. "But he escaped."

Matteo looked down the street. "That was close."

Lina turned to confront Léon. "Are you okay?"

Léon looked at his hands. There were minor cuts on his fingertips. The blast had charred the sleeve of his coat, but his expression remained unchanged. "I'm fine," he responded. "We can keep moving."

81

They reached the abandoned bakery building on Greifswalder. There was no electricity, and the interior was silent. It was difficult to see from the outside. It appears safe.

Lina immediately removed her bag and set it on the old wooden table. "They may have found out where we are. As the documents spread, the reaction will become more intense. We cannot expect everyone to stay silent. However, our circumstances have also changed... We are no longer just transporting information; we are altering its course."

Matteo looked at his watch. "We have twelve hours ahead. Whatever happens will be determined."

Ernst approached and asked, "What should we do?"

"We need to establish the Geneva connection with the cardinal..." Lina responded. "...without losing time."

Matteo nodded. "I noticed an old telegraph office two blocks from here. We can use this line inside."

Léon checked his arm. The burn on his elbow had stung. "I'll go," he said. "I'll be quick." Then he walked out the door, leaving. A brief silence followed.

82

The atmosphere inside the old bakery had changed. Léon telegraphed an encrypted message to the cardinal in Geneva, stating that distribution had begun in Berlin.

Lina spread the map across the table once more. She used a pen to cross out each marked neighbourhood one by one. Each mark represented the point at which the distribution was complete.

Matteo remained at the window, keeping watch. "Wilhelmstrasse is still quiet," he explained.

While Ernst was gathering the files on the other end of the table, he remarked, "It's not just Hitler; Goebbels has also vanished. But we know Himmler is active in Berlin."

Three quick, repeated knocks came at the door.

Anton raised his hand to silence everyone. He quietly approached the door and drew his weapon. "Who is it?" he asked; his voice was low.

A clear voice came from behind the door: "In this city, only the silent die now."

Anton hesitated before opening the door. A man in his fifties stood outside. He was drenched by the rain. He wore a dark raincoat and hung a small cross around his neck. In his hand, he held an old leather bag. He drew a breath before he spoke. "My name is Josef," he replied. "I've been following you since the moment you set foot in Berlin."

Lina stepped forward. "Why did you follow us? Who sent you?"

"No one," Josef replied. "No one sent me here. I decided myself." He opened his bag and pulled out a crumpled page. The pages resembled Vatican documents. The bottom left corner displayed the seal of Cardinal di Forlì. "It came into my hands last week," he said. "That's when I understood everything."

Ernst moved forward to scan the document. "This page could only have ended up with someone inside the Concordium."

Josef nodded slightly. "That individual was me. But I'm no longer there."

For a few seconds, no one spoke. Josef explained he had worked in the Berlin branch's archive for five years. "The archive contained encrypted telegrams, internal memos, and meeting minutes. Every day, they placed documents in front of me, but I never had complete access to their contents. Last week, they started sending some files straight to Himmler's desk, bypassing my involvement.

They overlooked my role. I wasn't taking orders; I was just observing."

Lina fixed her gaze on Josef's face. "Then why come now?"

Josef reopened the bag. He carefully placed three files on the table. "These are the last documents I have," he explained. "Everything else is being erased."

Lina opened the first file. It contained Goebbels' handwritten notes. The second file came from the internal security archive and included flowcharts for information control and marked tables showing who received what. Josef delivered the third document to Lina directly. In the centre of the page was a single line, written in dark ink:

"All executive authority has been transferred to Himmler. The Führer's role is only to announce decisions."

Ernst repeated the line aloud. "Hitler now merely announces orders…"

Josef nodded. "He just spoke now. Everything originates from Himmler's desk."

Lina examined the files. Her face was expressionless, and her gaze remained fixed on the documents. "This isn't just written proof," she clarified. "This is an internal testimony."

Josef spoke without hesitation. "Please do not include my name on the documents. Not written or spoken. However, the content needs to be published. People should know this."

Lina nodded without looking away from the document. "Your name will appear nowhere. However, these files will appear in the next print run."

83

The first reaction in Berlin happened in the early morning hours. In Alexanderplatz, four people began walking, each holding a page from the documents. Neither speaking nor shouting, they remained silent. They just walked. Ten minutes later, plainclothes officers apprehended them. The intervention was brief, but the words moved quickly. They spread throughout the city.

When Lina approached the table, Ernst was holding a newspaper. "La Croix", he said. "This morning, the Paris edition crossed the border. The headline *'Fear is changing sides'* is the real highlight." He folded the newspaper. "Even if people don't understand the text, they've started talking about the headline. For the first time in this city, people are not afraid."

Matteo turned on the radio. After a crackle of static, a broadcaster's voice emerged. A female announcer read out a single sentence: *"This morning, unauthorised documents were reported to have been distributed in the Kreuzberg and Mitte districts, and it has been declared that publications based on non-governmental sources pose a threat to public order."*

Léon moved to the window. He gently drew back the curtain. The crowd on the streets was not protesting. But they were present. "People are gathering," he announced. "However, they are not being directed. They're coming on their own. This is not a protest but an awakening."

Lina quietly stood up. "The second print run will begin tonight. While we are inside, the streets will not be quiet. Nobody can act alone anymore."

84

Léon was sitting in the chair next to the radio. He carefully unfolded a small piece of paper and examined each line. The response from Geneva contained an obvious message.

"The Pope will maintain silence. The cardinal expressed unequivocal support for the continuation of the operation. Mussolini's removal has been decided. They will publish the royal decree tomorrow morning."

There was a brief pause in the room. Lina took a deep breath and spoke slowly. "This does not mean the job is done. But there is no going back now."

Matteo, still facing the window, asked, "Anything about Germany?"

Léon shook his head. "No. Not a single note."

Ernst said, looking out the window at the silhouette of the street, "Goebbels has cancelled his Radio Ministry meeting this afternoon. Another person replaced him, but they didn't provide a name. The record said, *'We will arrest anyone who reads these documents and silence anyone who speaks.'*"

Matteo stood up, rubbing the back of his knees. "Goebbels still wants to maintain control. But the ground is slipping beneath him."

For a long time, the stove had been out. The inside was getting colder. The stone walls had absorbed the outside chill and muffled all sounds inside. Fog on the windows, with moisture dripping down, mirrored the uncertainty that had settled in.

Lina sat at the head of the table. The pages in front of her held the prepared texts for the second distribution. This time, some lines included specific names: Himmler and Goebbels, meeting notes from Wilhelmstrasse, signed documents, exact dates...

Ernst leaned back against the wall. He held one page in his hand and read quietly. "We're printing with these names, then?" he asked.

Lina replied without raising her head, "Yes. Hints are not enough anymore. If we remain silent, they will claim everything is a lie. If we give them names, they will attack us. But, at the very least, we will uncover the truth."

Anton, who had been waiting by the door, raised his collar and repositioned the bag on his shoulder. "We can't stay here much longer. If we're caught, not just us—every copy will be destroyed."

Lina turned her head. "The press is ready, right?"

Ernst performed a quick calculation while still looking at his notes. "We can print about three hundred copies in four hours."

Lina paused and nodded. "That's enough. If the second edition hits the streets, they will lose control."

85

Two men on the opposite sidewalk suddenly moved as they took a few steps. They wore hats and tucked their hands into their pockets. They were running. Fast and determined.

Léon shouted without hesitation, "Take cover!"

The gunshot that followed ripped through the cement. The bullet hit the wall on the left. Sparks flew from the stone.

Anton and Léon crouched and returned fire. Guns cracked. The men abruptly changed direction and disappeared around the corner.

Lina darted into the narrow alleyway on the right. Matteo was right behind her. Ernst, Léon, and Anton were in the background. Two more shots rang out from behind, but they missed—they were simply random. Their steps quickened as they turned the corner. They looked back and noticed the men moving away.

Five minutes later, they arrived at the old tram depot. The building was quiet, and they had chained the door shut. Léon removed a pair of pliers from his bag. He grabbed the lock and twisted it firmly, breaking the chain. The door creaked open. They stepped inside. Nobody spoke. Their respiration remained uneven.

Anton stood to the side, checking his knee. "Only a scratch, nothing deep," he said.

"They didn't plan that attack," Léon said quietly. "They were alert but not directed. There was no coordination."

Matteo turned to face him. "How can you be so sure?"

"If they had orders, they would not have let us leave... They no longer receive orders from above. Whoever is on the field is acting independently."

Ernst lowered his head. "When fear grows, obedience fades. Fearful people do not obey orders. They draw their weapons first."

Lina spoke without removing her gaze from the cracked wall. Her voice was calm, but her tone was firm. "This is evidence of disintegration. Control has deteriorated. We no longer face an organisation. Now we're dealing with remnants—those who no longer follow orders but still carry weapons."

86

During the four hours spent inside the tram depot, Berlin broke the silence. From the outside, it no longer appeared to be a disciplined capital but a city where something suppressed had broken. There was no noise, but it was not entirely silent. It was the silence of a city waiting.

Ernst paused as he read one of the morning's printed documents. He leaned in and marked a sentence with his pen. "The sentence... It is based on Goebbels' handwritten notes. Hundreds of people are now looking at this line."

Lina approached. She leaned against the page edge and read the sentence: *"The people should be ruled not by enough truth but by enough lies and fear."*

No one spoke for a while. The sentence hung in the air.

Matteo stretched his back and rose from his chair. "Now, the documents have beaten that fear."

At that moment, the hangar door opened. Anton entered. As he unbuttoned his coat, he commented, "Those who gathered at Alexanderplatz are still there. They've not dispersed. Their numbers have quadrupled. It's now over 4,000. They are silent but do not move. They're waiting."

Lina asked directly, "Police?"

Anton shook his head. "No intervention. No orders either. The police chief is missing. The chain of command has broken down."

"The radio broadcaster announced that some Wehrmacht units in Berlin had withdrawn earlier this morning. The Ministry of the Interior has requested emergency powers for the capital," Léon said.

Ernst took off his glasses and rubbed his eyelids. "That's Himmler. He's attempting to gain direct control."

Lina enquired quietly, "Where's Goebbels?"

Anton responded immediately. "He left the radio station several hours ago and was last seen at the Tempelhof Airport. He was only with two others. No military escort."

Without taking his gaze away from him, Matteo asked, "Waiting for a plane?"

Anton gave a slight nod. "I am not sure. But he wants to leave before the city completely collapses. A familiar situation... Leave without a trace before the chaos reaches its peak."

Lina turned her attention back to the table, saying nothing else. She opened her bag. She extracted the documents for the new edition and counted quietly. Then separate them into groups. Each bundle denoted a different street and door. "These copies must go out right now," she said. Her tone was calm but firm. "Not just squares... Homeowners must also notice them. This text will act as a threshold for everyone who reads it. They'll either stay inside or come out." She put the last file into an envelope. Then he gave it to Anton. "Take it. Start the distribution."

Anton took the envelope. He nodded. As he neared the door, he paused for a moment. He looked back over his shoulder. "This city won't shut down with the night," he said. "They will not be silent until morning. This time, there is no turning back."

87

Goebbels' black car slowly neared the edge of the Tempelhof Airport runway. The headlights were off. The plane was ready: a tiny civilian type with two engines. Mechanics had shut down the engines, but the plane's body remained heated and ready to go. There were three of them: Goebbels, his personal secretary, and a plainclothes bodyguard. Nobody spoke. The aim was clear: Austria.

The tower announced, "No clearance for takeoff; the runway is not secured."

Five minutes later, another vehicle approached the runway's edge. The driver switched off the headlights. The doors opened silently. Four men went outside. They wore black uniforms. No insignia. However, the weaponry they carried clarified that they did not require orders to fire.

The man in front moved his submachine gun closer to his body from beneath his coat. They came to a stop a few metres in front of the vehicle. The windows remained closed. There is no movement inside.

One of them stepped forward. He lowered his firearm and spoke. His voice carried neither a command nor a request. "The flight will not depart. The city may still be open. But you are not."

Goebbels replied promptly. The window lowered gently. For the first time, hearing his voice triggered a trembling. "I want to speak."

The man bent his head slightly. He said, "No. You've silenced others. Now the voice belongs to someone else."

A brief hush followed. They quietly removed the automobile from the runway and returned the aeroplane to the hangar.

At that point, Berlin remained standing. But Goebbels wasn't. His sentence was gone. Only the words of others remained.

88

In the late afternoon, the broadcast from Berlin Radio's main headquarters was abruptly cut: a sudden burst of static, followed by total quiet. It lasted a few minutes. The radio's light was on, but there was no sound.

Then a male voice appeared in the air. It was clear yet raspy. The tone contradicted established protocols: calm but disorganised.

"This broadcast is not official. However, we will validate the publicly available materials. No one can hide the truth."

They were all straightened by the radio equipment in the hangar.

Ernst leaned forwards. "Someone has entered the building," he informed me. "There is no authority. But on the air... a live broadcast."

Léon turned his head. "No one could have accomplished this while Goebbels was in charge. But he's left now."

Lina took a brief step backwards. With her gaze fixed on the ground, she murmured quietly. "Concordium has collapsed." There were a few seconds of stillness. Then she raised her head. "So has the Nazi Party."

89

Alexanderplatz normally calms down after sunset. The streetlights would turn on, and the tram's sounds would fade. But tonight was different. Small groups had coalesced into a well-organised mob. There were no banners. Nobody chanted slogans. But everyone was walking quietly and orderly.

Lina looked down from the top windows of the ancient bakery. The crowd was moving toward the centre of the square. "This isn't a protest," she stated calmly. "This... is a march for reckoning."

Ernst appeared beside her. "They have the documents," he added. "Neither of them is speaking. But practically everyone has one of those pages. Silence is now more powerful than speech."

Matteo spoke from behind. His gaze remained on the map spread out on the table. "And everyone knows what's being asked and who it's being asked to."

The crowd migrated to Friedrichstrasse. Their numbers had grown to the tens of thousands. No police barricades. There were no directives issued at the street entrances. The chain of command had disintegrated. Berlin was on an unbridled yet calculated march.

The phone rang. Ernst answered instantly. "Yes?"

Anton's voice came from the opposite end. His breathing was rapid, but he talked clearly. "Distribution is complete. The materials have reached four major districts. However, there has been a development."

"What happened?"

"Himmler recently entered the radio building. Someone cut the broadcast. Then, they read his declaration."

Ernst stood up. "What did it say?"

"To ensure national security, a temporary transfer of authority has been implemented. The chain of command will be reorganised. The state protects the public from misinformation."

Léon turned his head. "That's Himmler declaring he's taken control."

Lina spoke after a brief quiet. "Yes, an attempt to save himself, nothing more."

Matteo pointed to the bag on the table. Inside were documents they had not yet dispersed. "Nobody is taking orders anymore. Each of them is simply attempting to avert their own death."

Ernst asked gently. "Hitler?"

Anton's voice was low and clear: "He has not appeared. Not included in the broadcast. Not in the press. No orders. Just silence."

Lina returned to the window. The hushed crowd continued to move. They didn't speed up or slow down. Their direction was obvious. "This city no longer belongs to one man," she stated. "This city now takes orders only from itself."

90

Berlin Radio resumed its broadcasts. The announcer's voice was calm. He carefully chose his sentences.

"The state is aware of marches taking place throughout the city in reaction to leaflet distribution. To avoid panic, no forced intervention will be implemented. However, the public is warned that any unlawful behaviour that endangers public order is being thoroughly monitored. Some of the provided documents have been validated, while others are still under investigation."

The room went silent.

Ernst spoke without lifting his head. "They don't deny it. However, there is a threat. This is a silent acknowledgement and final warning."

Lina stood up. "Tonight, Concordium collapsed in Germany; not only with paperwork but also with people. But this is just the beginning. Vienna, Munich, and Rome are the three cities listed."

Matteo stepped near the window. "We truly see that Berlin has fallen completely."

Lina replied without turning her head. "We'll see it in the morning."

91

There have been no new announcements for several hours. The city was calm, but not in a tranquil way; rather, it was silent with expectation. Everyone was waiting for something to break.

Ernst cautiously brought the coffee cup in his hand to his lips. "If there's still no announcement after this silence", he said, "then it means there isn't a structure left capable of speaking to the people."

Matteo checked the radio's frequency. The morning broadcast was ready to start. A few seconds later, the announcer's voice appeared. The tone was familiar—the usual official reserve. However, the text was unfamiliar. The sentences centred on familiar names.

"The Berlin Department of the Interior has announced that, as of 6:00 a.m., this morning, a restructuring has been started within the party's internal chain of command. All powers of the leadership cadre in the Reich Chancellery have been temporarily suspended. The decision was made to ensure the continuity of public safety and the preservation of civil order."

The atmosphere in the room shifted instantaneously.

Léon corroborated what he had heard. "Reich Chancellery... suspended." He then remained silent. The sentence's impact was clear without further comment.

Ernst removed his glasses. He retrieved a handkerchief from his jacket pocket and wiped the lenses. "Legally, it may not be a coup. However, they effectively silenced Hitler from within."

Lina kept glancing out the window. She spoke without taking her eyes off the street. "And now everyone knows it."

At that point, the black telephone on the table rang. Léon responded: a brief talk. He hung up quietly. "Geneva called. They delivered the cardinal's note."

Lina turned. "What did he say?"

Without breaking eye contact, Léon read:

"Europe can now speak for itself. We will simply listen."

Matteo had laid out the newspapers Anton had brought that morning across the table. He read the headlines aloud.

- Volksbote: "Who stayed silent, and who spoke?"
- Berlin Volkszeitung: "Are the orders over?"
- Berliner Tageblatt: "The Führer did not speak. The city responded."
- Deutsche Allgemeine Zeitung: "The truth is emerging from the Vatican's shadow."

Ernst emphasised that these are not state-written headlines. "These are sentences said by people. The press only published them on paper."

92

Lina greeted Léon as he entered the bakery via the back entrance. His coat was still damp. He looked fatigued, but his expression was clear. "How is it?" Lina asked.

Léon stated, "No one is in police custody. They released everyone detained last night."

"Himmler?"

"Nothing to be seen; however, a statement bearing his signature has reached the city administration: *'All internal cells connected to Concordium have ceased operations.'*"

Ernst moved closer. "So, a type of manoeuvre: he is attempting to save himself."

Léon continued after a brief pause. "Yes. However, there is no record of *a single name*. No statement, no orders."

Lina's voice dropped but hardened: "Magnus."

Léon lowers his head. "There is no official order for his arrest. There is no known location, no witness and no trace. It's as if someone erased all the files, as if he never existed."

A brief hush followed. Outside, it was snowing lightly. Inside, you could hear only the stove cracking.

Lina looked at Léon and continued, "But he exists. And still does. If someone remains silent, that does not imply he does not pose a threat. He's still dangerous."

93

Meanwhile, in Rome

Rome began the day with extraordinary attentiveness in the early morning. People were already gathering in Piazza Venezia, even though the sun had not yet touched the palace's stone walls. No one had distributed calls or flyers. People filled the square. Participants did not queue up, hold banners, or chant slogans. However, anyone who thought Rome was silent was badly mistaken. For the first time, the city spoke for itself and did not take commands from anyone.

At 9:00 a.m., the herald read the royal decree aloud in the square. They used a clear, concise, and decisive tone. There were no exaggerations.

> *"Prime Minister Benito Mussolini has been dismissed for violating the constitutional order. By royal authority, a provisional government will be appointed in his place."*

The text summarised the end of an era in a few lines. However, the reaction of those in the square to the reading of the edict caused the true upheaval.

Years of suppressed rage, buried remorse, muted fear, and deep tiredness emerged on faces as those words resonated. Even the Blackshirts sprinkled around the audience stood in corners, unsure what to do. Some could not talk, and others stood silently together. However, that morning, a few were too full to be quiet.

"We've been listening to lies for years!" screamed an elderly guy in the middle of the audience. His jacket had dropped off one shoulder, and his eyes were bloodshot.

"They drenched our hands in blood and then stabbed us in the back!"

Behind him, a young man advanced. He ripped the poster of Mussolini in half with both hands and flung it on the ground. His face showed disappointment rather than wrath. "We won't march for him anymore!" he screamed. "He's not one of us!"

Another man began picking up shredded bits of the poster from the ground. His hands trembled, so he had to bend down slowly. He gathered the shreds in his palm and raised them to his face. "He turned us against each other," he explained, his voice barely audible. "That's what he was for from the beginning."

A few steps distant, there remained a throng of Mussolini's supporters. They stood shoulder to shoulder, upright, resembling a configuration that no longer existed. However, the mob was no longer around them. People close by had turned their backs. They whispered *"Betrayal"* among themselves, but no one dared to say it aloud.

At daybreak, Rome experienced neither victory nor sadness. The city was awakening. They could no longer ignore the silenced voices. People eventually removed the propaganda posters from the walls. A young woman removed a poster of Mussolini from a wall in one motion. The paper fell to the ground, trampled by dozens of feet. Nobody bent down to look.

The shredded faces of the posters merged in with the stones of the square. Silence was no longer considered usual. Rome spoke again with each shredded poster and every stride taken. Not with the eyes or the body, but via the voice. Every crackle signalled the end of an era.

That dawn, Rome stopped waiting for orders for the first time. Everything repressed from the start emerged, without a single word.

94

Meanwhile, in Berlin

The radio's glass tubes had gradually warmed up, and the old device's faint electrical hum hung in the air. Lina adjusted the dial to the right. The static faded. The announcer's voice was inconsistent, but his words were clear enough. There was no terror in his tone, but the subtle tension that arises as history changes was clear.

"Although the Vatican-sourced documents have not been released directly, the Papal Council has confirmed their contents. The Pope has not made a statement. However, Cardinal di Forlì's written declaration has been made public: 'Structures that enter God's house in secret will dissolve in the light. Concordium is not a faith but the institutional form of fear.'"

Lina nodded slightly and sat upright in front of the radio, her gaze concentrated on the dial. Her lips moved, and her speech was gentle yet distinct.

"It's done," she said. "It really happened."

The words altered the ambience of the room. Ernst, hands clenched over his knees, nodded slowly. His eyes were thoughtful. "In Rome, Concordium's backbone has been broken," he said. "Both politically and morally."

Léon gazed out the window. Even before it appeared in print, the impact of radio news spread among the public. He turned his head and spoke. "The church is no longer silent. Cardinal di Forlì speaks clearly."

Lina turned away from the radio and faced the room. Her eyes exhibited neither astonishment nor excitement, but a form of calm clarity. "We had been silenced," she said. "Rome is currently unwinding itself. But there is a roar emanating from within."

95

At first impression, the Reich Chancellery seemed abandoned. The hefty iron gates leading to the large stone building's garden were chained from the inside. There were no patrols or guards in the front courtyard. Complete silence had replaced the sound of footsteps that had formerly resonated down the marble corridors. The military unit briefing rooms, press conference hall, and secretarial offices were all vacant. They did not permit even the cleaning team that morning.

A brief but powerful pronouncement released the day before had halted the whole governmental apparatus in one stroke: *"Temporary Transfer of Authority"*. The statement had no signature. But it bore the Reich's seal. That stamp broke the chain of command. It was no longer obvious who held the decision-making authority. Bureaucrats sat at their desks, file drawers unopened and typewriters untouched. Although the phones rang, they remained unanswered or disconnected.

Everything in Berlin stopped that morning, but time passed.

Ernst sat at the edge of the table, meticulously arranging the morning paper. The headline, plain and straightforward, appeared in bold capital letters.

"Chancellor Silent. Party Scattered. People Speak."

The rest of the page was free of official remarks. Observational accounts, brief interviews, and speculative comments filled the rest of the page. No one could talk with assurance anymore.

Lina stood at the window. She looked outside, but the morning fog blocked her view, making the streets of

Berlin appear like a dream. Without looking at the page, she said quietly, "Hitler is alone. This caught him unprepared."

Matteo was twisting the tuning knob on a small vintage radio. Fragments of music and distorted voices punctuated the static hum. Finally, the frequency stabilised. The announcer's voice appeared precisely at 8:00 a.m. Muffled but controlled:

"According to SS sources, an assassination plot against Heinrich Himmler was uncovered last night. It is claimed that the plan originated from units loyal to Joseph Goebbels. Goebbels is in custody. Himmler left Berlin late last night. His current whereabouts are unknown."

Anton had sunk into his chair. Without closing his eyes, he spoke from his seat, "Himmler is fleeing."

Ernst removed his glasses. He quietly placed them on the table. His eyelids drooped, making it difficult to concentrate. "Everyone left behind is frozen, waiting for orders. However, no one is giving them orders anymore."

Lina said with strain on her shoulders but a cool tone, "Leadership is no longer being debated. Everyone is acting alone. They're just trying to save their own names."

Quiet descended over the room. It was not the result of a lack of something but of an extreme withdrawal of everything. There was no hope or rage—only piercing clarity. There are no requirements for eye contact. Everyone understood the same thing. Berlin's heart didn't stop, but it lost rhythm. The withdrawal muted the nervous system. Orders belonged in the past. What remained was a shattered governing framework, like frazzled nerve fibres pushing in opposite directions.

At that point, no one mentioned a leader.

January 8, 1936
Berlin

On the second level of the Reich Chancellery, Adolf Hitler was alone. Throughout the day, there were no sounds from the inside: no footsteps, no creaking chairs, and no phone ringing.

Around 7:00 a.m., the guard at the end of the corridor received a brief instruction: "No one will enter today." With that sentence, the door was closed—and never reopened.

There was an extraordinary silence throughout the building. The central office, which normally resonated with the clacking of secretaries' typewriters in the morning, was quiet that day. They did not give out any work lists, and they did not establish any meeting spaces. The Reich Security Office issued no orders. Calls to the Ministry of Foreign Affairs and Propaganda went unanswered. The administrative heart of Berlin had stopped pounding. The Reich Chancellery had become a static, frozen environment.

By noon, precisely 1:00 p.m., resignations came in from regional Nazi Party headquarters across the country. Telegrams started arriving at headquarters one by one. Each provided a different explanation: health issues, neighbourhood pressure, and personal burnout. However, every message had the same sentence:

"We are no longer in a position to speak on behalf of the nation."

With that single sentence, the party's provincial lifeline was severed. Local officials, unable to accept commands, were unwilling to decide on their own. None of them considered themselves strong enough to start a new procedure. Instead, a quiet retreat started. They closed the doors, abandoned their offices, and locked the archives. The Nazi Party was disintegrating from within.

In Berlin, significant newspapers such as *Völkischer Beobachter, Der Angriff,* and *Berliner Lokal-Anzeiger* experienced an unusual delay early in the day. They postponed the publication of daily newspapers. News editors made urgent phone calls to learn more about the issue but could not reach any government authorities. Around 4:00 p.m., the first unofficial report appeared.

"Führer isolated in his private quarters."

An interruption disrupted the radio's normal programming. With a trembling voice, the presenter made the following brief announcement:

"An unusual silence reigns across Berlin-based government offices. All meetings at the Reich Chancellery have been suspended. The public is urged to remain calm and composed."

The special broadcast began at 7:00 p.m. The presenter picked his words slowly, starting after a few seconds of stillness.

"To the people of Germany... This is the gravest moment in modern German history. Today, January 8, 1936, at approximately 4:20 p.m., in the Reich Chancellery building in Berlin, the Chancellor and Führer of Germany, Adolf Hitler, was found dead in his private quarters. According to preliminary government reports, the cause of death was a self-inflicted act."

The news reached every area of Germany. People gathered at coffee shops, train terminals, and public places. Hundreds of people sat in front of their radios, heads lowered, hands on knees, unmoving. The broadcast continued:

"Sources from the Reich Chancellery report no signs of attack or assassination. The room's condition leads investigators to believe the Führer killed himself. State security forces are currently ensuring security. There is no situation that poses a threat to public order. The authorities urge the public to act with dignity and resilience."

That same evening, at 9:00 p.m., the Berliner Morgenpost and the Frankfurter Zeitung released special editions. The front pages of the newspapers had only three words:

"Hitler Tot Aufgefunden." [1]

For the first time, printers printed subheadings uncensored. Paperboys in Berlin exclaimed, "The Führer is dead!" People rushed for the papers in bewilderment, followed by horror.

However, the mood inside the Reich Chancellery remained constant. The windows remained closed. The light in the Führer's room came back on just before midnight but then went out permanently. No one announced anything about the body. Nobody saw the corpse. No sound came from within.

But Germany had heard. That night in Berlin, no anthems or slogans were yelled. The city, which had once echoed his name, now listened to its own silence.

---

[1] Hitler Found Dead.

97

The Vatican Palace was undergoing remarkable preparations in the early morning hours. At 9:00 a.m., the Vatican Radio Service got a two-page official document from the Papal Press.

Encrypted telegrams went to prominent Catholic media sources throughout Europe. The Pope's name did not appear in the statement. Cardinal di Forlì, the President of the Papal Council, signed the document. The text was straightforward, plain, and irrevocable.

"To invoke the name of God in clandestine power games is to betray God's silence. Concordium has defiled that silence. Now they shall be judged by their silence."

That sentence broke the centuries-long relationship. Concordium, a secret entity, was no longer recognised by the church. The church withdrew its recognition.

98

Simultaneous press briefings took place in Paris, Zurich, and Vienna that morning. Thousands of Concordium documents were made available to the public. Unique collections were exhibited in several centres.

Researchers assigned an identification number to each document and placed it in a glass exhibit. Long lines of visitors formed. There was no censorship of the study of the documents. Officials made all text conversations, photos, telegrams, torture reports, collaborator lists, and financial transactions public.

99

January 10, 1936
Rome

By midday that day, there was activity in Mussolini's office at the Palazzo Venezia in the capital. It was quiet, with no display. But its significance was enormous. Authorities took Benito Mussolini into custody around 2:00 a.m. They did not publicly announce the procedure. In the evening, the Ministry of Justice released a brief statement:

"A provisional judicial process has been started on charges of undermining the constitutional order, using public authority for personal gain, and collusion with clandestine organisations."

The case was directly based on the Concordium documents and the Vatican's official stance. Mussolini did not prepare any defence. An independent judicial panel of three people oversaw the trial. The session was closed to the public. The defendant did not say a word. He made only the following statement, which was recorded on the official transcript:

"I only made my way through fear. When fear became silent, so did I."

The court announced the verdict at 8:00 p.m. that same day. The court sentenced Benito Mussolini to indefinite political exile for violating the constitution and forming alliances with secret organisations.

100

January 12, 1936
Napoli

Just before sunrise, there was peaceful preparation at the port of Naples. Everyone knew what had to be done, but nobody said anything. Three unidentified state personnel escorted a small civilian boat to the dock. There were no media representatives there. There are no curious observers. Nobody was present to see him off.

The boat left around 6:00 a.m. Malta is the final destination. Escorts were not provided.

Mussolini sat on the deck. He had no hat on. His hands clasped around his knees. He didn't make eye contact with anyone or look back at the shore.

101

January 13, 1936
Bavaria

The snow-covered side road remained silent. The night's darkness had not yet lifted in the Alpine pass that connected Bad Reichenhall and Salzburg. A black Mercedes approached the intersection, its headlights cutting through the haze of snow. They had changed the license plates to local civilian numbers. However, they had predetermined the route. The name inside the vehicle was being tracked: *Reichsführer SS Heinrich Himmler.*

There were four people in the Mercedes. Himmler's adjutant sat to his right. An SS-Untersturmführer and a liaison officer sat in the backseat, eyes fixed on the road. As the vehicle approached the intersection, a red and white barrier with a stop sign halted its progress. A black-uniformed detachment stood directly behind the barrier. The battalion was led by an SS-Sturmbannführer, with an SS squad of eleven men surrounding him. Everyone remained on active duty, but no one could accept orders with a clear conscience anymore.

The barrier remained unopened. The Mercedes slowed, and the engine shut down. Himmler rolled the front window down halfway. The cold air rushed in. He fixed his eyes on the officer in front of him and spoke firmly, "Clear the road immediately!"

There were no responses. The SS-Sturmbannführer moved forward. His gaze was dull but determined. His weapon stayed in the holster. He stated clearly, "You gave us orders. We pursued them. But we want to know what we were doing, Reichsführer."

The SS-Untersturmführer in the back seat grabbed his weapon. It was a reflex, though a fatal one. Chaos ensued in the moments that followed, leaving no one to explain what happened. Nobody knew who had taken the first shot. Gunfire echoed briefly before dissipating into the valley.

All four men in the Mercedes were shot in less than 30 seconds. Himmler was seriously injured in the chest and shoulder. No one offered help. When the SS-Sturmbannführer opened the door, Himmler didn't move. His face paled in the cold air, and his eyes were wide open.

That morning, before Berlin awoke, the Berliner Tageblatt's presses were already in action. The headline *"Himmler killed on Salzburg road - Reported dead after armed SS clash"* caused shockwaves across Germany.

The subheading acknowledged the gravity of the situation, stating that authorities apprehended Reichsführer Heinrich Himmler near the Bavarian border and that he died in a shootout inside his vehicle.

The article avoided presenting a series of claims as official facts. However, the simple message was: they stopped a Mercedes with altered plates on the Bad Reichenhall-Salzburg road. The four occupants exchanged gunfire, and all of them—Himmler included—were killed. The information gathered at the scene was based on both eyewitness testimony and leaked police reports.

Berlin Radio issued a brief announcement. When the female announcer announced Reichsführer Heinrich Himmler's death, her voice was calm. The incident happened outside of official protocol. The government has issued no official statement regarding the event.

102

Meanwhile, in Berlin

The last sentence of the radio broadcast lingered in the air. The subsequent silence was more than a technical glitch; it was as if the blood flow through the city's veins had broken, as if Berlin had lost its inner voice. Failing to resume the broadcast signalled not a break in the daily radio routine but the collapse of a massive structure. In that emptiness, everyone had the same thought: an era had ended. Nobody knew who had done it or how much it cost.

Lina learnt about the news from the boys at the end of the street, who were handing out the morning's editions.

One of them held up the edge of a newspaper and exclaimed, "Himmler's dead!"

She took the paper. As her gaze scanned the headline, her body moved mechanically towards the window. Her lips were still as she read the lines beneath the title. She made no sound.

Matteo was still sitting in his chair, motionless. He'd been sitting with his back to the window for a while, responding to everything in silence. He quickly glanced at the headline in Lina's hands. His expression didn't change. As if he had expected this outcome.

Ernst was at the corner desk, sorting through stacked files. He said quietly, "They acted by decision, not command. The unit is still in service. This is no longer about discipline but about responsibility."

Lina approached the window, holding the newspaper tightly in both hands. She looked outside. A crowd had formed on the sidewalk across the street. They wore heavy coats and boots. One of them was reading a newspaper aloud. The others listened silently. Their faces conveyed neither disbelief nor anger, only emptiness. Everyone finally realised that their plan had succeeded.

Lina said, without looking away from the people outside, "The command machine has broken down."

After a moment, Ernst responded. Without lifting his head from the documents, as if thinking aloud, he stated, "And when that machine stopped making noise, no one tried to fix it."

No one else in the room said anything. Nobody turned the radio back on. Nobody read any other lines from the newspaper. The crowd outside dispersed neither. The air on the street was dense but not chaotic. Nobody shouted anymore. Everyone was just listening.

For the first time, Germany turned inward, silently acknowledging that one of Concordium's most powerful protectors had fallen.

Part 8

Beneath the New Sky

103

January 16, 1936
Berlin

The interim session of the Berlin City Council opened with the sound of a bell, breaking the silence. There were no more Reich orders, partisan procedures, or the Führer looming over everyone. The prior regime's insignias remained on the backs of the chairs in the hall, but their faces were no longer turned toward those emblems; instead, they glanced at each other.

There were no obvious leaders among the attendees. No one sat in the front row. A secretary managed the session, who did not preside. The speakers kept their speeches short. The attendees read proposals directly and kept discussions brief. Silently, the attendees cast their votes. The statement, *"A provisional people's council will be established, the documents will become publicly available, a committee will create a new constitution draft, and in 60 days, ballots will be distributed for the first vote,"* reverberated throughout the chamber from the decision ledger.

Everyone understood the significance of the decision: this was more than just an administrative transition; it was, for the first time in decades, a basis on which people might freely express themselves.

Matteo, who was sitting in an old chair near the window, raised his head. His eyes had a somewhat brighter appearance. He let out a smile. "An election," he explains softly. "A real election."

Lina had been reading through an old file until that point. She took a brief pause before raising her head. She raised her brow slightly and said, exhausted yet firm, "The one thing Concordium feared most."

Ernst secured the pencil he had been holding to the file's edge. He took a deep breath and said with a bowed head, "People expressing their own opinions."

No one in the room said anything out loud. However, the Berlin wind seeping through the window seemed to reveal that suppressed feelings were surfacing, and terror could no longer find a quiet echo.

Concordium's order, established in silence, was now disintegrating because of speech. For the first time, those previously silenced would vote for themselves instead of others.

104

The Vatican's brief but symbolic message echoed not only within the stone walls of Rome but throughout Europe. The Papal Press Office made the statement on Vatican Radio in the early morning. Cardinal di Forlì signed a statement that simply stated, *"Light is visible when darkness is lifted. The light has come."*

These few words broke the centuries-long stillness around Concordium. Although the message mentioned no specific individual, political group, or state, everyone understood it. It was not a statement of an era's end; that era had already passed. This was only confirmation.

European publications featured the sentence on their front pages. They all featured the same headline: *"The Light Has Come."*

In Milan and Florence, civilians congregated in the early morning. The demonstrations were unplanned. There weren't any flags or organisers. However, everyone appeared to agree that nothing would ever be the same again. Soon, volunteer groups assembled in front of municipal buildings. People removed the old regime's symbols. Instead, handwritten signs read: "The word belongs to the people. The silence has ended."

The interim administration made its first official decision at midday. Italy's new executive council stated that national elections would take place in 1936. The preparation procedure started immediately. With popular support, the election will establish the groundwork for a new constitutional order.

This action was more than simply announcing an election date; it was a declaration of renewal. Participation rather than suppression, voice over fear, light over darkness... From the rubble of Concordium, Europe awoke with a fresh voice.

105

January 18, 1936
Berlin

The door creaked open. For a moment, cold air from outside entered the room. Anton stepped in. He was holding a brown envelope. The crimson wax seal on the envelope stated, *"Papal Council - the seal of Forlì"* and was immediately identifiable. "It arrived from the Vatican," Anton explained, his voice quiet but clear. "With Di Forli's seal."

Lina accepted the envelope without rising from her chair. Her fingertips traced the seal's lines carefully before opening it in one stroke. Inside, there was simply one page. The letter, written on thick paper, displayed unsteady but readable handwriting. The title, *"The Departure of Pater Magnus"*, caught her interest.

Lina slowly turned the page. Her eyes caught the line in the bottom corner. Without squinting, she read:

"...he left through the northern gate that night, leaving the other two behind. He carried the seal himself. Despite being alone, he would not remain alone."

The room fell silent for a moment. Léon sat in the armchair in the corner, staring at the blurred city silhouette reflected in the windowpane. He remained silent for a long time. "Pater Magnus is alive," he finally stated, as if he knew it already.

The sentence echoed throughout the room, heavy yet familiar.

Lina slowly raised her head, holding the paper between her two fingers. Her eyes shone with clarity rather than fear. "And he's moving," she added.

Anton straightened up. "But it remains difficult to track. Looking for him is like sweeping an empty forest."

With that sentence, the mood in the room shifted. It wasn't a threat, just a warning. Because if Pater Magnus was still alive and had left the Vatican with his own seal, it meant there was still a spark waiting to be lit within the ashes of Concordium.

And no one knew where the spark would land.

106

In one of the Vatican Palace's inner chambers, Cardinal di Forlì sat at his desk before dawn. The curtains were slightly ajar, and in the low light, the shadows of the Vatican gardens fell against the wall. He leaned over to the last page of the notebook in front of him. The fountain pen silently touched the paper before coming to a halt. The cardinal did not write. He said quietly but clearly, "Magnus is no longer a threat. But he is a reminder. Shadows will always exist wherever there is light."

Those words were never recorded in any official documents. No one wrote them. No one sealed them. But they existed.

Hours later, an official leaving the Vatican boarded one train to Berlin. He had no briefcase. He carried only a single phrase. Throughout the journey, he did not speak or take notes. However, when Lina heard the name, he conveyed an obvious message.

When the official discovered Lina in Berlin, he issued a one-sentence statement. He didn't explain what had happened or give any details. He simply looked her in the eyes and stated, *"It was the cardinal's word: Magnus is no longer a threat but a reminder. Shadows will always exist wherever there is light."*

Lina listened without lowering her head. Her eyes narrowed. This did not mean that the war was over. It simply meant that its form had changed. Pater Magnus' presence was no longer a planned event but an echo—a dark shadow cast from the past into the future. Shadows would always remain.

However, Lina was now on the side of the light. Nobody could stop that.

107

March 1, 1936
Paris—Gare de Lyon

The hazy light of a March morning filtered through the station's iron domes, and silence enveloped the bench where Lina, Ernst, and Matteo sat. Neither of them spoke. Their suitcases were closed, and the tags were still intact, but they were no longer carrying only clothes. The documents were gone. They broke the code, dispersed the archives, and revealed the secrets.

Europe had seen the body of Concordium and counted its components. Only a shadow remained: a man. He was now nowhere.

Ernst interrupted the silence. He spoke with his eyes fixed on the ground, his voice confident rather than hopeless: "We will not find him."

Lina responded calmly. "But we had to search."

Matteo turned his head slightly towards them. His voice was clear as ever, but there was an odd emptiness in it: "His absence is the only sign that Concordium has truly finished."

At that point, Léon appeared at the station's entrance; his face was neither urgent nor excited. He approached quietly, giving a slight nod. "Nothing. No trace, no letter, and no witnesses."

Lina stood up. She slung the bag over her shoulders. Her expression wasn't emotionless, but she had already decided. "Then we'll stop searching."

Ernst opened his lips. He paused, as if deciding what to ask. Then he asked, "So, is it over?"

Lina responded promptly. "No. We're going to stop. But his shadow will no longer guide anyone."

They began walking and looked down at the platform. Voices echoed throughout the crowd, asking for tickets, saying goodbye, and crying children. However, fear no longer muffled these sounds. They are free.

Everything left behind had once happened. Concordium originated as documents composed of lines, ciphers, and secret seals. Then it went dark—silent rooms, orders issued in terror, unseen hands.

Now it was just a memory.

The past is only a memory; it cannot rule.

Epilogue

June 19, 1936
New York

The twelfth-floor apartment, which overlooked Central Park, appeared to be frozen in time. The evening light filtering through the large windows carried no wind, despite the building's height. A stillness hung in the air, as if the silence itself halted all movement. A man stood up in front of the glass. His dark brown suit had no creases. His left hand was on a cane, and his right held a crystal glass with a few silent, melting ice cubes. He fixed his eyes on the green border of Central Park. He did not move, just watched.

Quietly, the door opened. The man who entered took cautious steps. The carpet absorbed the sound of his footsteps. He held himself straight and walked with a firm tread. However, the first words he spoke revealed a hidden hesitation.

"Europe has calmed. Officials announced the date of the Berlin elections. A museum has opened in Paris. Everyone has returned to their own affairs."

The man at the window didn't move. His head remained still. He made no response. He just kept watching, as if the entire world existed beyond the glass and nothing inside belonged to him.

The man who entered took a few more steps. Now, he selected his words with greater care. "Concordium has dissolved. Its name is now just an archival heading. It's over. All that remains are the people and memory."

This time, the man by the window spoke. His voice was firm, not because of its volume, but because of the assurance it conveyed. It was cold, but my mind remained calm. "Over?" he enquired. "Is that what you truly believe?"

Another pause ensued, but this time, something thickened—as if the two words made the air in the room heavier.

The man who entered swallowed. His next words were cautious and defensive: "Europe has completely unravelled. Everyone is now aware. The documents spoke. Nobody is listening to them anymore."

The man by the window tilted his head slightly. His entire face did not appear. However, his profile, jaw line, and the shape of the fingers resting on the cane all appeared familiar - very familiar.

"Concordium was not a name," he clarified. "Not even a structure. There was a need. Fear was the driving force. I've grown through fear. When fear shifts, another land reignites the need."

The man became silent. He lowered his gaze to the floor. He looked at the carpet. There appeared to be nothing more to say.

The man by the window spoke one last time. His voice is now clearer. Speaking not only to the person in the room but to the entire world:

"Europe is silent now, for us. We have said everything. We have written everything. Everyone has spoken. We have withdrawn from there."

He placed the glass on the windowsill. The glasses became foggy. He gripped his cane even tighter. Slowly, he turned. With that turn, the balance of the room shifted. Light transitioned to shadow, which led to the unknown. His face was still not fully visible. However, his identity was now unquestionable.

"Now, we simply wait."

The man who had entered raised his head. "Where?" he asked slowly and almost whispered.

The man looked, but they didn't exchange glances. The one word he said pulled every shadow in the room towards it. **"Here!"**

The other man whispered softly, **"Magnus."**

No other sounds followed. Beyond the window, in Central Park, children ran and dogs barked as the morning routine gave way to the evening.

No one knew who the man inside was.

Nobody could predict the moment he was waiting for.

But he was present.

He stood.

And he waited.

THE END

Printed in Dunstable, United Kingdom